Letters
to
Amelia

LETTERS
TO
AMELIA

a novel

Lindsay Zier-Vogel

Book*hug Press
Toronto 2021

Library and Archives Canada Cataloguing in Publication

Title: Letters to Amelia : a novel / Lindsay Zier-Vogel.
Names: Zier-Vogel, Lindsay, author.
Identifiers: Canadiana (print) 20210222166 | Canadiana (ebook) 20210222212
ISBN 9781771666985 (softcover)
ISBN 9781771666992 (EPUB)
ISBN 9781771667005 (PDF)
Classification: LCC PS8649.I47 L48 2021 | DDC C813/.6—dc23

Printed in Canada

The production of this book was made possible through the generous assistance of the Canada Council for the Arts and the Ontario Arts Council. Book*hug Press also acknowledges the support of the Government of Canada through the Canada Book Fund and the Government of Ontario through the Ontario Book Publishing Tax Credit and the Ontario Book Fund.

Book*hug Press acknowledges that the land on which we operate is the traditional territory of many nations, including the Mississaugas of the Credit, the Anishnabeg, the Chippewa, the Haudenosaunee, and the Wendat peoples. We recognize the enduring presence of many diverse First Nations, Inuit, and Métis peoples and are grateful for the opportunity to meet and work on this territory.

To Nana and Papa

1

When Grace wakes up, she's confused that the radio isn't on in the kitchen and that the apartment doesn't smell like coffee. She stares at the ceiling and remembers the waver of Jamie's voice, his tone sad, then gentle, then gone. How dare he. How fucking dare he.

Grace throws his toothbrush out while she brushes her teeth, then his soap from the shower, then his razor from the medicine cabinet. She feels pricking at the backs of her eyes, but she can't start crying, not now. *I am packing my lunch. I am pulling a shirt out of the laundry basket. I am getting dressed. I am locking the door. I am ignoring my landlady's barking dog.*

The July heat thickens the air, the humidity clinging to Grace's skin as she locks her bike next to the library—the library that doesn't look like a library, with its concrete edges geometric and triangular. People say it's supposed to be a peacock, and from certain angles, it looks like one, its head jutting out on a long neck, its concrete tail feathers fanning out against the sky. The main library is the body and the tail, but Grace works in the breast of the building—the Thomas Fisher Rare Book Library, where ivy frames the windows, softening the concrete. This morning there's a streak of bird shit stretching the full height of the reading-room glass.

She walks up the stairs, her legs like lead. Her phone buzzes in her pocket.

You've got this, her best friend, Jenna, has texted. *I'll call you at lunch.*

"Hey, Grace!" Patrick, the resident medievalist, calls out, holding the elevator door for her. He holds out a Starbucks cup.

"For me?"

He nods, handing it to her.

She's pretty sure it wasn't meant for her, but she accepts it, the bridge of her nose burning at his kindness. She coughs so she can wipe her eyes without causing alarm.

"You feeling better?" Patrick asks.

"Yes, thanks," Grace says. She had called into work on Sunday night to say she'd come down with the flu, knowing her boss's voice mail would pick up. She thought about leaving the same message Monday night, but on Tuesday, she got up, got dressed, and left for work. She made it only as far as Harbord Street before she started dry-heaving and stumble-ran back home. She steadied her voice as much as she could and called the library, leaving a message with Patrick, who told her to make sure to stay hydrated and try some toast, or maybe some plain rice.

Grace takes a sip of her coffee and Patrick talks about the class he's planning for the fall. "I could use some help pulling the material," he says as the elevator doors open to the reference desk.

"Sure," she says. "Of course."

Grace had been hoping to sneak in without anyone realizing how late she was—she had pressed snooze when her alarm first went off, then turned it off instead of pressing snooze again the second time—but the other two techs, Jeremy and Abigail, are sitting at their desks.

"Jamie see that double play last night?" Jeremy asks over his computer screen, pushing his red hair out of his eyes. "I still can't believe the Jays lost after all that."

"Yah," Grace says. There's a picture of her and Jamie from their trip in June to Saskatchewan on her desk, the bright blue sky radiating behind their smiling faces.

"I think my brother-in-law has some tickets he can't use if you guys want them."

You guys. Plural. "Great," Grace says.

Jeremy beams. He always got along with Jamie. "I'll email you the dates!"

"Janice was by looking for you earlier," Abigail says. "She left something on your desk."

Grace's heart starts to thud and she sees a pink Post-it from the head librarian next to the stack of indexing Grace didn't finish last week. *Please come to my office when you're in*, it reads. Her office? Shit. Grace uses the elastic on her wrist to pull her hair back into a ponytail.

"Janice?" Grace taps on the door frame with one knuckle.

"Grace—" Janice looks up from her computer. Her glasses sit on top of her head, holding back her blunt, grey bob like a headband. "Please close the door."

Grace's heart falls to her stomach. She's going to lose her job. This is it. She missed the last two days and Janice knows she was lying about the flu. She tries to recall how much she has in her savings account, and deducts how much she'll have to pay her landlady on August 1st. She could probably make it a few months, but after that? After that she'd have to fly home to Saskatchewan and live in her mom's old bedroom overlooking the back field and then what—

Janice gestures to the chair in front of her desk.

"I need your utmost discretion," she starts, and pulls out a shoebox. It's old—Grace has learned over the years to date cardboard—the edges are soft, but there are no signs of water damage or mildew. "We found this last week in the shelf read," she said. "Well, I found it."

"Oh," Grace says. Did she miss something in the stretch of boxes and books she was responsible for when they closed the library down for two weeks and looked for missing books and misplaced boxes?

Last year, Patrick found a manuscript marked as the library's millionth purchase that had never been catalogued, but this year, other than a few boxes that weren't filed correctly, and the copy of *Alice's Adventures in Wonderland* that had fallen behind another collection of Alice books, there hadn't been anything remarkable.

"I need to know you can keep this private."

"Of course," Grace says. Maybe this isn't about her being fired.

"I found some letters," Janice continues. "They were in a box of John Woodman's papers."

Grace nods but doesn't know who John Woodman is.

"The aviation writer. We acquired his papers in the late seventies. I don't think anyone's ever really looked at them, but I've been thinking of doing an exhibit on the Ontario Provincial Air Service. Anyhow, this box was buried under a bunch of other manuscript drafts."

"What's in it?" Grace asks, wishing Janice would get to the point already. The dull pounding of a headache is starting to collect between her eyes, and she needs a glass of water.

"Letters," Janice says, her voice conspiratorial. "From Amelia Earhart."

Grace has a vague picture of Amelia Earhart—a pilot, a feminist icon, dead, she thinks.

Janice looks at Grace with wide eyes and Grace composes her face to look more amazed than she feels. "Wow," she says, but it comes out flat, so she says it again with more enthusiasm. "Wow!"

"I have no idea how Woodman, or someone from his estate, would've gotten them. I can't find any connection, but here we are. Now, Purdue has all of Earhart's papers and they are not going to be happy about a little library in Canada having a bunch of letters, but they're ours. They were given to us," she says, her voice defensive. "I want the Fisher to get the credit here."

"Of course," Grace says.

"They seem to be between her and a beau. She was married and they aren't to her husband."

"Oh."

"It could be scandalous once they're out," Janice says.

Grace nods. She reads the private letters of famous people all the time and they're far more boring than anyone thinks. The only people who really think they're interesting are bookish PhD students and wild-haired profs who hole up in the reading room for months at a time.

"I need you to read through all of them, and write a summary, a few sentences, for each. When you're done, we'll scan them, and have a special site made. We'll do a full PR campaign. I want scholars coming to our portal. I want everyone coming to our site. The stats are going to make the university very happy." She beams. "We are going to put the Fisher on the map."

Grace nods.

"You can't tell anyone," Janice says. "Not Jeremy or Abigail, or Patrick. Not your parents or your friends. Not even your boyfriend."

Grace feels the tingle of potential tears and blinks. "Of course."

"And you're going to have to do it around your other work. I was trying to come up with a fake project for you to do, but the others would sniff it out immediately. You can work on them when you're at the reference desk, or in the reading room, so long as it's quiet, but please keep them locked in your filing cabinet." Janice hands Grace the shoebox. The cardboard is softer than she had expected. "Can you believe it?" she says conspiratorially.

"It's very exciting," Grace says. She's going to have to look up Amelia Earhart back at her desk.

"Thank you, Grace. I knew I could count on you."

Grace takes the box back to her desk and checks her phone. She rereads the text from Jenna. Two and a half hours till lunch. She can make it. She tries to tidy up, organizing the pile of indexing she still hasn't finished, putting pencils back in the drawer, crumpling up Janice's Post-it note. She glances at the clock. She's got fifteen minutes before her shift at the reference desk starts.

Jeremy is at the reference desk and Abigail is in the reading room, so Grace opens the shoebox and pulls out an envelope. It's smaller than most envelopes are now, and the flap has been torn open. Grace unfolds the brittle paper inside. The handwriting is loose and easy in faded blue ink that slants slightly to the left—a bubbly cursive with lots of space between each word.

> Dear Gene,
>
> Sorry I've been in such a mood lately. I've been trying to do the Honolulu-Cali flight for months and we're still months from figuring out the logistics and it's putting me in a foul mood. GP scheduled my lectures and I'm wall to wall for the rest of the year. (I should really get someone else on that. I've had to start drinking cream so I don't waste away.) All this to say, I don't think I'll be able to get up to Boston next weekend. Rain check?
>
> Love,
>
> A.E.

Grace refolds the letter, slips it back into its envelope. She doesn't know much about Amelia Earhart except that she flew planes and Hilary Swank played her in a movie they filmed in Toronto a few years ago. She puts the letter back with the others—there are at least sixty of them, maybe more. She pulls out another.

> Dear Gene,
>
> People ask me all the time what my favorite flight was. I'm supposed to say the Atlantic flight (I loved my plane, but that flight was nothing short of harrowing), but my absolute favorite flight was in my little Avro Avian. Have you ever flown one? Do if you ever get the chance. They're

just so light and responsive. After I finally submitted my
Fun of It draft, right after the Friendship flight, GP
wanted me to jump on the lecture circuit immediately, but
I insisted I needed a break and took off in my little gray
moth. I just followed roads and rivers and ended up in St.
Louis, and Muskogee, and Fort Worth, and one day I had
to land on the main street of a teeny little town in New
Mexico—Hobbs, I think it was called. It was the most free
I've ever felt, maps safety-pinned to my pants, my cheeks
so wind-burnt, not even cold cream could heal them. I
looked like a racoon, but the happiest raccoon you've ever
seen. It was right before we met, just weeks before.

I have no idea when, or how we'd make it happen, but
we should find a little two-seater and go somewhere for a
few days, a week. If anyone asks, we can say it's airline
business, and I'm sure we could stay at Carl's ranch in
Colorado without it being a big to do. Wouldn't that be fun?
Flying, just the two of us together. Let's do an open air
cockpit so we can really feel the wind. Closed cockpits are
such a thing now, and don't get me wrong, I'm grateful—
my cold cream consumption has gone significantly down
and it's a relief not to have permanent circles around my
eyes, but I love the screaming wind.

I've been doing lecture after lecture, two a day, and then
hopping on a train for the next stop for two weeks straight
now. On Saturday, I did three talks back to back to back
and could barely whisper by the end. I shouldn't complain,
but it is tiring and not always very fulfilling. Mostly, it's
keeping me from flying. You know what I miss most? That
moment when you're flying up through the middle of a
cloud (who ever said they have silver linings has never
flown through one) and then when you reach the top and hit
the sunshine. Is there a more glorious moment? I can't even
count how many times I've tried to write about the clouds

from above, terrible, terrible poetry that NO, you cannot read!

Even if we can't fly together any time soon, that you understand it is enough.

I love you,

A.E.

Grace does a quick Wikipedia search, but the entry is long and she's scheduled to be at the reference desk.

Once she takes over from Jeremy and can Google things properly, she learns that Gene is Gene Vidal, a former pilot, an athlete, the dad of writer Gore Vidal, and GP is Amelia's publicist-turned-husband, George Putnam. Apparently, her marriage to George was a "marriage of convenience"—he was rich, and flying wasn't cheap—and it says he proposed six times before Amelia relented.

According to Wikipedia, Amelia's middle name was Mary, she was born in 1897, she grew up in the Midwest, and had one sister named Muriel, but the family called her Pidge. Amelia set flying records. She wrote books. She crossed the Atlantic twice, once with two male pilots when she wasn't allowed to touch the controls because she was a woman and women weren't supposed to fly, and then a few years later, solo. She was an early supporter of the Equal Rights Amendment, and a feminist before the word *feminist* really existed. She lived in Kansas, in Boston, in California, in New York, and was building a cabin in Colorado.

She disappeared in 1937, the entry says, during an attempt to circumnavigate the globe. She was declared dead in absentia two years later after failed attempts to find her body. Grace looks at a map of Amelia's final flight on which all of her stops are plotted—Oakland, Miami, Puerto Rico, Venezuela, Brazil, Senegal, tracing the equator until Papua New Guinea, where there's a dotted line over the Pacific Ocean and a handful of tiny islands, like specks of dust on her computer screen.

Apparently, no one knows what happened to Amelia and her navigator, Fred. They disappeared and that was that. Grace keeps reading, but there's a lot of technical information about radio navigation—kilohertz and beat frequency oscillators and different types of antennae. She skims it until she gets to the search mission—unsuccessful despite the U.S. government's millions of dollars. Underneath, there's a list of theories about her death—the crash-and-sink theory that they ended up in the Pacific, another that they found a tiny island and lived there for a few days, or weeks, no one really knows. And another that she was captured by the Japanese Navy—it was the cusp of the Second World War, after all.

Grace's research is interrupted when she has to show an elderly prof how to look up eighteenth-century allusions to vomit on the reference computer.

When she's back at the desk, Grace pulls up photos of Amelia. She's got curly hair cut short, and tousled—more bedhead than famous person. She squints and half-smiles into the camera, more impatient than coy, it seems. She stands in front of propellers, with goggles perched on her forehead. She is tall and slim, boyish.

She looks up Gene and on his Wikipedia page it says he and Amelia met in 1929 while they were both working at the Transatlantic Air Transport company, trying to make air travel safe and palatable to the American public. He was married, and Amelia married George in the thirties, but there were rumours they were lovers from when they met until her disappearance. Based on these letters, it looks like the rumours were true. He smiles from the screen—a wide open smile, his hair dark with the same severe part that all the characters have on *Mad Men*.

Abigail steps out of the elevator with a full trolley of boxes and Grace quickly clicks the browser closed. Abigail is not one to keep things to herself.

"How are you feeling?" Abigail whispers. She doesn't have to whisper, there's no one here, but it's a force of habit.

The missing rushes back in, like a high-speed train through her chest, and it takes Grace a moment to realize Abigail means the flu she lied about, not Jamie leaving. "A bit better," she manages.

Abigail nods sympathetically, then says, "Farouk has a reading tonight if you're feeling up for it," she says. Farouk is her boyfriend, or at least that's what she calls him. Grace isn't sure that's what he'd call himself.

"Thanks," Grace says as brightly as she can. "I'll see how I'm doing at the end of the day."

Abigail pushes the truck into the reading room and Grace can feel her throat closing. She pushes open the door marked STAFF ONLY and runs to the bathroom. "Fuck." Her eyes are puffy. She splashes water on her face and puts her hands on the sink, trying to get some air in. "Fuck," she says to her reflection.

There was no lead-up, no indication Jamie was going to leave. But last Saturday morning, while Grace was standing at the kitchen sink, trying to pick dried Cheerios off a bowl with her fingernail, he said, "I don't know if I love you anymore."

The kitchen went still and Grace's sternum cracked like a plate.

She stood at the sink, water pouring out of the tap and asked him to repeat himself.

He wouldn't.

"Say it!" she insisted, her hands dripped onto the floor, two puddles on either side of her feet.

"I'm sorry, Grace. I'm so sorry."

He was joking. He had to be joking.

His eyes weren't joking. They were so, so sad. In fact, leaning against the kitchen counter, his arms folded across his chest, his Adidas T-shirt, the one that had tiny little holes in it from the broken washing machine at their first apartment, she realized she'd never seen him sad before, not like this.

"So, what, this is it?" she asked.

His silence said yes.

He emptied three shelves in the living room, three drawers in the bedroom dresser, and a bunch of hangers from the front hall closet. The apartment went from theirs to hers in less than an hour.

Lucy, the CanLit specialist, walks in. "You okay?" she asks. "You look pale."

Grace waves her hand, trying to find the words.

"Right. You had the flu. My wife had it last week. It's a doozy. And in the summer. What a rip-off, eh?"

Grace nods.

"Why don't you head home," she suggests. "I'll cover for you."

"Are you sure?" Grace asks. "I'm supposed to be in the reading room for the afternoon."

"Of course."

"Thank you," Grace says, feeling the tears fill her eyes. She blinks them back.

"No problem at all," Lucy says, turning to the bathroom stall. "Just go home and get some rest."

2

Grace lies on the couch and watches three episodes of *The Office*. When she looks at her phone, she has five voice mails and eleven texts from Jenna.

> *You okay?*
>
> *Tell me you're okay.*
>
> *CALL ME BACK ASAP!*

Grace texts back. *Sorry. Left work early and turned my ringer off. I'm fine.*

> *Thank god. I've been freaking out.*
>
> *I'm fine. Seriously.*
>
> *I'm bringing dinner. I've got a meeting till 5, but I'll cab over right after.*
>
> *I'm really okay.*
>
> *I'm coming. And DON'T CALL HIM. Promise me you won't.*

Jenna arrives with burritos and a bottle of wine.

"I got a shrimp, and a veggie, extra guac on both," she says, and puts the wine in the freezer. "They didn't have a chilled one that was drinkable."

She sits next to Grace on the couch and Grace can smell the fancy product in her hair. She's still wearing her work clothes and her heels were kicked off at the door.

"How're you doing?" she asks.

Grace stares at the coffee table—the coffee table she and Jamie had found at an antique store down on Queen Street after they first moved in together. "Not great."

Jenna goes to hug her, but Grace puts up her hands. "Don't." She will break if Jenna hugs her.

"You went to work today, though. That's something."

"And left early," Grace says. "After bawling in the bathroom."

"Take the wins. Baby steps," Jenna says. "You hungry?"

Grace shakes her head.

"You have to eat something."

Grace watches her unwrap the burritos and accepts the veggie one. She can't fathom having a single bite, but she knows Jenna won't leave until she does.

They met in first-year university, their dorm rooms down the hall from each other. Jenna broke up with her high school boyfriend during Frosh Week and Grace brought a Deep'n Delicious cake to her room, and they've been best friends ever since.

"I still can't believe he's gone." Grace presses her palms against her eye sockets. "How do you go from folding laundry together to just leaving? I don't get it."

Jenna shakes her head.

Fireworks spark on the backs of Grace's eyelids. "And I know it's stupid—I'm thirty-two for god's sake—but he unfriended me on Facebook," she says.

"He did not!"

Grace nods. "I thought it was just a glitch at first, but I checked again. He unfriended me." She lets the tears slide down her cheeks.

"Fuck that," Jenna says. "I'm unfriending him." She pulls out her phone, but he's already unfriended her. "Bastard. Fucking asshole."

Her rage only makes Grace cry harder.

"I'm sorry," she says. "I'm so sorry. She gets the wine from the freezer and puts an ice cube in each of their glasses. "Oh Grace. Fucking fuck. I'm so sorry. This is the worst."

"It's the worst," Grace says, accepting her wine.

"Like, the actual fucking worst," Jenna says.

They clink glasses.

"I still don't get it," Jenna says.

"Me neither," Grace says.

"Like, how can you just fall out of love with someone?"

Grace's chest aches. She is tired, so tired. Fucking Jamie. "That's it. That's what he said."

"What did your mom say?" Jenna says, taking a sip of her wine.

"I still haven't told her," Grace says. "You know how much she loves him."

"Want me to call her? I'll tell her."

Grace shakes her head. "I'll tell her. Not yet, but I will."

"Eat," Jenna insists, refilling Grace's wine.

Grace takes a bite of her burrito.

"Not sure if you're ready for a tiny silver lining?" Jenna pauses and Grace offers a small nod.

"At least you don't have to deal with his mom anymore," Jenna says. "She was always way too involved in everything he did. He never stood up to her."

"True. And I won't have to see his entitled private school friends again."

"They were the worst."

"They were the worst. Fuck their Bay Street I'm-so-rich bullshit."

"Like, come on. You're grown-ups. Stop with the stupid frat boy parties already."

Even though Grace has barely touched her burrito, Jenna pulls out the Deep'n Delicious she brought over on Sunday when Grace called her with the news. There's still enough for two pieces.

"I'm good," Grace says.

"No, you have to eat some. It's tradition. It will make things better. It's scientifically proven."

Grace rolls her eyes but accepts the fork.

"It's true. Remember my breakup with Nate? That was fucking horrible. And Andrew? God, I was a shell of a human after."

Except now Jenna's life is perfect—she's married to Eric, who is the nicest guy ever, with the loveliest family, and they have a house in the Beaches and spend two weeks every year in Turks and Caicos. Grace's life used to be perfect, too, just a few days ago, but now she's single, with an apartment she can barely afford, and a hole in her chest that will never heal.

"How am I ever going to date again?" Grace tries to stop a sob.

"That is not what you need to worry about right now. Right now, you just need to focus on eating cake, and then sleeping. Tomorrow is a new day."

Even though Grace insists she's fine, Jenna cleans up, and waits for Grace to brush her teeth and put on her PJs.

"No Facebook, okay?" she says.

"Promise."

"For real."

"Okay, okay."

"Call me in the morning," Jenna says.

"I will," Grace says.

"And get some sleep."

"I will," Grace promises. She doesn't go to bed after Jenna leaves, though. Instead, she goes through the books Jamie left behind, trying to find a clue, something, anything. When she can't, she finishes the cake and opens her computer, unable to avoid the pull of Facebook, the tiny circle with Jamie's face, the "add friend" button, a list of all their mutual friends. Eighty-nine mutual friends. She stares at the screen until her eyes blur. She finishes the bottle of white Jenna left in the fridge.

You got this, Jenna texts her.

Grace brushes her teeth, pulling Jamie's toothbrush out of the garbage, then throwing it back in.

3

In the morning, Grace ignores the voice mail from her mom, and the empty Deep'n Delicious cake tray on the coffee table, and wishes she hadn't slept on the couch.

I am turning on the water. I am holding the shampoo. I am rinsing my hair. If she narrates exactly what she's doing—*I am locking the door. I am walking along the sidewalk, right foot, left foot*—she can keep Jamie's absence from hijacking her lungs.

After Grace slips her leftover burrito into the staff fridge, Abigail asks if she has plans for the weekend. Grace pastes on a smile as best as she can and makes up something about brunch plans then tries desperately to think about anything except the text messages Jamie isn't returning, the voice mails she's been leaving on his phone, piling up like dirty laundry in the bottom of a closet.

She tries to swim at lunch, thinking the pool will be healing, but there's something about the weightlessness of the water that undoes her and she has to empty tears out of her goggles at the end of every length. At least, she tells herself when she climbs out of the water, her limbs heavier than they should be, people will think her eyes are red from the chlorine.

He's gone he's gone he's gone, every footstep back to the library.

Grace blinks at the sky and takes a deep breath. She has four more hours to go.

Back at her desk, she checks her inbox for an email from Jamie she knows won't be there.

There's nothing. Of course there's nothing and before she can open Facebook, she pulls out a letter from her filing cabinet and unfolds the delicate paper. The ink is black this time, but the scrawl is still bubbly and loose.

Dear Gene,

Thank you for the silk scarf. It's beautiful. I haven't taken it off since it arrived in this morning's post. You know when you're flying across the Midwest in, maybe, late August or September, and the sun is just rising and the fields are ready to be harvested? It's that exact color, that goldish green-brown. It is stunning. I love it. You wrote that you considered red, and I do love a pop of color, but this brown is my favorite.

I found some driving gloves I thought you'd love the other day—they were so soft, a buttery tan leather. They would've looked so good with that tweed jacket of yours, the one you were wearing the last time we were at the St. Regis, but I couldn't figure out if they'd be too small, so you'll just have to imagine them, and next time I see you, I'll be sure to measure your hands. Ha ha.

I want to get this in the post, so I will sign off here.

Love,

A.E.

Grace pulls up a blank Word document. *Undated correspondence from Amelia Earhart to Gene Vidal,* she types. *Thank-you letter for a brown silk scarf.* But it's a beautiful letter, a love letter. She tries again. *Love letter from Amelia Earhart to Gene Vidal, referencing flying, Midwest fields, driving gloves.* But that's no better, not really.

She reads the letter again and a knot of tears get stuck in her throat. She and Jamie used to give each other gifts, little things, like the jar of pickles he gave her when they were first together after she mentioned missing her grandmother's dills. She was so touched that she cleaned the jar when it was empty and used it to hold loose change by the front door. The first gift she had given him was a Joe Carter bobble-head she found on the curb. It wasn't in the best shape, but he loved it and kept it on his desk at work. She wonders if it's still there.

Before they moved in together, she'd come home to a small bag of kumquats or figs waiting for her on the porch, or a box of truffles sitting on his dresser at his apartment. And after they moved in together, she'd find a tin of shortbread, or fancy cheese, or a shirt she had been admiring in a window on College, but never would've bought for herself.

She can't pinpoint when the gifts stopped. Had they just gotten too comfortable with each other? Had that been the seed that grew into this?

"Is anyone available?" Janice calls from her office door.

"I am," Grace calls back before Jeremy can get his headphones off. She presses save on the Word document, even though it's nowhere close to done.

Janice asks her to scan photos of a famous physicist for a professor in Nebraska. The physicist's photos are black-and-white, with scalloped edges and smiling families bundled against the winter. They stand in the snow in front of wooden houses, somewhere in Northern Ontario, the bright sun bleaching out their faces. Names are labelled in pencil on the back, but Grace can't make out any of them.

Oh my god. I just heard the news. I'm so so sorry. You were one of the good ones, the most solid couples we knew.

Grace stares at her phone, at the message from Paula. Fuck.

Jamie might have taken over our couch, but I want you to know I'm always here for you. I'd never choose between you and J.

Their couch? Grace assumed he was staying with his mom, not with friends.

Paula knows, Grace writes to Jenna. Paula was Jamie's friend's girlfriend, now wife. They weren't friend-friends, but Jamie and Mark always hung out, so they spent enough time around each other to be more than acquaintances.

She hates that people like Paula know, that they're sending text messages speculating about why and when, picking her relationship with Jamie apart, looking for clues from the last time they went out with them the way she always did when a couple she knew broke up.

Ugh, Jenna writes back.

Thanks, Grace writes back to Paula. But doesn't press send. Fuck it. She doesn't want to be friends with her anyway, especially not now that Jamie is crashing with them. Besides, what would they even do? Sit around on the couch that Jamie is sleeping on while Mark watches baseball and Grace listens to Paula talk about real estate prices in Toronto?

She scrolls through her contacts and wonders who else knows, if there's anyone she should tell first, get ahead of the story, as Jenna would say. But what is the story she wants to tell? The story is that Jamie left her. That he doesn't love her. She can't text that to anyone. She starts deleting old work colleagues she hasn't talked to in years, and university friends she hasn't been in touch with, except for over Facebook. She realizes as she scrolls that most of her contacts are actually friends of Jamie's. He always had so many friends, from high school, from the sailing club when he was younger, from university, from work, from the one year he trained for a triathlon. When Grace started dating Jamie, she had friends, most from university, some from work when she was at the main library, but Jamie was always meeting up with people, renting cottages to visit, planning bike trips to the island, meeting for supper in Little India. It was easier to join them than make her own plans, and so eventually his friends became hers by default.

She has Jenna, of course, and Carolyn, who is doing her PhD and studying for her comps and TA-ing. Grace checks her phone. The last text Carolyn sent was three weeks ago—a photo of a pile of books next to a beer. *Raging Friday night*, she wrote.

Hey, she texts Carolyn. She doesn't know what else to write, so she leaves it at that, not expecting to hear back for days.

But Carolyn texts back right away. *I'm drowning in Chaucer. Fucking Chaucer. (Okay, I kind of love Chaucer.)*

Jamie and I broke up, Grace types, then deletes. *I've got some news*, she tries again, but erases it. *Firkin this week?*

Carolyn replies with a yellow thumbs-up. *You free after work today? 5:30?*

Grace sends back the thumbs-up emoji, and instead of stalking Jamie's Facebook page, she deletes all of his friends from her contact list.

The Firkin is dark and smells like stale beer and bad choices. Carolyn waves Grace over to a booth behind a line of undergrads in jerseys watching the Jays game, yelling at the umpire and drinking pitchers of Moosehead.

"Hey!" she says, standing to give Grace a hug. "Whoa, you okay?" she asks before Grace even sits down.

"Do I really look that bad?"

"No, no. You just, you look tired."

"It's Jamie," she says, trying to keep her voice even.

"Oh, shit," Carolyn says. "Lady, I'm so sorry. Alex and I got into a doozy of a fight on the weekend. He wants me to move in, and I told him, once again, that I'm not going anywhere until these comps are done. Like, give me a break already. Can't he already see how stressed out I am?"

Grace blinks. "It wasn't a fight."

The server comes over in a black golf shirt and too much enthusiasm. He lists off the specials and Grace stares at the beer list.

She can feel Carolyn's eyes on her but doesn't look up.

"Two pints of Keiths, please," Carolyn says.

"And how about some appetizers? We've got great poutine, nachos, sweet potato fries—"

"We're good," Carolyn says. She waits till he's back at the bar, chatting too loudly with another server. "Okay, what's going on?"

Grace flips a coaster over and over again and tells her.

"Jamie?" Carolyn looks around the bar like he's going to appear out of the walls. "*Jamie*-Jamie?"

Grace nods.

"Are you serious?"

They pause as the server slides their beers onto the table without saying anything.

"He left," Grace says.

"When?" Carolyn asks.

"Last weekend."

"Last weekend? You should've called!"

"I—I couldn't," she manages, trying to compose herself her face, her voice. "Sorry," she says. "I'm fine."

"A, you don't have to apologize and B, you're not fine."

"Okay, I'm not. My boyfriend of seven years left me. What's wrong with me?" Her voice is a small howl.

"There's nothing wrong with you."

Grace takes a sip of her beer.

"Nothing," Carolyn repeats. "Jamie's the dick here."

But Grace isn't ready to hear someone else hate him, not yet.

"Who leaves without notice? What a fucking asshole."

Grace spins her coaster around on the table, wishing Carolyn would stop. "I've been trying to just get through the week, you know? But then I got a text from Paula, remember her? Mark's wife?"

"The one who always dressed up as a sexy nurse for your Halloween parties. Who does the sexy Halloween costume anymore, I mean, come on!" Carolyn says rolling her eyes.

"He's crashing with them. And I just hate that he's telling everyone." She presses a crumpled tartan napkin against her eyes.

"You ladies all right?" the server asks in his radio-announcer voice.

Grace stares at her beer.

"Two mac and cheese and a pitcher," Carolyn says.

Grace balks. "I'm okay," she says. "The pint's fine."

Carolyn shakes her head. "A pitcher," she says to the server, who nods and turns to the bar. "He just said he wasn't in love with you anymore?"

Grace nods, wishing she could change the subject, talk about literally anything else. She'd rather hear about English Department drama, or Alex's new sculpture, or Chaucer. She wishes they could just talk about Chaucer.

The mac and cheese arrives with the pitcher and Carolyn refills Grace's pint glass.

"You know, there was always something about him I didn't trust," Carolyn says over a forkful of macaroni.

Grace looks up from her beer. "Pardon?"

"He was always just a bit too much, you know?"

But Grace doesn't know.

"Remember when we all rented that cottage and then at the last minute, he invited a whole bunch more people? There was something about it that seemed weird."

But it wasn't weird. He was generous. He was just trying to make sure no one was left out. Grace finishes her beer.

"I've got to go," she mumbles. "I've got a big project at work and need to get in early."

"Oh, shit. Shit. I shouldn't have said anything," Carolyn says.

"It's fine," Grace says, even though it's not. She pulls out her wallet, but Carolyn won't let her pay.

"Grace, I'm really sorry."

But it's too late. Grace lets her hug her, then walks out of the air conditioning into the early-August heat. How dare she shit-talk Jamie.

He was generous and kind and always so nice to Carolyn, even though neither of them ever liked her pretentious boyfriends, and never said anything about how she'd go on and on about whatever obscure texts she was reading for school. But then he's also the Jamie who fell out of love with her, didn't say anything for months, then up and left without hesitation. How can he be both?

4

Dear Gene,

*Director of the Bureau of Air Commerce—well, doesn't
that have a lovely ring to it? Congratulations, my love! I'm
canceling all my plans this weekend and will celebrate with
you in D.C.!*

See you soon!

Love,

A.E.

P.S.: If the rumors are true, TIME *magazine wants you on
its December cover!*

*P.P.S.: Please say hi to Eleanor for me. I owe her a letter
and a dinner!*

Eleanor—Grace looks it up. It must be Eleanor Roosevelt. Then she
types in *TIME Magazine* + *Gene Vidal* and finds that the rumours *were*
true—he's on the cover of the December 1933 issue.

"Who's that?" Abigail asks.

Grace starts. She didn't hear her. "I don't know. A prof today was asking about old issues of *TIME* and I just looked one up." Grace pulls a file folder on top of the letter as discreetly as she can.

"What are you doing tonight?" Abigail asks.

"I don't know yet." She usually spent Friday nights drinking Manhattans with Jamie, or out with his coworkers at the pub by City Hall.

"Jeremy and I are going for beers. You should come!"

Going home to an apartment that is only hers is terrifyingly lonely, so she joins Abigail and Jeremy. They talk about Janice being a taskmaster and Lucy's new haircut, and speculate if the history professor who comes in every Thursday is gay or not, and discuss Patrick's retirement status. They're waiting for Patrick to retire, even though Grace doesn't think he's as old as they think. She's seen pictures from Christmas parties from ten years ago and he looked the same then as he does now—slightly ancient, with his furious white hair and long white beard. He looks like a caricature of an eccentric librarian, except he was a priest for thirty-some years, but then he fell in love and that was the end of that.

Grace wishes she could ask him what it was like to leave the priesthood—not the big, huge epic things like the crisis of faith, but the mundane things, like having to pay rent, or getting a mortgage, or wearing jeans, or going on dates. She wants to know how he met his wife and what it was like to be a husband all of a sudden, not a priest, but she doesn't know him well enough and the only things they really talk about other than work is the weather and Saskatchewan. When he was a priest, they shipped him to Regina for a while, and though he doesn't ever talk about what he did there, he likes talking about the sky and the discarded pianos people left by the side of the highway.

After Jeremy leaves for what he thinks might be a date, Grace stays and they're joined by Abigail's grad school friends. Grace is wearing the wrong dress and the wrong sandals and has no tattoos or piercings or master's degree. They talk about bands she doesn't know, and radio stations she's never heard of, and even though Grace wants to leave, she knows it's still better than being at home.

34

Abigail's friends leave for another bar, but Abigail wants to see if Farouk is at a house party in the market, so she links arms with Grace and another girl, who has a blue streak in her hair, and they move down the sidewalk like an amoeba.

Grace is swept up in the ironic unicorn cake, the shots, and the joint that gets passed around. She can't tell if she's having fun, or if she's just drunk, but a guy wearing a Ramones shirt gets her another beer and leans against the door frame and asks if she knows the birthday girl. He's so close she can smell his breath—slightly sour, but also not terrible. She shakes her head. "You?" she asks.

"She's dating my roommate," he says. He talks about a show he went to the night before at a dive bar underneath a convenience store and she imagines kissing him. Could she? Would he kiss her back? But it's Jamie she wants to kiss. She feels the tell-tale prickle behind her nose and feels her eyes start filling.

"She's taken, Jory," Abigail says, putting her arm around Grace. "Where is your guy—Jon? No, Jimmy? What's his name again?"

"Jamie," Grace slurs. She waves her hand and Jory disappears into the kitchen.

"What the fuck does that mean?" Abigail asks, imitating her waving hand.

"He's gone," Grace says.

"Like moved to a different city gone?"

"He left me," Grace says.

"Shit! For someone else?"

Grace wants to say yes, but she shakes her head. "He doesn't love me," she says, and Abigail's face fills with so much pity Grace feels like punching something.

"Dude, that's awful," Abigail says. "That's so shitty."

Grace nods, hating herself for saying it out loud.

"Hey, Jory," Abigail calls out in the direction of the kitchen. "I lied. She's not taken!"

But she doesn't want anything to do with Jory. "I've got to go,"

Grace says, wishing she wasn't so drunk, hoping Jory with the Ramones shirt and the nice lips didn't hear Abigail. "I've got an early morning."

She knows Abigail doesn't believe her, but she leaves the house and hails a cab anyway.

Lady Gaga plays on the radio and she opens her window to dilute the smell of air freshener. Abigail is the last person she should be telling about Jamie. What was she thinking? She stares at College Street passing by in a blur and takes a deep breath to keep from vomiting in the cab.

5

Grace tries to avoid Abigail on Monday and manages not to cry until noon, though she spends her lunch sobbing in an empty seminar room. She washes her face in the bathroom and puts on eyeliner, figuring she can't let herself cry if she's wearing eyeliner. She texts Carolyn and makes plans for sushi later in the week. Plans she thinks she'll probably cancel, but it's still nice to have something anchoring the week.

Right before the end of her shift, Janice corners her while she's hauling a wheeled truck full of manuscript boxes to the elevator.

"So," Janice whispers, expectantly, "are the letters juicy?"

"I've only read a few but they're interesting," Grace says, even if she's not sure they really are.

"Oh good," Janice says.

Grace tries to recall everything she read on the Wikipedia page and tells Janice about Amelia's first plane—a yellow Kinner Airster she bought in California on her twenty-fourth birthday—and that her father was a drunk, how she never drank a drop of alcohol, and that for a brief while, she had a clothing line and used bolts in place of buttons.

"This is all in the letters?" Janice asks.

"Oh, well, maybe. I'm not sure. I haven't gotten to a lot of them yet—I was doing some retrievals for Professor Katz, and then I had to help Jeremy with some stuff and Lucy needed me to do some indexing."

"Of course. Of course. It's a big undertaking. You just let me know how I can support you."

Grace nods, then takes the box of letters to the reading room for her shift.

Dear Gene,

I've always wanted to go back to Newfoundland. It's really beautiful (in a stark and barren sort of way), like Ireland, or Scotland, but with a fraction of the people. I didn't spend much time in Harbour Grace—just popped in for a quick nap—but I spent more time than I ever wanted to in Trepassey. It's not exactly a cosmopolitan hub. I can't tell if you'd love it or hate it.

I didn't ever do any fishing in the ocean—the fog was too thick, and I spent so much time on the plane being batted around by the wind that the last thing I wanted to do was hop in a boat and bob all over that long, narrow bit of the Atlantic. But if you walked inland a bit, there were these amazing streams just teeming with trout. It was impossible not to catch one.

And I must admit, eating fish that tasted like fish was a lot better than eating eggs that tasted like fish—apparently, they feed their chickens fish, so everything has a fishy taste. Slim hated fish, so all he ate was chocolate, and of course whisky. He was pickled the entire twelve days we were stuck there.

I left my curling iron behind, so maybe we could go and find it (ha ha!), or the Mother Hubbard monstrosity I had to buy in town. It was voluminous, from my neck to my wrists, all green gingham. Oh, I was something to behold!

If we do make the trek (would we? Could we? It probably doesn't make any sense, but I do think we could pull it off without the press finding out), we should probably pack our own provisions. Even though the trout was fresh, the only other thing on the menu was potatoes, cabbage, and turnips, and I know how much you love turnips. Oh, and boiled lamb stew.

The one thing that was charming, even if the lamb stew was nearly impossible to choke down, was their silverware—all gathered up from shipwrecks. And there was the fanciest, most ornate detailing in these little wood houses perched on the rock. They make rugs, too, rag rugs, out of the linens that wash ashore from boats. A bit morbid and dark, but resourceful too!

Could you say hi to Doc for me when you're in New York? We had to reschedule lunch a few weeks back (some storm coming in from the Atlantic had him in a tizzy!) and we haven't found a time that works since.

Love you,

A.E.

Newfoundland. That's where she and Jamie were supposed to be going in a few weeks to celebrate their seventh anniversary. She's never been, but Jamie had been to St. John's a few times for competitions where engineering students race three-hundred-pound cement toboggans. Jamie had already started making one of his trip-planning Excel documents—a hike up to the top of Signal Hill, whale watching, visiting the easternmost edge of Canada, drinking beer made out of icebergs in a nearby fishing village.

Newfoundland. Fuck.

She blinks hard and makes herself reread Amelia's letter. Trepassey. She looks it up. It's south of St. John's, right on the ocean, though she supposes most of Newfoundland is right on the ocean. There's a photo of a plane with big pontoons and wings stacked on top of each other—the *Friendship*, the caption says. Amelia, Bill, and Slim were grounded there for almost two weeks, the website says, the fog too thick to fly to Wales.

What about Newfoundland? she types into her phone to Jamie, then deletes.

She stares at Amelia's script and opens a Word document.

Undated letter from Amelia Earhart to Gene Vidal. Reflections on Trepassey, Newfoundland prior to transatlantic flight. Should she put in the part about the trout? The shipwreck silverware? *Invitation to travel back with Gene to find curling iron, and see trout-filled streams,* she types. It's not enough, it's not nearly enough, but she presses save and puts the letter back in its envelope.

She stares at her computer screen, a little red pin stuck in Trepassey, and her chest threatens to split wide open. One more letter, she tells herself, but when she pulls it out, the thin paper almost translucent, she realizes it's another letter about Newfoundland.

"Jesus Christ," she says under her breath, but decides to keep reading so she can be done with these Newfoundland letters already.

Dear Gene,

I just got your letter and tore it open on the front steps. Okay, okay, we don't have to go up to Trepassey to go trout-fishing (it is a bit rural) but what about Harbour Grace? It's in Newfoundland, too, and it's really quite charming. It's right on the ocean, and the hotel there has some of the best tomato soup I've ever eaten. I still dream about that thermos of tomato soup I had in the cockpit.

It was such a blur—Bernt and Eddie flew the Vega there. They're great pilots, both of them, and I trust them more than most, and know I needed the rest, but still, part of me wanted to just fly it anyway. It reminded me of being stuck in the cockpit of the Friendship *with Bill and Slim, sitting there like a sack of potatoes.*

Canadians are really so very polite. More so than Americans, and even Brits, I'd say. Or maybe they are just more reserved. There was no grabbing at my sleeves, or crowding around me so I couldn't breathe. They just let me be, let me have a nap at the hotel, filled my thermos, then sent me off. Oh, and the accents there! They are wonderful! A bit Irish, but also not. Sometimes I couldn't understand what anyone was saying and I'd just smile and nod and they'd smile and nod.

I've wanted to go back and see that runway again—really take it in. When I left, things were one way, and when I landed, everything was different. That runway was the turning point. The last moment I had of my previous life (that sounds so dramatic and isn't really true. My "previous life" ended when the Friendship *landed in Wales).*

Enough about me. I'm so glad you're going on that road trip with Gore. It'll mean the world to him. I drove across the country with my mom in '24 and I still think about it all the time.

Write me when you're back. Maybe we can find some time to meet up in the city, or even meet up in Chicago for the weekend?

Love,

A.E.

Grace looks up Harbour Grace and opens a new Word document to write the synopsis, but gets an email from Janice inviting the staff out to the pub around the corner.

Jeremy pokes his head into the reading room. "You coming for drinks?" he whispers. "Come on, you've got to come!"

Beer is not what Grace needs, but she wants to get away from these letters about Newfoundland, so she concedes.

"To a solid shelf read and a great academic year ahead!" Janice says, raising her glass and announcing that the first round is on her.

Grace makes her mouth into a smile and lifts her pint in the air. At least she managed not to get stuck sitting near Abigail.

She sips her beer and shoots the shit with Patrick. It feels okay, like maybe things might go back to normal, but then Lucy's wife joins them and seeing Lucy's head lean toward her makes Grace's ribs ache, so she pretends to get an emergency text from her landlady and leaves before she finishes her drink.

6

Grace sits in the reading room, sharpening pencils and glancing up every now and then to the prof in the corner. He's a regular and knows the rules. She doesn't have to worry about him. It's the new grad students in the fall who will need to be watched, but there are a few more weeks until they start trickling in, with their contraband pens and water bottles.

She sharpens another pencil, then checks her phone under the desk. Janice went on a tear when she saw Abigail on her phone at the reference desk earlier in the summer and they've all had to be more discreet about it since.

Thanks for the sushi, she texts Carolyn. Grace had braced herself for more apologies and awkwardness, but it was fine. Carolyn mostly talked about the classes she was TA-ing in the fall, and the prof she was working with who was bringing one of her favourite UK writers over to do a guest lecture.

My pleasure, Carolyn texts back. *Next week is mayhem, but another lunch date the week after that? Wednesday?*

Sure, Grace replies.

She glances at her inbox and sees Jamie's name pop up. It's the first email he's sent since the day he left, backpack slung over one shoulder, a duffel bag over the other. Her pulse starts to pound in her throat. She clicks it open.

Can I come by to pick up the rest of my stuff? That's all it says.

The adrenaline surges into rage. That's it? That's all he's going to write?

Fine, she types. *Friday. After work. Love, Grace*, her thumbs type automatically. She frantically hits the delete button and scrolls down to see what he wrote. *Jamie*. He never writes his full name. He usually signs off *J*. She deletes her name altogether and leaves the end of the email empty, bottomless.

She puts her phone down and tries to swallow a jagged sob, but she can't and before she can even get a breath in, she runs to the staff bathroom. She leans her forehead on the metal door of the stall, cold and solid, and tries to breathe through the broken glass in her throat.

Grace can't sleep on Thursday night and ends up taking half a Benadryl at midnight to knock her out, but then she sleeps through her alarm and spends the day groggy and barely able to keep her eyes open at her desk. It would've been better to be exhausted than dealing with this Benadryl hangover.

She picks up milk and peanut butter from the convenience store on the way home and gets bread from Harbord Bakery. "We've got rye and challah and whole wheat, I think one loaf of the white left," the woman behind the counter says. There are remnants of bright pink lipstick in the deep, vertical creases of her lips.

Jamie always got rye, so Grace orders the challah, except she forgets to get it sliced and it's so soft it's impossible to cut. She ends up ripping off a piece, covering the soft yellow centre with peanut butter.

She checks her phone again, but there's nothing from Jamie, just a string of unanswered messages Grace sent him in a fury—*Fuck you.*

You're a spineless piece of shit.

You fucking coward.

She keeps scrolling. The last one he sent says, *Pizza tonight?* It's from when she thought he still loved her.

The buzzer goes off and the landlady's dog barks her usual hysterical greeting. Grace starts to go downstairs, but can hear him opening the front door. She doesn't know where to stand, so she goes into the bathroom and shuts the door.

Jenna texts. *You sure you don't want me to come over?*

I'm okay, Grace replies, even though she's not sure she is.

His footsteps up the stairs, his knuckles against the apartment door. "Grace?"

She stares at the hand towels folded in threes. She can hear his keys, the door opening.

"Grace?"

She doesn't want to leave the bathroom. She wants to stay in here until he clears everything out, until he's gone. "Coming," she manages and doesn't let herself look in the mirror.

He's standing in the living room in the Oakland A's shirt his brother gave him for Christmas. His hair is longer than it was the day he left, and Grace can smell his shaving cream. It smells like every morning for the last seven years.

"Hey," Grace says. Her voice sounds strangled.

"Hey."

And they stand there.

"How are things?" he asks, fiddling with his keys.

Grace says nothing. She is one of those fish at the very bottom of the ocean with see-through scales—her heart, her lungs, the bile rising from her stomach, visible.

"Sorry. Sorry, I don't know what to say," he says.

"How're Michael and Paula?" she asks, even though she doesn't care.

"Okay," he says. "I'm moving, though. I found a place down by the water."

45

"A place?"

"A condo."

"You bought a condo?"

"Just renting," he says.

Grace turns to the kitchen "Do you want a drink?" She pulls out the gin without waiting for an answer.

"I'm okay, thanks."

But she already has the ice cubes out, and needs something to do, something so she can keep her back to him. Jamie, the man she was in love with for seven years. Jamie, who needs a haircut and has a tiny dot in his earlobe where he had an earring in high school, the one mark of rebellion. Jamie, whose shoulders, calves, jaw she used to know.

It had only taken a few months for them to become Jamie-and-Grace, and after five months, Jamie asked her to move in together. He had opened a new door of being an adult—of budgets, grocery-shopping dates, and security. It was Grace's first grown-up relationship and she could finally be done with boys who didn't clean their bathrooms, or wash their sheets, and lived off pizza and Subway sandwiches.

She loved the way she felt around him—moored, secure, and like she didn't ever have to be someone she wasn't. She felt chosen and special, beautiful, even, though she wasn't even close to the prettiest girl he'd dated.

He didn't understand her insecurities. "But I don't want to be with them, I want to be with you," he'd say, and she would push back, testing the limits of his love, but it was there, it was always there. "I just love you," he'd say, and she started believing maybe it could be that simple.

She stopped questioning his love and started trusting the solidity of their two-ness. Their relationship became a room-filling fact, solid and immoveable, like the table in Nan and Pop's dining room in Saskatchewan, except it wasn't at all. It had vanished in a single Saturday.

Shame flashes through Grace and she pours more gin in her glass than she means to.

He tells her she can keep the couch and the coffee table. She wants him to take the kettle that doesn't whistle anymore, and his whisky glass, but is afraid if she opens her mouth either a jagged-edged sob or a torrent of profanities will take over, so she drinks her gin and tonic and says nothing.

When he walks into the bedroom, Grace steadies herself between the front door and the living room.

A jangle of hangers in the closet.

Grace wonders if he's going to take the hangers, too, or just his clothes. Either way, there'll be room now to bring the bin of winter clothes up from the basement and if there's still room, she can always hang up her T-shirts so the closet isn't empty.

"Have you seen my razor?" he asks from the bathroom.

She doesn't tell him she threw it out. He doesn't ask about his toothbrush.

Jamie moves to the kitchen next and stands in front of the fridge with the frying pan in his hand.

"It was from your mom," Grace says before he can even ask. She opens the cupboard and hands him his whisky glass.

"Thanks," he says and tucks it inside a toque.

When they first moved in together, they'd crank Motown every Saturday morning after they'd read the paper and clean together. Jamie would stop whatever he was doing and dance with her for *Signed, Sealed, Delivered*, then they'd walk to the market to get croissants, and come back and marvel at their clean apartment as if someone else had come and cleaned while they were gone. She didn't ever think they wouldn't be in love, though she can't remember the last time they had a Motown cleaning party. She can't remember the last time he stopped sweeping to dance with her, or kiss her neck, or reach for her hand—

She finishes her drink and the gin blurs the edges of the room.

He lifts a box of pots and Grace misses him so much her entire body aches.

"Are we going to talk?" she asks.

"Talk?"

"About this, about you leaving."

"I don't know what there is to talk about," he says, his voice sad and slow.

Everything, she wants to yell. Your unhappiness. Why you didn't say anything until it was too late. But the words stay stuck in her throat.

"I want you to be happy," he says and Grace wants to slap him, her palm erasing his mouth, his eyes snapping into focus—what does he care about her happiness? Her rage frightens her and she holds on to her elbows.

"When—" she asks, then steadies her voice. "When did you stop loving me?"

"It's not like that."

"You don't love me anymore. It started sometime."

"I don't know."

"At your work party?"

He shakes his head.

"At my parents'?"

"I don't know, Grace."

"You didn't love me then?"

"I didn't say that."

"Tell me when."

"I don't know."

"Is there someone else?" she asks. "It's Aarti, isn't it?" Aarti was his high school girlfriend. Well, high school and university. They broke up only because she left for grad school at Harvard. She's impossibly beautiful and has a PhD in biochemistry.

He shakes his head. "She's engaged."

"That doesn't mean anything."

Grace pictures Jamie and Aarti, with her glossy, shampoo-commercial hair in a fabulously styled condo with a white sectional and HBC blankets. Grace only met her once, at the thirtieth birthday party for one of Jamie's high school friends, but she used to check Aarti's Facebook page when it was public, open for anyone to sift through. Eventually she changed the settings and Grace only ever saw pictures of her if Jamie left his Facebook open—skiing in Vail, or in front of the Eiffel Tower, or from a *Harvard Magazine* article about women in tech where she looked glamorous somehow in a lab coat.

"There's no one," he says.

"And I'm supposed to believe you?"

"There's no one, Grace," he says again, and she knows that even if she did go through his inbox, his texts, his Facebook messages, she knows she wouldn't find anything.

"You left me then, for what? For no one?" And now she wants there to be someone, Aarti, or an impossibly perfect girl who knows how to walk in heels and blow-dry her hair. Someone who gets manicures and goes to the gym and does hot yoga.

"I went looking for engagement rings," he says, refusing to meet her eyes. "At first I thought it was just because I couldn't find the right ring and I went again a few days later, but—"

"But what?"

"I couldn't."

"You couldn't find one?"

"I couldn't do it," he says.

"You were going to propose."

"I thought it was what I wanted. I thought—"

"When?" Grace asks.

"Just before I went to visit Connor."

That was in February. "You've known since then?"

"I didn't *know*-know."

"You knew," she says, her voice a howl. "Jesus. So what were last five months, then?"

"I didn't know for sure," he says. "I wanted to want to be with you. I did. I thought this was it. I thought it'd be you and me, but I couldn't get a ring."

He didn't love her this whole time, not when they were in Saskatchewan in June, not when she went with him to his work barbecue. Not all those times she hung out at Hemingway's with his horrible high school friends. Not when he talked to her mom on the phone, not when they had sex—god, how many times have they had sex since February?

"I'm sorry I've hurt you. I really wish—"

"You're not fucking sorry. You're the one who fell in love with me," Grace yells, wishing he would fight back, swear, call her a bitch, yell, something. But that's not Jamie. Jamie is even, steady. "You said 'I love you' first. It was your idea to go on a second date, on a third. It was your idea to move in together. Your idea to come to Saskatchewan for Christmas that first year. It was all your idea." She hates herself for buying into his confidence, his assuredness. "You can't just up and leave after all that."

But of course he can. He's always been all in, or all out. It was his engineering brain, they used to joke, but Grace didn't think their relationship could be shut off like a switch, too.

He looks at the edge of the counter. "I'm sorry, Grace. I'm really sorry."

Grace always thought that he was incapable to lying, it's one of the things she loved about him, but it turns out he was a master of lying to himself. And now there's nothing to be done anymore.

It takes him four trips to fill the back seat of his mom's car with garbage bags of clothes, boxes of books, and the pots and pans.

"Bye, Grace," he says after he's taken down the last load. He opens his arm like he might hug her.

Sadness floods her limbs and she wants to collapse into him. It's so much work to hold herself up. It's so much work to just stand here. But then he sideways-hugs her, his arm around her shoulder like an awkward dad hugging a teenage daughter.

"Do you want to talk to Lana about taking my name off the lease or should I? I'm not sure if I need to be there, or if you can just do it," he says.

Grace refuses to answer and holds out her hand for the key.

She listens to his footsteps down the stairs, Lana's dog barking at the screen door opening, then closing. She stands on the balcony after he's driven off. The hum of the air conditioner drowns out the cicadas. A moth thumps against the door, its wings beating against the glass, desperate to get to the light in the bedroom.

"Go down to the streetlamps." They're big round globes that look like the moon. "Go. Go." She brushes it away from the door and over the edge of the railing.

He's gone, she texts to Jenna, and before she can type out anything else, Jenna calls.

"You okay?" she asks.

Grace sobs. She can't get the words out—*ring*, and *engagement*, and *gone*. She cries and cries and Jenna says she'll come over.

"No, no. I'm okay. I mean, I'm not, but I am." She manages to tell her everything—the frying pan, the whisky glass, the five months of not loving her.

"Fuck him," Jenna says. "What a fucking coward."

He is. He's a coward.

"He doesn't deserve you," Jenna says and Grace thinks for a split second that maybe she's right.

Just before she goes to sleep, Grace gets an email from Jamie with nothing in the subject line. She opens it, hoping for something, anything, but it's a forwarded email with the plane tickets, their seventh-anniversary trip to St. John's. All of her sadness and all of her grief is replaced with a deep, deep rage that spews out of her hot and molten.

"Fuck," Grace yells at the screen. *Fuck you*, she texts him. "Fuck you," she screams into his voice mail. Fuck you fuck you fuck you fuck you.

She calls Jenna back. "Newfoundland," she chokes out.

"Oh shit. Your trip!"

"What the fuck am I supposed to do?"

"See if you can exchange your flights," Jenna says. "Use them to go home, or we could go to New York in the spring, maybe?"

"Maybe," Grace mumbles.

"Or fuck, I'll come with you. Send me the dates, I'll try to get off work."

Grace calls Air Canada in the morning, but they won't let her change the name on Jamie's ticket, and the refund they offer won't even get her halfway to her parents' house in Saskatchewan.

"Fuck it," she says to her computer screen after she hangs up, and decides to use her ticket despite him, or maybe to spite him. She's already booked the time off and telling Janice her trip is cancelled would mean telling her about Jamie. She'll do it, she'll just go. Her first solo trip in years.

The next morning, she rereads the two letters Amelia wrote about Newfoundland and the line about it being beautiful *in a stark and barren sort of way* strengthens her resolve.

"You'll love St. John's!" Lucy promises. "Where are you staying?"

"A little B&B on, I forget what street, just up from the main downtown street." It was the first one that popped up when Grace Googled *St. John's accommodations.*

"You and Jamie are going to have the best time," Lucy says, and Grace doesn't bother correcting her.

7

Grace is surprised St. John's doesn't smell like the ocean, but is grateful that the oppressive heat of Toronto has been replaced by a cool, ever-present breeze. There's no beach in the city as far as she can tell, just a harbour on the far side of a twelve-foot fence and two docked tankers, huge and imposing. Grace knows nothing about ships, except someone, maybe her dad, once told her that there are highways in the water, and that there are still pirates.

The cobblestone sidewalks are steeper than she expected, and she walks up and down and up and down, her calves screaming. She passes a stretch of rainbow-coloured houses—turquoise and yellow and green and cherry red—that are called Jellybean Row. She turns right on Water Street, where the air still doesn't smell like the ocean, and walks by restaurants serving seafood pasta, pubs promising fiddle music, and tourist shops with twirling racks of postcards. Grace goes into one on the corner, a bell ringing overhead. There are boxes of maple fudge, towers of maple syrup cans, and bags of chocolate labelled Puffin Poop. There are baskets filled with stuffed moose and stuffed beavers. There is an entire wall of Mountie printed aprons.

Grace feels guilty for leaving without buying anything, so she picks up a tea towel with a silkscreened map of Newfoundland for her mom.

"A local artist makes them," the woman behind the cash tells Grace. Her accent is so lovely Grace wants to stay there for the rest of the afternoon.

"Bill in the bag or would you like it?" she asks.

"Bag is fine," Grace says.

The woman smiles and Grace lingers, hoping she'll ask where she's been and what she's seen, but the woman turns and straightens the tea towels.

It's only five—too early for supper and Grace still has a few hours to kill before bed. She'll charge her phone, then find some food, she decides, following Water Street for a while longer.

Grace sits at the end of her bed so she can see a glimpse of the ocean—a sliver of blue-grey in the corner of the window—while she eats a peanut butter sandwich and opens the wine she tried to chill in the bathroom sink.

She'd decided to splurge on lobster at a restaurant next to an Irish pub, but when it arrived with beady eyes and enormous claws, she realized she didn't know how to eat it. She ate the potatoes and the waiter eventually took pity on her and told her to use the nutcracker to break the shell open at the knuckle. She didn't want to think of lobsters as having knuckles, but he took the claw and cracked it open for her. The meat was red and white and delicious and she tried to do the same to the other claw, but her hands were slippery with butter and the shell wouldn't crack. Eventually, she gave up and asked for it to go.

It came in Styrofoam that Grace threw into a garbage bin on the walk back to Pat and Mike's B&B and she bought some bread and peanut butter at a corner store instead.

She knows if Jamie were here alone, he wouldn't let himself be trapped in this tiny potpourri-filled room. She feels pathetic, then feels the rage or grief—it's hard to tell the difference—trickling back in, like pins and needles down her arms and into her fingers.

She opens her email, half-hoping to see something from Jamie, but there's nothing from him, of course there's not. She takes a sip of lukewarm wine and opens an email from Lucy's cousin.

Anna hosts the weekend morning show on CBC and has sent a list of places to see, and restaurants to try, and offers to have her over for supper or happy hour, or take her for a hike along the East Coast Trail. A hike seems too ambitions, but Grace figures she could handle happy hour. It's just a drink—an hour, tops, she tells herself. And anything is better than sitting alone on this flowered bedspread eating peanut butter sandwiches with lukewarm wine. She writes Anna back. *Let me know if I can bring anything.* I, singular. It feels like the first time she's done anything alone in seven years.

The next afternoon, Grace heads up the hill from Pat and Mike's, practising what she's going to say if Anna asks why Jamie's not with her. She could say "Sorry, my boyfriend couldn't make it" and keep it vague so it's not clear if he couldn't make it tonight, or on the whole trip. Or maybe "Plans changed"?

Grace follows her phone's map to a little cul-de-sac. It's only a twelve-minute walk from downtown St. John's, but it feels like she's in the suburbs—a basketball in the centre of the road, towering trees that seem ancient, and flowers she doesn't know the names of climbing up trellises. These aren't the colourful wooden row houses from a few blocks away, though they are still wood, with siding and awnings stretching over front porches in striped green and white.

There's a note stuck to the screen door with masking tape. *Come around the side*, it reads in a messy scrawl.

"Hello?" Grace calls, poking her head around the back of the house.

A woman in a tank top, her red hair in an unravelling braid, sits at a picnic table, flicking through her phone, a wineglass next to her. Grace was expecting someone much older and more formal, more khakis than cut-offs.

"Grace!" Anna says, standing. "I'm so glad you made it!" She opens her arms and hugs her.

"Hi," Grace manages. She hasn't been properly hugged in so long it feels strange.

"Come, sit! I've got a white started, but there's red if you'd prefer. Or beer. I'm pretty sure Hugh picked up beer yesterday."

Grace didn't realize Anna had a husband, or that she had kids. Her eight-, maybe nine-year-old daughter April has a friend over and they play a game that involves jumping through a sprinkler and climbing up the rope ladder of one of those play structures every suburban backyard has. There seem to be rules and an order to the game, but Grace can't make sense of any of it. Anna's son, Marcus, is older, maybe twelve or so. He sits at the table with them, reading a book that seems way too complicated for a kid his age.

Grace braces herself to explain why Jamie isn't here, but Anna doesn't seem to notice. She pours them both wine and brings out a plate of cheese and crackers and homemade pickles.

"Where've you been so far?" Anna asks. "What've you done?"

She hasn't done much, but Grace tells her about climbing the hill to the fort she already can't remember of the name of, about getting lobster for supper, though doesn't say she didn't manage to eat it. She tells her about wandering along Water Street, and about stopping in at a pub with fiddle music, even though she didn't really stop in, and just heard it from the sidewalk.

"Okay, we'll get you a solid list," Anna says. "No more subpar lobster. There's a place that you just have to go to—Raymond's—they're probably booked solid until the new year, but you can usually get in for a cocktail, or sometimes to even eat at the bar. It's worth it. It's so worth it. Or—do you have a car?"

Grace shakes her head.

"Okay, well, if you do get a car, the Mallard Cottage is a good place, too. Oh, and you should go to Ferryland. It's not a far drive, but it's beautiful, and you can order a picnic. They bring one out to you. It's really just magical."

Grace takes notes on her phone, even though she's never rented a car by herself and isn't sure she should really be spending money on expensive meals out.

"Can we eat yet?" April yells from the sprinkler.

"There're snacks in the fridge," Anna says, but April insists she's hungry for supper. "Let me see when your dad's coming home," she says, checking her phone. "Fuck," she says, looking at the screen.

"Swear jar!" Marcus yells with clear delight.

"S-word or F-word?" April shouts.

"F-word!"

Anna rolls her eyes. "I'm going bankrupt with this goddamn swear jar."

"Swear jar!"

"Kid's going to buy a brand-new bike and I'm going to end up in the poor house." She winks at Grace. "'Kay, Hugh's not going to be home for supper, but you'll stay, won't you?"

Grace wants to object—it's too much. She barely knows Anna and April has a friend over, but Anna insists.

"You can make the salad," she says. "Marcus, see if there are any cherry tomatoes that are ripe."

Supper is loud and chaotic at the picnic table outside. April refuses to eat her salmon burger and makes a cheese sandwich, and her friend, in solidarity, eats both a sandwich and a salmon burger. Anna adds to Grace's list of things to do and see that she'll never get through— Shakespeare in Bannerman Park, a swimming hole just south of the city, a hike along the East Coast Trail that is filled with blueberries. "We went last weekend and we couldn't carry them home, there were so many. Oh, and you have to listen to *The Fisheries Broadcast*, right, Marcus?"

He rolls his eyes.

"It's the best—it's so Newfoundland. Whenever I'm travelling, I stream it on my computer and instantly feel like I'm home."

It's dark by the time they're done supper, and a second bottle of wine. The kids go inside and stars start to appear overhead.

Grace finishes her glass. "I should head back," she says, stacking plates.

"Don't worry about the dishes," Anna waves Grace off, but she carries as many as she can into the kitchen.

Hugh arrives home just as Grace is ready to leave. He's tall and looks exactly like Marcus, with sharp cheekbones and a face full of freckles. Anna kisses him hello and it's so easy, and so intimate, Grace's throat tightens.

"Hugh, Grace. Grace, Hugh," Anna says.

Grace makes herself smile.

"Stay!" he says, shaking her hand. "Any friend of Lucy's is a friend of ours!"

"I really should go," Grace says. "It's late."

"I'll run you home," he says.

"I'm really okay to walk. It's a nice night."

"No, no!" Anna insists. "Easy-peasy!"

She hugs Grace goodbye and Grace feels like she's known her for years, not the last four hours.

"Thank you," Grace says. The words seem too small for such an easy, wonderful night. "Thank you so much."

Grace follows Hugh to the driveway and climbs into the passenger seat. CBC blares out of the speakers before he has a chance to turn it down.

"Sorry," he apologizes. "I was waiting to hear if the story I was working on tonight was going to get a promo for tomorrow." He starts backing out of the driveway. "Where's your husband? He was coming, too, right?"

"Boyfriend," Grace says. "Ex-boyfriend." She hasn't said it aloud before now. "We—we broke up a few weeks ago. Well, that's not true. He broke up with me. He left." Her words are dull and heavy.

"Oh, shit, I didn't realize."

"It's okay. It's fine," Grace says, her heart thudding in her neck. "Well, no, it's not. It's not fine. I'm not fine. It came out of nowhere, and poof, seven years, down the drain."

"My god. I'm so sorry."

She should stop. She knows she should stop, but she can't. "We were supposed to be here for our anniversary and had planned everything we were going to do—Quidi Vidi Village, some old lighthouse, a place to kiss a cod and get screeched in, an art gallery I don't remember the name of—"

She talks until she runs out of words and the tick of the turn signal fills the space between them. Grace stares at the dark windshield, fighting the salt-sting of tears and wishing she could stuff all those words back in her mouth.

"I'm so sorry," he says, pulling up in front of Pat and Mike's. "If it's any consolation, Quidi Vidi Village is a total tourist trap and really isn't worth it."

Grace fumbles with her seat belt, hating herself for ruining the whole evening. She finally felt normal for a moment, but now she's back to being a pile of nerve endings.

"Thanks for the ride," Grace says, trying to keep her voice light. "And sorry, about, about all that."

She scrambles out of the car before she starts crying.

"It's really no trouble at all," he calls after her and waits till Grace is inside before pulling away from the curb.

8

The next morning, shame burns in Grace's throat. Why did she have to wreck the whole night? She sends a thank-you email to Anna. *And please tell Hugh I'm sorry. I'm fine, really.* And she will be today. Today will be fine. She will be fine, she tells herself, pulling her hair back into a tight ponytail.

Grace rents a car and tries to get a picnic at Ferryland, but they're booked all day, so she stares at the map Mike sent her with, the wind threatening to tear it from her hands. The highway goes all the way down to Trepassey, the place with the trout streams Amelia wrote about to Gene. Seeing the name of a town she recognizes feels like a good omen, so she decides to see it for herself.

Grace rolls down the window and sings along to Fleetwood Mac and tries not to be freaked out that there are no hydro lines, no telephone poles, and no bars on her phone. The ditches are filled with thistles and Queen Anne's lace and occasionally signs for worms and fishing licenses. Grace tries not to picture her little red rental car accordioned into a moose. She tries not to panic that she didn't pay extra for roadside assistance.

Before she left this morning, Pat made her promise to watch out for moose. "They'll total your car," Mike said before Pat shushed him. She called Grace "duckie" and told her to be safe. "Just keep an eye out," she said and squeezed Grace's arm. Grace thought they were being overprotective, but the highway is lined with caution signs that have aggressive moose silhouettes and she wonders if she should've stayed in the city. On some stretches, there are lights that promise to flash if there are moose nearby. Grace doesn't know if she can trust them or not, though, so she spends the drive scanning the shoulder of the road, wishing Anna had mentioned the moose before encouraging her to rent a car.

Grace chastises herself for forgetting her water bottle and eases the car off the highway at the first gas station she sees. Everything is covered in a layer of dust and the cans of Orange Crush in the unplugged cooler are ancient. She grabs a bottle of water and the guy behind the counter asks where she's going.

"Trepassey," she tells him, handing him a five-dollar bill.

"Named after the French verb, *trepasser*, to die," he says, counting out her change.

"Oh," Grace says, leaving behind the receipt and hurrying back to the car. Does "trespasser" really mean "to die"? She tries to look it up on her phone, but there's no reception.

Trepassey doesn't seem particularly dire when she passes the sign into town—there is a playground and a liquor store and pots of marigolds everywhere. She drives to the harbour and puts the car into park. She expected to see ropes tethering boats to long wooden docks, but there are no docks here, just a single fishing boat heading out to the mouth of the bay, the long finger of ocean that pushes its way into town—a narrow stretch of blue that would've been the runway for the float plane Amelia wasn't allowed to fly.

She keeps driving and finds a museum overlooking the harbour—a small house with peeling blue boards and a faded stencilled sign. The door is locked, but the windows are open, curtains slipping outside and licking the wind. Daisies grow in clumps around the perimeter and Grace is careful to step over them to look into the front window. All she can make out is a glass case of teapots and silverware.

Grace walks across the street to the post office to see if they know when the museum opens, but the woman behind the desk says it's not opening this summer. "They're going to move the whole museum down the road to a new building, but no one knows when," she says, moving a pile of envelopes to a plastic grey bin behind her. Grace turns to leave, but the man in line behind her asks where she's from. She doesn't really want to talk, but he's standing between her and the door and she can't leave without being rude.

"Toronto," she says.

"All the way from Toronto," he says, pronouncing the last *t*. "What brings you down here?"

"I'm doing some research," she says before she can stop herself. "About Amelia Earhart." It's not entirely true, but it's also not completely a lie.

"Oh, a researcher from the Big Smoke."

Grace shifts and offers an uncomfortable half-smile.

"Flew in on the *Friendship*, bright orange biplane, then got fogged in for days. Our fog is legendary, right, Norma?"

Norma smiles from behind the desk. "Sure is."

"My gran met her," the man continues. "She's gone now, otherwise I'd bring her over so you could interview her for your"—he waves his hand—"research. She went to the school up on the hill and she used to tell the story about how furious the nuns were that Earhart showed up wearing pants."

He says that while Amelia and the other two pilots waited for the fog to lift, Amelia would walk along the tops of picket fences with her arms outstretched. "She was quite the legend because of it. If you need any more information, I can give you my email."

"Thanks," Grace says. "It's just preliminary stuff for now."

But the man writes his name and email down on a scrap piece of paper that Norma hands to him. "Here you go." His name is Herb, according to his Hotmail address.

"Thanks," Grace says, folding it and putting it into her pocket. She feels guilty for lying, for letting him think she's a researcher, not just a library tech running away from her lonely Toronto apartment.

"Email me if you have any questions. I do know a lot about the area," the man says.

Grace wants to ask if there are trout streams nearby, but before she can, Norma tries to sell her on a place in town that serves a hot lunch. "You're going to be needing some food before the drive back," she says.

"I've got lunch in the car," Grace says. "But thank you."

Grace sits in the front seat of the car. It's quiet. So quiet. She debates for a moment going back in and asking about the restaurant, but turns the keys in the ignition and pulls back onto the one road that leads out of town. Just before it turns into the highway, Grace pulls over to the shoulder where there's a good view of a far-off lighthouse. There's a small, narrow beach, with ropes of kelp and shattered sea urchin shells. The beach isn't sandy but made up of tiny smooth stones that look like black sesame seeds.

Grace sits on a pile of driftwood and opens the paper bag Pat sent her with. No one's made her a lunch since her dad used to in grade school, and she's so touched by the corned-beef sandwich wrapped in waxed paper, the apple, the pair of Chips Ahoy cookies, she feels the burn of tears at the backs of her eyes. She blinks hard and stares at the horizon—it isn't as clear as it is back home on the edge of Lake Ontario. Here, the blues alternate light, dark, light, dark, and the top line is hazy.

She chews her sandwich and takes a picture of the beach with her phone. Jamie would insist on driving to the lighthouse if he were here. He'd want to meet the lighthouse keeper and see the light and ask how it worked.

She tries to shake him out of her head. This trip isn't about him. This is her trip. She crumples up the waxed paper and wonders if Amelia and Gene ever did come back to see the trout streams and eat the eggs that tasted like fish. She wonders if Amelia ever did collect the curling iron she left behind.

The edge of her sandal is wet and she looks down. There is water creeping up to the driftwood. The tide, she realizes, so used to lakes that she's startled, and even a bit scared of the moving shoreline. She doesn't want to leave, but she's afraid of how fast the tide will rise and, besides, she's terrified of driving that moose-filled stretch of road without cell service in the dark. She takes one more picture of the ocean, then climbs back in the car and turns on the local CBC station. A man with a thick accent reports on which licenses can catch turbot this week and she lets *The Fisheries Broadcast* carry her back to St. John's.

9

Grace sleeps through her alarm, and debates staying in, but she only has the rental car for one more day, so she gets dressed, and packs a raincoat, just in case.

As she's walking out to the car, Pat hands her a paper bag.

"A little lunch, duckie," she says.

"You didn't have to," Grace says.

"It's nothing fancy."

"Thank you."

"Where're you off to today?" Mike asks.

"I'm thinking I might drive up to Harbour Grace."

She did some research last night and read that when Amelia flew across the Atlantic from Trepassey, she was just a passenger because of those sexist jerk pilots who didn't believe a woman could fly, but when she crossed the Atlantic from Harbour Grace, just an hour from St. John's, she flew solo, which feels like a much more significant flight.

"Mike's dad has a cousin over in Bryant's Cove, on the other side of the strait," Pat says.

"Not much to see in Harbour Grace," Mike says.

He's right. Grace looked on the city's website last night and it looks small.

Pat shrugs. "Well, enjoy your day. Mind the moose."

Mind the moose, Grace repeats to herself in the car, trying to get Pat's accent right. "Mind the moose," Grace tells the steering wheel. She can hear the accent in her head, but it doesn't sound right when she says it aloud.

She puts her lunch on the passenger seat and asks Siri to find the fastest route. There's really only one way and Siri guides Grace out of St. John's, where the clouds hang low over the highway, the asphalt flanked by evergreens and shipping containers. The city is replaced by small lakes and ponds and gullies. Grace has never seen a gully before now, has never even heard the word, but they're everywhere—tiny little patches of water on the far side of the ditch.

It's another fifty kilometres before Siri will say anything, so Grace turns on the radio. The local station is having a Van Halen marathon.

"Right now, hey! It's not tomorrow," she sings out the open window, though she's not sure if those are actually the lyrics. It doesn't matter if they're right or not and there's no one to correct her.

Trees, lakes, moose signs, ponds, more gullies, and more Van Halen. The landscape looks way more like Ontario than she would've thought and the Atlantic feels a million miles away.

When Siri tells her she's arrived, Grace parks the rental next to a wood-panelled station wagon and crosses the damp grass to a statue of Amelia Earhart standing in front of an airplane that—Grace glances at the plaque—isn't hers. She reads the plaque at the foot of Amelia's statue—commemorating her being the first woman, and the second person, to ever fly solo across the ocean.

She's taller than Grace, her boots reach up to her knees, the laces criss-crossing up her shins. Her cheekbones are sharp, her jaw angular. The buttons on her coat are the size of quarters and she stands so easily, so patiently, as fog rolls in from the other side of the highway.

"She's a pilot, you know," a kid says, climbing onto the base of the statue.

Grace nods.

"Hannah, get over here," a woman yells to the pig-tailed girl. "I said get over here. I'm counting to five!" The mother counts but the girl doesn't move.

"She's dead now," the girl tells Grace. "Her plane crashed."

"I don't think they know what happened to her plane," Grace says.

"Well, they only make statues of dead people, so she has to be dead." The girl swings around Amelia's legs, making faces up at Grace.

The mom apologizes, yelling at Hannah to finish her lunch, but the girl refuses to let go of Amelia. Grace wants to come up with a retort, but she doesn't have one, and the kid is only six, maybe seven. It hardly seems fair.

Grace leaves the statue and crosses the parking lot to the visitor's centre. She tells a teenager with a *Welcome to Harbour Grace* shirt that she's looking for Amelia. "Earhart," she adds, and he hands Grace a binder with badly photocopied pictures tucked into plastic sleeves. In the first photo, Amelia's standing next to the Vega, her eyes dark circles from the bad copying job. The kids crowding around her have smile-shaped shadows instead of mouths.

Grace flips through the binder—Amelia standing on steps with a bunch of official-looking men in suits, Amelia signing a document, Amelia standing in front of her airplane. There's one where Amelia is wearing a pale blouse, her smile serene. She looks like a fifty-year-old socialite, not a thirty-five-year-old pilot about to fly across the Atlantic. Grace wonders if a summer student slipped the photocopy into the wrong plastic folder but when she checks the label at the bottom, it says it's Amelia. It says the photo was taken at the Cochrane Hotel. That must be where Amelia had the nap she wrote about in her letter, where she got her Thermos filled with tomato soup.

"Just west on Water Street, before the cemetery, but it's called Hotel Harbour Grace now," the teenager tells Grace when she asks. "Take a right out of the parking lot."

Grace is expecting something grand, something classy, but air conditioners shudder out of opaque windows and the lobby smells like smoke and old margarine. It's hard to imagine Amelia here, on the worn carpet, next to the cheap wallpaper, with the stink of rotting fish wafting in from the harbour.

The front desk is empty and there's a pair of older ladies with jiggling arms playing the VLT by the bar. The dining room is set with red tablecloths and laminated menus. Grace wants to see if they still serve tomato soup, but the restaurant is empty. She could just walk over to the kitchen and ask, but it's easier to imagine the soup than to hear they haven't served it in years, or, worse, have to eat her way through a bowl of watered-down Campbell's.

She knows it's not the Newfoundland way, but she slips out, ducking under the green awning, and gets back in the car.

Grace stops in at the Conception Bay Museum next—a must-see, according to the official Harbour Grace website. It's a red-brick building on the water that used to be a pirate fort. The first floor is all pirates and fishing paraphernalia—nets and sextants and maps. On the top floor, there's a whole room dedicated to the town's airfield. There's a leather flying coat that isn't Amelia's in a glass case, replicas of various instrument panels, a bunch of model planes suspended from the ceiling. The red one, Grace reads, was Amelia's. It looks sturdier than the biplane from Trepassey, but still more like a toy than a plane that could cross an ocean.

On the TV in the corner, Grace watches a man in coveralls spin the propeller of a plane and then the camera cuts to Amelia, standing bluish and tall, her cheekbones smoothed out by the film. She shifts her weight. She touches her lips with her fingers. The only sound is the VHS tape chugging forward and Grace is afraid it'll catch.

The wind picks up, licking the edge of Amelia's shirt, turning the collar of her coat in on itself. Her curls are blown back from her forehead, and she looks a lot younger than thirty-five. The propeller becomes a circle instead of a blade, and the video skips ahead to a bobbing landscape—the ground dark, the sky a few shades lighter. And then the plane—her Vega—cuts across the screen. The camera stays trained on its tail until there is no plane, only sky, and the scratch and dust marks of old film and Grace realizes she is holding her breath.

A teenager in a pioneer dress, with Converse on her feet, stands in the doorway. "Sorry, we're closing for lunch," she says, not at all apologetically.

"Oh," Grace says. "Okay." She wants to watch the tape again. Just once more, and she debates saying they've sent her from the University of Toronto, that she's doing research, but she can't handle the lie and she doesn't think the teenager would care anyway, so she leaves, and follows the teenager down the stairs, past the pirate display, and steps out onto the sidewalk.

Siri loops Grace around the city to Lady Lake Road, gravel crunching under the tires of the rental.

There's no parking lot, just a patch of scrubby grass and a few half-crushed Labatt Ice cans. Grace puts the car in park and grabs her raincoat. She'd expected the airfield would be paved but no, of course it's not. It's long and narrow and the grass has been cut recently. There's a plaque attached to a rock at the top of the airfield—*Amelia Earhart May 30, 1932*. The grass is soft with rain and dotted with clover—purple pompoms scattered throughout the green.

Grace pulls her phone out and checks the Wikipedia page she had pulled up the night before. It took fourteen hours and fifty-six minutes for Amelia to make it across the Atlantic and land in Northern Ireland. Almost fifteen hours before she set her plane down in a cow field that is now part of a golf course, where the fourteenth hole is named "Amelia's Landing." It seems impossible that you can putt on the same grass where history was made, but Grace supposes there are much stranger things happening on historical sites than golf.

She stands at the top of the airfield and pictures Amelia's Vega rolling down the green. She wants to run the length of it, but is afraid someone will see her, so she just stands and stares.

It starts raining, just spitting at first, and Grace shoves her phone in her pocket, but soon it's pouring and even with her raincoat, she's soaked before she gets back to the car. She sits in the front seat and eats Pat's bologna sandwich, staring at the rain-blurred field. It feels strange to be at the exact airfield from the video in the museum, this exact stretch of land she saw in black-and-white not even twenty minutes ago. It's strange to see what Amelia would've seen—the same treeline, Lady Lake just across the highway, the ocean close enough to smell. Grace pictures Amelia's riding boots tied up to her knees, like the ones on her statue, goggles pushed to the top of her flying hat. She wants to go back to the museum and wait until the teenager reopens it so she can again watch the Vega barrelling down the grass, its wings eventually catching wind.

Grace Googles *Amelia Earhart + St. John's* after she drops the rental car off and discovers there are newspaper clippings at the art gallery-museum-archive building that is made of glass and perched on top of a hill.

There's a whoosh of quiet as the door closes behind her and it smells comforting—like dusty paper and damp books. She waits for the librarian to finish up with another patron, an older man with a cane.

"Amelia Earhart, 1932 and '35, Trepassey and Harbour Grace," she whispers to the librarian when it's her turn.

The librarian is small and slight, with a sweater on over his collared shirt. Grace wishes she had thought to be bring a sweater, too. She should've known the archives would be cold. They always are. He hands her a pencil and tells her to have a seat. The room has the same big tables as the Fisher, old spines lined up on shelves, a jar of sharpened pencils at the front desk. Instead of looking onto traffic on St. George Street, there is a bank of windows that looks onto the harbour. Sun bounces off the water and there's a huge red-and-black tanker on its way in or out, it's hard to tell.

The librarian comes over to her table and hands Grace a plastic container with *The Western* written on the top and points her to the microfiche.

She should be better at threading the film than she is. The librarian hovers behind her and Grace's hands start sweating. "I'm okay," she says. "Just been a while."

"Careful with the edges," the librarian says.

I work at a rare books library, Grace wants to snap. I am responsible for handling cuneiform tablets—I can figure this out.

And she does, eventually.

The Western was a paper for the west side of Newfoundland—she can't imagine it exists anymore. She scrolls through the ads—tins of Gillett pure flake lye, gin pills for the kidneys—but she can't find anything about Amelia. Still, she jots things down on scrap paper, trying to look like an academic, until the librarian goes back to his desk.

She keeps scrolling until she catches Amelia's name under World News. The article calls her Mrs. Amelia Earhart-Putnam and says that she spent one night in St. John's before her Harbour Grace flight. Grace glances out to the harbour. She saw this too—walked the same steep sidewalks, maybe even saw the street with the brightly coloured houses. The article goes on to say that she made the Atlantic crossing *through storms, rain and fog.* That's it, that's all. She flicks through the Wikipedia page she's bookmarked on her phone and cross-references it. There is nothing in the microfiche about how part of the Vega's engine was on fire, that there was ice on the wings, forcing the plane into a tailspin, that Amelia barely righted it before crashing into the Atlantic.

Grace returns to the microfiche. There's a small square about historic storms in London, and *The Poultry Corner* with tips about keeping your goose and gander together over the winter, but nothing more about Amelia.

She winds the film back up and walks back to the front desk. "Do you know where she stayed when she was here?" she asks the librarian. "Which hotel it was?"

"Here?" he asks. "In St. John's?" It sounds like one word when he says it—*Sinjawhns.*

Grace nods.

"Don't think she was here," he says.

"In 1932, she stayed over before flying out of Harbour Grace," Grace says. "The article said."

He taps the end of a pencil on the desk. "I'll take a look, but I've never heard that before. We're pretty good at holding tight to any celebrity contact." He laughs.

Grace goes back to the microfiche and rethreads the film. She scrolls through the ads, the birth announcements, the *Farmer's Almanac* predictions.

The librarian comes over. "She didn't stay here. She was in Saint John, though—no apostrophe-s—in New Brunswick."

Grace looks at him.

"*S-T*, here. There, they spell it out—*S-a-i-n-t*. You wouldn't believe the number of people who get it wrong," he says.

"Oh." Amelia hadn't seen beach-less harbour, or walked past the Queen Anne's lace that grows just about everywhere, its leggy stems and tiny white flowers like a firework caught mid-explosion.

"But I found some photos you might like," the librarian says. "From that Harbour Grace flight." He loads up the film and leans back so Grace can take a look.

The first photo is labelled *Man standing between Earhart and photographer appears to be Newfoundland Prime Minister Richard Squires*. In the second photo, Amelia stands under an arched doorway flanked by two men in overcoats. All three of them are looking at the camera, but none of them are smiling. She looks stiff—tired of talking, maybe, or maybe impatient to get up in the air before the weather changed.

In the last photo, Amelia stands behind the propeller, hands in the pockets of her flight suit, easy, relaxed.

"Fun fact," the librarian says, "these were all taken by a woman. Uncommon in the thirties, as I'm sure you know. Elsie Holloway took over the portrait gallery up in Harbour Grace during the First World War. Quite a trailblazer herself. We have quite a few of her photos here.

"Oh, and I found a copy of a telegram, too," he says. "Not from

Earhart, but for her, from '27." He threads the microfiche and scrolls through until he finds it. "Here it is," he says, moving out of the way.

It's from George—GP from her letters, though according to Wikipedia, he was just her publicist when she was in Trepassey.

SUGGEST YOU GO INTO RETIREMENT TEMPORARILY
WITH NUNS AND HAVE THEM WASH SHIRT, ETC.—
STOP

"She got fogged in, didn't she?" the librarian asks.

Grace nods and likes that the librarian knows she'd know that.

"You know they have a museum," he says.

"I went down earlier this week," Grace says. "They're closed this summer."

"Not much there, anyway," he says, "though the lighthouse keeper is worth the trip. Lovely fella, been there for years. Dying art, the lighthouse keepers. The lighthouses are all automated now."

The librarian leaves Grace with the photos and the telegram and she goes back and forth between them. *Elsie Holloway*, she writes down on a scrap of paper, wishing she had thought to bring a notebook.

Grace skips past the formal pictures and stares at the one of Amelia next to her plane. She looks just to the left of the camera lens, her silk scarf around her neck in an easy knot. She is slightly taller than the wing behind her. The propeller is so big it stretches out of the frame and her Vega, a dull grey in the photo, but red, bright red, in real life—a beacon of bright against the overcast skies.

She sits with the photo of Amelia and her Vega until she's too hungry to sit at the table any longer, her stomach growling embarrassingly. When she finally gets up, the tanker ship has almost reached the edge of the harbour and the sun has disappeared behind a thick wall of clouds.

10

In the morning, Grace's window is thick with fog, the same fog that kept Amelia grounded in Trepassey for days on end. It's her last day in Newfoundland and Pat and Mike insisted over breakfast that she go up to Cape Spear. She was planning on going back upstairs and crawling into bed, but she can't admit to that, so she lets them call their cab driver friend, Bob, who drives Grace to the far side of the harbour and then up a set of switchbacks to the easternmost point of Canada.

Bob doesn't say much on the ride over, and it's a relief to be able to just sit and stare out the window without having to be cheery, or polite, or list off everything she's done on her trip so far.

"I'll wait here," he says, pulling into the parking lot behind a tour bus. "No rush."

"I can call you maybe, or find another cab back?"

"I've got a book," Bob says, patting the glove compartment. "Take your time."

The lighthouse is half buried by the fog, and there are a bunch of plaques Grace doesn't bother reading, and a pair of ancient-looking cannons three kids climb while their dad takes their picture. There is a fine rain suspended in the fog and Grace's raincoat isn't as waterproof as she thought. Her shoulders are wet as she walks to the fenced-off point—the easternmost edge of the country.

Grace stands at the edge, the rock face plunging down toward the Atlantic, the grass scrubby but somehow still growing. The fog is too thick to see the ocean.

This is the first trip in seven years where she is going to be the only one to remember everything she saw, everything she did. There won't be anyone to remind her of the smell of fish and freshly cut grass in Harbour Grace, the rain that pooled on the plaque with Amelia's name on it, Pat's bologna sandwiches, the salmon burgers at Anna's, the lobster she couldn't eat. This trip is hers, only hers, and the weight of it feels terrifying.

Somewhere below her, a gull screams. The fog is claustrophobic and she just wants to see the water.

Grace backs away from the edge and walks to the lighthouse gift shop, where a pair of tourists in matching yellow ponchos spin the postcard stand—jumping whales and icebergs and laundry hanging on a line. She picks out one with the Cape Spear lighthouse for Jenna and buys her dad a jar of bakeapple jam. She had it for the first time yesterday morning with one of Pat's scones and even though Pat said it was a berry, it tasted like apricots and honey.

Bob walks through the door. "Sorry, I've got to head back into town," he says.

"Sure, of course," Grace says. "Coming."

He ducks back out the door and Grace writes Jenna's address on the back of the postcard. She wants to write about Anna, and *The Fisheries Broadcast*, and Pat and Mike, and the gull screaming, the cannons that doubled as jungle gyms, the drive to Trepassey, the airfield in Harbour Grace—

So much fog! she scrawls and hands it to the woman behind the desk for a stamp. "It might take a while to get to Toronto, but it'll get there," the woman promises. "Canada Post might not be fast, but it is reliable."

The fog is even thicker when Grace leaves the gift shop, Bob's car buried in the far end of the parking lot.

"Sorry," Bob apologizes back in his cab, his lights on. "My daughter's not feeling too good and I've got to go pick her up at school."

Grace hadn't pictured him as a dad. "Of course," she says, buckling her seat belt. "Drop me off wherever."

He's more talkative on the way back to the city, telling Grace about his daughter, Alexis, his ex-wife, his dad who's still disappointed he's driving a cab and not fishing.

"Even gave me his boat, but what am I going to do with it? Cod's only just coming back and you've got to really love the sea to be out on it daily. Pair of boys got caught in the tides just last week and never came home. I can't do that to Alexis. I just can't."

He turns up the hill from Water Street. "Mike says you're leaving tomorrow."

Grace nods. It's the last night that she's "duckie" and no one knows anything about Jamie. She still has to pack, but agreed to go for a drink with Pat and Mike. They insisted no trip to St. John's is complete without a pint at The Ship—it was also on Anna's must-do list—and Grace doesn't feel like she can sit around in her room for the whole night.

"Ten's fine," Bob says when they pull up to Pat and Mike's.

"Ten?" A ten-dollar cab ride gets you three blocks in Toronto. They've been gone for hours.

"It's fine."

She gives him a twenty. "You stuck around," Grace insists, opening the door before he can give her change.

"All right then, I'll run you up to the airport tomorrow," he says.

"Okay," Grace says. "Thank you."

"Check, though, in the morning. Flight could be cancelled depending on the weather."

Even though she can't afford another night, Grace hopes the fog stays thick and impenetrable and grounds her plane.

The fog has lifted by the time Grace has packed her suitcase and settled up with Pat and Mike. She checks in too late to get a window seat, and her seatmate—a businesswoman in a blazer with a laptop that the flight attendants tell her to close before takeoff—is not impressed when Grace leans over her to watch the runway tilt, then disappear, the sky rushing up to fill the window. The plane swings east, over the city, with its roofs jammed up against each other and fences separating backyards. Even with the houses, it's still mostly trees and water.

It takes no time to climb through the clouds and reach the blue sky on top. The plane casts a smear of a shadow against the clouds underneath. Every now and then, there are gaps in the white, revealing green-and-brown squares—wheat? corn? Grace has no idea.

She flicks through the photos on her phone—the sesame-seed beach, the instrument panels at the museum in Harbour Grace, the row of brightly coloured houses, the thick smear of fog at Cape Spear. Grace goes through the in-flight movies, but realizes there won't be time to watch a whole movie, so she looks through TV shows and clicks on an episode of *Whose Line Is It Anyway?*

Midway through a sketch about pumpkins, Grace's ears pop and the pilot comes on and says they're starting their descent. But she's not ready to go home yet. She's not ready for this trip to be over. She holds on to the hope that the runways at Pearson will be full and they'll have to loop around the airport a few times before landing, around and around until the fuel almost runs out, buying her more time away from the life that is waiting for her in Toronto.

11

Everything is the same when Grace gets home. She doesn't know why she expected it to be any different, but she wants the apartment to feel transformed somehow. Other than the pile of mail, and the milk she forgot to throw out souring in the fridge, nothing is different—same couch, same ugly kitchen tiles, same dog barking downstairs, same bed—at least she made it before she left.

The muggy air fills her apartment and she cranks the air conditioner in the bedroom and turns on all the fans to swing their wide faces left and right and back again. She calls her parents to tell them she's home, knowing they'll be at the Legion playing bingo with Aunt Lorraine.

She calls the Thai restaurant up on Bloor, and when she gives them her number, they ask if she wants the regular.

"Yes, please," she says, grateful she doesn't have to make any decisions.

But when it arrives, there is way too much food. It was their order, hers and Jamie's, and now she's drowning in green curry and lemongrass chicken and tom yum soup. The missing floods her limbs and she suddenly wants to tell him about Cape Spear, and the supper at Anna's, about the man at the post office whose grandmother met

Amelia in Trepassey, and the band that played at The Ship on her last night, and how they said, "Wishing you calm seas and tight lines" at the end of *The Fisheries Broadcast*. But she can't.

We need to take a break from communicating, he texted after she screamed into his phone about the flights to St. John's. What he meant was, "Stop calling me. Stop texting me."

She texts Jenna instead. *I'm home.* She watches her phone, waiting for it to ding with Jenna's response.

She finishes the soup and starts washing the dishes.

Welcome back, Jenna texts. *Good trip?*

Grace starts writing about The Ship, Cape Spear, Bob, Anna, the *Broadcast*, but erases it and calls her instead. It goes straight to voice mail.

Sorry, watching a movie with Eric, Jenna writes back. *Talk tomorrow?*

After she takes a load of laundry down to the basement, Grace moves out to the balcony, where the air conditioner hums and the conversations of people walking up the street drift up to the second floor. It's still muggy out and even though it's nine o'clock, the August sun hasn't fully set. She leans back on the faux wicker and stares up at the oak leaves. The neighbour's tree must be a hundred years old, the branches shading most of their balcony. Her balcony.

She knows she should stay off Facebook—all the happy couples with their brand-new houses and their baby bumps and their trips to Europe, and she knows she shouldn't type Jamie's name into the search bar, but she does. She presses the return button.

He's updated his Facebook profile photo. It's the picture of him in San Francisco, the Golden Gate bridge stretching elegantly behind him. It was from the trip they took to see his brother, Connor, and he smiles under his Oakland A's hat, squinting into the sun. He's smiling at her. She takes a photo of the screen with her phone and sends it to Carolyn. *WTF*, she writes. *I took this photo.*

Dick, Carolyn writes back.

Grace stares at the computer screen and wonders if he's using the same photo on a dating app—the apps they used to mock their friends for using. But maybe he is on one now, it's not impossible. And who wouldn't want to date him? He's an engineer, he makes good money, he's objectively attractive. He has his stupid condo down by the water.

She debates creating a fake profile to look for him. *Do you think I should?* she texts to Carolyn.

TERRIBLE IDEA! she texts back. *STEP AWAY FROM YOUR COMPUTER. DO NOT PASS GO DO NOT COLLECT $200.*

Grace knows it'll undo her if she finds Jamie on OK Cupid, so she types *Harbour Grace Amelia Earhart video* into Google. The YouTube clip is washed out, even more than it was in Newfoundland, and Grace didn't realize the top of Amelia's head was cut off for the beginning of the film. She tries to turn the volume up, to hear what Amelia's saying, to hear her laugh twelve seconds in, but there is no sound, of course there's not, there's no colour, either—it was before sound and colour could be captured on tape. Grace wishes she knew if Amelia was nervous, or just impatient with the sun sinking and the weather so changeable.

The man in the Fokker jacket turns the propeller, spinning it around and around, tighter and tighter, and then there's the heel of Amelia's shoe as she climbs up into the cockpit of the Vega and she's off, wheels up, over the Cochrane Hotel and gone—

Grace watches it again. And then again. It's strange, watching these two minutes and six seconds here, on the balcony, not in the museum down the road from the airfield.

It's been four weeks and two days since Jamie left, but in the morning, time falls in on itself and the Band-Aid of St. John's and being called "duckie" in Pat's lilting accent rips off. Everything feels raw and Grace is alone with the loneliness that roils in her gut.

The air is humid and thick, and she starts sweating before the screen door slams behind her. One of her bike tires is flat, and it's too late to find the patch kit, so she walks to work, wishing for the hills of St. John's instead of the flat stretch of Harbord Street. In St. John's, every house near the harbour has a concrete anchor in the basement to make sure it doesn't slide down the hill in a big storm. Bob told her that on the drive to the airport. She thought he was joking and waited for him to wink in the rear-view, but he didn't. She can't imagine living in a place where the winds are so strong they could drown a house in the harbour.

Grace is waiting to cross the street when it hits her again—Jamie's gone. And she is a house sliding down the hill.

The moment she sees the huge concrete peacock, her limbs feel instantly lighter. She's relieved to be back where there is structure and routine and to-do lists. She's even looking forward to the pile of indexing she didn't get to before she left.

The elevator door is almost shut when Janice calls for Grace to hold it. Grace really wanted to take the ten-second trip in silence, but her hand is already holding the doors open.

"You're in early," Janice says, shoving her umbrella in her purse. She asks how Newfoundland was and Grace gives her the Coles Notes—lobster, ocean, coloured row houses, the moose signs. She doesn't mention Trepassey or Harbour Grace. She doesn't mention going alone.

"And now, back to the letters," Janice says conspiratorially. "Send me a few synopses by the end of the week."

The door of the elevator opens to the reference desk.

"Sure, of course," Grace says, wanting to get back to her desk and reread the Trepassey letter again now that she's seen that long finger of ocean pushing into town, the Harbour Grace letter, too, to see if there was anything about clover growing on the airfield.

As soon as it's quiet, Grace pulls out the cardboard box from her filing cabinet. Trepassey was stark and barren in a beautiful sort of way. The accents *were* wonderful. *I was there. I saw it, too*, she thinks. She pulls out the next envelope, thick, cream-coloured paper, and is careful to mark where she pulled it from with a slip of paper.

Dear Gene,

*That was a most wonderful Saturday. It truly could not
have been more perfect, even with the rain.*

Let's do it again, shall we? The weekend of the 24th?

A.E.

Their love seems so clear, so clearly encompassing, it makes Grace's heart ache against her ribs. She and Jamie never wrote each other letters, not once. Emails, in the early days, and texts, sometimes a heart or a smiley face at the bottom of a grocery list, but that's it.

Grace glances at the framed photo of her and Jamie on her desk. It's from her parents' farm in Saskatchewan and the blue sky stretches endlessly above them. She angles it away so she can't see it and turns to her computer to look up a photo of Gene. There's an ease to his stance—one hand in a pocket, a huge smile—and Grace can almost see him breaking out into laughter.

She's got three more minutes before her retrieval shift, so she pulls another letter out.

Dear Gene,

*I'm sorry we got cut off. I don't know what happened there.
You were asking about the* Friendship. *Everyone made such
a big deal about it, but I really just sat there like a sack
of potatoes. The view was lovely, but I didn't get to fly at
all. And after we landed, all anyone wanted to talk to me
about was what I'd packed (very little obviously—a pair of
scarves and a toothbrush) and what I wore (Major Worley's
fur-lined suit, though that wasn't glamorous enough for the*
New York Times*). Bill and Slim despised me afterward for
all the accolades I got for their work. It didn't matter that I
told every single reporter that I hadn't flown the plane, that
they had. After the parade back in New York, I never saw*

either of them again. (I've never told anyone this, but just before we took off, I found hooch stashed in the cockpit that I poured into the ocean. And Bill thought he was a better pilot.)

People often ask if I was scared (who has time for that?) but no one asks me what the best part was. The best part of that entire trip was visiting Toynbee Hall. It's what the Denison House is modeled after. I got to meet all the kids and speak with Maude, who was running it at the time. It made me miss the Denison House and though it seems silly now, I actually thought I was going back to them at that point. I had no idea what was waiting for me when the ship arrived back home.

I still miss those kids, though some of them won't be kids anymore. I wonder if Farrah ever figured out long division? I wonder if Deming still plays basketball? I wonder if Adil's parents ever got their money back from their horrible landlord. I know it sounds crazy, but sometimes I feel like I have a parallel life. In it, I'm still at the Denison House, in my room on the top floor, organizing basketball tournaments and helping conjugate verbs and writing referral letters. I'm driving to the beach on the weekends, and having bonfires and shucking oysters and digging for clams. Taking the odd plane up for a toodle. Money doesn't matter, reporters don't matter. Those were some of the best days of my life. I miss them.

I keep wanting to stop in and say hi the next time I'm in Boston, but it'd end up being such a to-do, and then they'd have to spend all this time wrangling press and photographers and reporters, and it'd be a burden for them that they just don't have time for.

I'll send a note, and a check and keep missing them from afar, I guess.

I should sign off before this becomes a tome.

Love,

A.E.

Letter from Amelia Earhart to Gene Vidal, Grace types into a Word document. *Reflections on the* Friendship *flight, her visit to Toynbee Hall and her time at the Denison House.* But she has no idea what either of those places are.

She glances at the clock. She's late, so she tucks the letter back into the box, careful to lock the drawer, and rushes to the reference desk.

"Sorry," she says to Jeremy, taking the chits he's collected from the reading room. "I'll go and get these."

She takes the elevator to the sub-basement and pushes a book truck to the Banting and Best papers. She loads up the truck with boxes forty-three through forty-six, then pulls out her phone and looks up Toynbee Hall and Denison House. They were settlement houses, created in London and Boston to counter systemic poverty in largely immigrant communities and provide social and educational programming. Amelia was a social worker at the Denison House before her flight in the *Friendship* and Grace imagines her crouching next to a kid, trying to figure out math questions. She pictures her in a gym, ref-ing a basketball game. It's strange to think of Amelia as anything but a pilot—

"Grace?" Lucy comes around the corner of the stacks.

"Oh, hey," Grace shoves her phone in her pocket.

"Abigail said if I ran into you to let you know there's a big request from some lit prof."

"Okay. Thanks for letting me know," Grace says,

Lucy pauses. "Are you okay?" she asks, her face sad and expectant.

Fuck. Anna and Hugh must've said something. But she can't go there right now. She can't open up that door, that Jamie-sized door. "I'm fine," she insists. "Great," she adds, and pushes the box-filled cart toward the elevator.

12

When Grace admits she's been mostly eating peanut butter sandwiches, Jenna and Eric start bringing food over—Tupperware filled with homemade pasta, and lasagna, salads from Eric's garden, with dressing tucked in tiny mason jars, once even an uncooked pizza on a cookie sheet with instructions about oven temperatures and baking times. It's all so lovely and kind it makes Grace weep while she eats, on the couch, with a glass of wine, or two, or more, she doesn't bother keeping track, watching old seasons of *The Office*. It's strange, eating alone, but she's getting used to it and each day Patrick remarks on how delicious her lunches look.

She needs to tell her parents about Jamie, but every time they talk, she manages to dodge it, and she throws herself into work, going in early and staying late. She writes synopses for Amelia's letters about her job as a gravel-truck driver, and the auto-mechanic course she took in her early twenties, and the oil geyser she took photos of in California. The more letters she reads, the more amazed she is by Amelia's independence, her insistence on working, on defying cultural norms. Even now getting married and having kids is expected, and it would've been especially so in the twenties and thirties.

One morning, Lucy is also in early and stops her in the staff room to ask her for help with a new project. Usually Grace loves working on Lucy's projects—it's a break from the monotony of the reading room retrievals–reference desk circuit—but she'd rather be working on Amelia's letters. Janice said she had to keep up with her usual tasks, though, so Grace locks Amelia's letters in her filing cabinet and starts sorting through the bequeathed papers of a famous botanist—everything from mail, to half-filled-in tax forms, to early publications, to the most delicate drawings of prairie plants. She separates the manuscripts from the first editions, the letters from the printed-off emails.

She clears her desk and sorts through forty years of Christmas cards, then starts in on the photos. She organizes them like she's playing solitaire—all of the photos from 1949 in a line, all of the 1950 photos in another. By the time she hits the mid-sixties, the botanist's face begins to rise through all the strangers'. A long, narrow face, with light hair that was braided at first, then mostly short, getting lighter and lighter as the photos move from black-and-white to colour.

Every year for the last seven, Jamie made Grace a red velvet birthday cake. It started as a bit of a joke—Grace mentioned in passing that she'd never had one and Jamie took it as his personal challenge to make her one, and then it was a thing. But when she wakes up on her thirty-third birthday, Grace realizes that she doesn't miss the red velvet cake at all. That, in fact, it was a gesture that was more about Jamie than it was about her.

"Fuck red velvet cake," she says to her reflection in the bathroom while she brushes her teeth.

When Grace's parents call to wish her a happy birthday, she opens the package they sent, slicing the tape open with a steak knife to find a new pair of goggles, a book with inspirational quotes, and a jar of her dad's pickled carrots.

"Thank you!" she says.

"Happy birthday, sweetie," her mom says back.

Before she can psych herself out, she takes a deep breath and tells them about Jamie.

"Oh, Gracie," her dad says.

"But you two just got back from Newfoundland," her mom says.

Grace hates that she lied to them by omission, but she still can't tell them she went alone. She leaves the timeline vague.

"Everything seemed fine when you were visiting in June," her mom says.

"I thought so, too," Grace says.

"Well, what happened, then? He was just, well, so even and steady," her mom says. "He must've had some sort of breakdown or something—"

"Mom, he didn't have a nervous breakdown," Grace says.

"It just seems so unlike him—"

Her mom offers to come for a visit, but Grace doesn't have the energy to entertain her. She tells her she's okay, that work is busy and keeping her occupied, that Jenna and Eric keep sending over supper.

Her mom tells Grace about her aunt's fiancé, the one before Uncle Richard, who left her days before their wedding. "And look at her and Rich, so in love. Still, after, what, twenty-nine years now. Almost thirty. That wouldn't have happened if she had stayed with Ed."

I don't care about some years-ago guy named Ed, Grace wants to tell her, but instead she checks her email and flips through Facebook, letting her talk until she tells Grace she loves her.

"We both love you, Gracie," her dad says. "Happy birthday, kiddo."

"Let us know if you need anything."

"Actually, do you have Nan's potato salad recipe? I'm going to make it tonight."

After she hangs up, Grace walks down to the fancy butcher in Kensington Market and gets hot dogs, then makes her nan's potato salad recipe. "Don't forget the pickle juice," her mom said when she read out the recipe over the phone. "Those three tablespoons make it or break it."

Jenna and Eric come over in the late afternoon and help Grace rearrange the furniture in the living room and carry the broken kettle and a box of books Jamie didn't take with him down to the curb.

"It looks so much brighter in here," Jenna says. It does look different, and a little more like hers, with a blown-up photo of Jellybean Row hanging in the living room.

Grace pours them each gin and tonics and they eat out on the balcony. The potato salad tastes just like her nan's, and her dad's pickled carrots are delicious, but she burns the hot dogs on the barbecue.

"They taste like campfire," Eric insists. "If they're not a bit burnt, why bother."

"I told my parents finally," Grace tells them and they all clink glasses.

"And? How'd Cheryl take it?" Jenna asks.

"Not great, but not the worst. I was expecting tears."

"From you or her?"

Grace laughs. "Her. But they were okay. And I'm just so relieved it's done!"

When Eric takes their glasses in to make another round of G&Ts, Jenna asks about her trip. "We just got your postcard!"

"It was great," Grace says, willing herself to leave out the lonely parts.

"Your pics on Facebook were amazing."

"I met up with a coworker's cousin and she gave me this great list of things to see."

"And you rented a car!"

"It was her suggestion. I'm glad I did. It's really beautiful there." Grace almost mentions Amelia, but Eric comes back out, the screen door slamming behind him.

He hands her a G&T and Grace wonders how Amelia used to celebrate her birthday. With a solo flight somewhere over the Midwest, or a trip to the ocean, maybe.

An ice cream truck rolls slowly up the street, its song tinkling up to the balcony.

"Should we?" Grace asks.

"Um, that is not even a question. Of course we're getting ice cream," Jenna says and Eric runs down and gets them all chocolate dips.

A few days after her birthday, Grace is in the middle of Season 4 of *The Office* when her phone buzzes. Jenna, she figures, or maybe Carolyn, but when she glances at her phone, she sees Jamie's name.

You around?

Grace almost takes a screenshot and sends it to Jenna, but then remembers she's out with a client.

Yah.

Can I pick up my bike stuff? The pump and patching kit. It's in the closet.

Grace didn't think there was anything left of his after Eric and Jenna helped carry the last of it to the curb on her birthday. *Ok*, she writes back.

I'm out front. I don't want to ring the bell.

Here already? Jesus. She pauses Michael Scott mid-rant and doesn't let herself think as she heads downstairs to open the door. August is leaning toward fall and the evening air is cool as she lets him in.

"Hey," he says, his bike helmet under his arm.

"Hey."

The landlady's dog barks as Jamie follows her up the stairs. Then Jamie is in her apartment. It's strange and disorienting.

"Should I—?" he gestures at the closet door.

"Yah, go for it," she says. Her words feel self-conscious and she stands awkwardly in the living room, embarrassed by the empty tube of Pringles on the couch.

He pulls a small box down from the top shelf. "Sorry, I forgot it was here."

He's gotten a haircut and is wearing his grey Adidas T-shirt, the same T-shirt he wore the day he left. Does he know that? No, of course he wouldn't think of that.

He stands there with the box in his hands and Grace expects to feel the flush of rage fill her limbs, but it doesn't come. She stands there without the prickles of tears or the flood of anger. She feels stronger than she has in weeks. It's just Jamie, with helmet hair, and a hole in the shoulder of his shirt. He seems smaller, like he takes up less space.

She shouldn't, she knows she shouldn't, but she asks anyway. "Do you want a beer?"

"Okay," he says.

They sit on opposite ends of the couch, and don't talk about everything falling apart, or about Jamie's new condo or Grace's trip. She doesn't even know if he knows she went to Newfoundland. He wishes her a happy belated, but doesn't ask what she did. Instead, they talk about his brother's new girlfriend, and the bike lanes that are going up on Bloor Street. They drink beer, and then have another, and Grace feels mature, being able to drink beer with her ex.

She has a flash of Jamie sitting next to her at Wrigley Stadium, beaming over his Carlos Peña jersey. She remembers the look on his face when he stood waiting for her on her porch when they were first together, with a brand-new bike after hers was stolen, a bow tied to the handlebars. She wonders if he remembers that.

She's never understood how exes could be friends—she always thought there'd be too much hurt, and too much history, but sitting here, with her legs tucked underneath her, she realizes there's something comforting about sitting with the person who knew her from twenty-five to thirty-two. He witnessed her last seven years and there's something reassuring about it.

It's getting late, and she knows he should go, but it's so nice to finally just talk instead of crying or yelling that she pours them shots of pumpkin spice vodka someone brought over as a joke gift, and then they drink what is left of the scotch his stepdad gave him for Christmas last year.

"It's late," he says, and stands.

She nods and walks him to the door. She feels a trill travel up from the pit of her belly, and then they are kissing, hard and hungry, and she is taking off his shirt, and her shirt is off, and they are still kissing as she walks him backward to the bed.

Everything is blurry, like a film in fast motion, and familiar, his body is so familiar, so here, right here, her hands on his shoulders, she knows these shoulders, and the only thing that matters is his mouth on her neck, on her belly, her body rising to meet his.

He doesn't stay the night, which makes Grace angry at first, but she knows she couldn't have handled having coffee like they used to. She knows it'll be easier to get on with things if he's not there in the morning.

She wakes up with a raging hangover. Fucking pumpkin spice vodka—what was she thinking? She climbs into the shower and before she has time to replay last night, she vomits on the floor of the shower. She lets the water pound against her eyelids until the hot water runs out.

She texts Jenna, who responds with the wide-eye emoji. *You okay?* she writes.

Yah. Shockingly.

You sure?

I mean, it was a little sloppy. She really hadn't thought she'd ever kiss him again, let alone sleep with him, and keeps expecting to feel remorse, or regret, but she doesn't. She doesn't feel rage either. She wishes she hadn't been so drunk, but also knows it never would've happened if she had been even slightly more sober.

Maybe this is the closure you needed, Jenna texts.

Yah, Grace writes back. And she thinks maybe it is.

13

Grace replaces the photo of her and Jamie on her desk with a photo from Newfoundland—the big, huge sky, the never-ending ocean, the tiny slip of a lighthouse in the distance. Abigail notices and asks if Grace wants to go for lunch, but there's no way she's going to get into everything with her again, so she makes an excuse about having to do some retrievals for Janice.

"It's for an upcoming thing," Grace says. "Some RCMP flying thing."

"Well, I'm here if you ever need to talk," Abigail says, her head tilted and her eyes hungry for gossip.

Grace hopes no one else can hear their conversation, but Patrick is bent over the spine of an old book, and Janice's door is half closed. Jeremy is at his desk, but he's got headphones on.

Grace nods. "Thanks," she says, and wishes she hadn't gotten wasted and told Abigail about Jamie. Now that she's told her parents, she could make it more public. But no, she doesn't want everyone at work feeling sorry for her. *Separation of church and state*, she thinks, and takes Amelia's box down to the sub-basement, where she can read letters without being interrupted. She sits between the stacks with Lucy's new acquisitions—tiny handmade books by a local poet. The books are fragile, their spines all greens and blues and muted purples, like lined-up Easter eggs.

She flips through the letters she's read, and finds a few she hasn't. There are three more complaining about the lecture circuit, and another short one about changing Saturday plans to Sunday. And then Grace finds one about Toronto. She scans the first line again in case she misread the looping handwriting, but no, it definitely says Toronto. She feels a hum behind her breastbone, the way it does when someone famous has a tie to the city.

Dear Gene,

I had a really vivid dream last night but all I can remember now is that I was in Toronto. Have you been? I'm guessing probably not. Pidge went to school there for a while, and I was there in 1917 for a couple of years. It wasn't the best time to visit (that's an understatement. They were deep into the War, with soldiers training and heading overseas, and coming back wounded, if at all. The War was barely an idea in Boston, but it was in full swing in Canada). Some parts of being there were horrific. Some parts I still cannot bear to remember. (Oh, the screaming, howling, the pain, the nightmares the soldiers had. They still haunt me.) But there were lovely parts too—strange how that works, isn't it?

It was frightfully cold that first winter, but the skating was wonderful. I had a beau up there (was he really a beau? I don't know. We didn't talk much about it. It was too strange to talk about "love" when we were surrounded by so much horror) and he took me to hockey games, which were marvelous.

It's where I first saw a plane. I know much has been said about that red plane I saw during the Exhibition, the red plane that—what did I write in The Fun of It?*—*

"whispered in my ear" as it dove for the crowd, then pulled up. There are a bunch of those "formative moments" that people, journalists, etc., want to hang on to. Like the roller coaster Pidge and I built in our backyard in Atchison. They like to say that the feeling of flying on that rickety apple box set me on my course forever, and it's not to say it wasn't fun, but we also built a carousel that summer, and put together the bleached-out bones of a cow skeleton, and built a lean-to out of branches and moss that I tried to sleep in overnight. So yes, I built that roller coaster, but it's in the story because it fits the narrative. Maybe if I were a doctor, the cow skeleton would be the childhood story everyone would tell. (Or if I had joined the circus, the carousel one!) But that red plane in Toronto really did speak to me.

It wasn't easy to get to, but after that, with any free time I had, I'd go up to the airfield north of the city. They wouldn't let me in a plane, of course, but it just felt good to be around them. Their hum, and roar, the spinning propellers, how the pilots would swing their legs up and over to get into the cockpit. I hadn't done it yet, but I knew exactly how it would feel to scramble up a wing, to spin a prop, to swing my leg up and over.

All this to say, I realized this morning that I want to go back. I want to see it without all the hospitals and soldiers with missing limbs. I want to wander through the university campus without the tents set up for the air force. I want to wander by the lake—it's on a lake, did you know that? I had no idea until I had been there for a few months!

It's strange, isn't it, all the places we keep close, even though it's been years sometimes since we've been there.

Love,

A.E.

Toronto. This is where Amelia fell in love with flying. This is where it all started. Grace flushes with a combination of excitement and pride and she can't believe she hadn't thought to look it up before.

She Googles *Amelia Earhart + Toronto + hospital* and finds a photo of Amelia dressed up as a nurse's aide. She scrolls down and discovers the hospital Amelia worked at is just south of the library. Grace locks up the letters and walks into the early September heat without telling anyone where she's going. Toronto. She was here. Amelia was here, walking on these very same sidewalks. Grace walks west on Harbord, then south, to the building that splits Spadina Avenue like a rock in a river. This was Amelia's Toronto, except instead of nervous first-year engineers painted purple following a guy with a trumpet and the smell of 7-11 hot dogs, there were First World War soldiers who hadn't mastered walking with crutches or the turn of a wheelchair wheel.

The imposing, Gothic building isn't a hospital anymore. It hasn't been for years. It's been under construction forever, the ivy stripped off the brick now and circled in a chain-link fence. According to the sign tied to the fence, it's going to house the Architecture Department when they're done with it. Grace stands in front of the fence and watches a digger claw at the ground.

This is where Amelia worked ten-, twelve-hour shifts, according to Google.

Grace knows it's crazy, but down here, even with the bulldozers and the excavators, Amelia feels close by, like she could run into her on the sidewalk, or maybe see her turning down Willcocks Street, her long strides, her arms swinging.

A biplane that looks like it has no business still being in the air shoots straight up into the sky, leaving behind an arrow of smoke. It peaks then goes tumbling down toward the lake, spinning over itself, engine off. Grace holds her breath until the pilot pulls upright before hitting the water, the trail of smoke like a peal of laughter. People clap, and Grace reminds herself to breathe.

The air show marks the end of the summer in Toronto. She hasn't ever been, but Jenna and Eric are in Sudbury visiting family, and the pool is closed for Labour Day, and she couldn't stand to spend the day at home, so she biked down to the water and found a small patch of grass, the highway grumbling behind her. There are risers set up right in front of the water, but they're blocked off for air show VIPs. She's definitely not one of them, with their Tilley hats, and sunglasses clipped on top of their normal glasses, and multi-pocketed shorts. They carry binoculars and fancy cameras and wear T-shirts from other air shows.

This is where Amelia fell in love with flying—right here on the edge of Lake Ontario during the Ex. Maybe even right here, where Grace is sitting. The lake stretches out blue and peaked with whitecaps, as another biplane flies straight up in the sky.

There's a lull in the sky, and then the ear-splitting roar of the Snowbirds.

Everyone lifts their hands like visors over their eyes, squinting, searching the sky for the nine planes that rip the sky open with a roar that comes instantly from everywhere. They are angry-looking, these jets, all angles and sharp corners as they split off, each veering into its own corner of the sky.

Two planes come roaring back—Grace sees them before she hears them—low over the water, so low she thinks she might be able to see the pilots. One of the planes is upside down, its wheels sticking up into the sky like a dog playing dead. It can't be more than a few feet from the other plane.

Do the pilots even bother looking down at the Ex, with its rickety roller coasters and Ferris wheel and whack-a-mole booths? Do they see the lake, or all the Tilley hats lined up along the edge of the water, the ribbon of Lakeshore Boulevard separating the fairgrounds from the lake?

Six of them shoot across the sky in a diagonal line, then fan out like overlapping playing cards, reorganizing near the CN Tower. It's like synchronized swimming, except with planes instead of sequined bathing suits. They split off like falling tulip petals, drooping back toward the earth. They dip down over the lake, then shoot straight up into the blue, all six of them disappearing like shards of glass glinting in the sun, leaving behind their signature thunder.

14

Grace sits on the bathroom floor. She's been tired, so tired, but it's been rainy and October has been grey and miserable, she blamed it on that, but she stares at the pregnancy tests lined up like pencils on the first day of school. Positive, all of them.

She missed a period, but figured it was just stress and didn't think much of it, but then she still didn't get it, so she bought a pregnancy test just for peace of mind. When the first one was positive, she didn't believe it, so she bought six more. And now there are seven tests lined up on the bathroom tiles—far too many blue plus signs in tiny plastic windows for it to be a false positive.

Pregnant. The word is so strange. She always thought her Grade 9 gym teacher was exaggerating when she told Grace's class that it can take only one time—the night Jamie came over to get the box full of Allen keys and inner tubes. Getting pregnant on one night of breakup sex—what are the odds? One in a thousand? One in a million? It was one night and the sex wasn't even mind-blowing. It was drunk and sloppy, and now she's pregnant. Except pregnant is what responsible people are—women with mortgages and blazers in their closets and wedding rings. She's thirty-three, a library tech. A single library tech, for god's sake, with crappy Honest Ed's pots and a dresser full of worn-out jeans.

She climbs into the shower, staring at her belly, which has never been flat, but also doesn't look any different. Or does it?

She closes her eyes and lets the water pound against her eyelids.

Grace sits in the doctor's office, staring at a sailboat mobile above the examining table. The green boat twirls every time the door opens or closes. Grace focuses on the sailboats, trying not to panic about the wine she had last week with Carolyn and that other night a month ago when she went over to Jenna's place and Eric made enchiladas and she drank margaritas until she was too drunk to bike home.

The doctor walks through the door, holding Grace's chart to her chest. The green boat spins.

"Congratulations!" she says, beaming.

Grace's stomach bottoms out like she's jumping off a diving tower, limbs suspended and flailing, every thought eclipsed by the roar of falling.

"And the lucky dad?"

"He'll be thrilled," Grace lies.

Dr. Lavin doesn't say anything about termination, and assures Grace the wine and the margaritas were fine—"It happens all the time before women know they're pregnant," she says. She tells Grace to take folic acid and avoid alcohol and drugs and raw cheese and deli meat and Grace nods, letting the advice wash over her, trying to maintain the face of a happy mom-to-be.

"Are you nauseous at all?" Dr. Lavin asks.

Grace nods. "It just started," she says. She woke up yesterday feeling carsick and hungover all at once, and ended up vomiting next to one of the leafless cherry trees by the library.

"It'll pass," Dr Lavin says. "Call the office if it gets to be too much and I'll send over a prescription."

The linoleum tile squeaks under Grace's boots as Dr. Lavin gives her a referral to the OB who delivered both her kids and hands her a stack of pamphlets.

"Remember the folic acid," she says. Every boat on the mobile twirls as she leaves the room.

The receptionist congratulates Grace on her way out and Grace stuffs the pamphlets about breastfeeding and SIDS and miscarriages in her backpack. Outside, the skies are still grey and Grace sits on a bench next to an elderly man with a schnauzer. The dog sniffs her boot and the man eats a bagel, sesame seeds spilling on his legs like confetti. Grace stuffs her gloves in her pocket and pulls out her phone, scrolling through the As, the Bs, the Cs until she gets to the J's. *Jamie.*

"I'm pregnant," she'll say. Or maybe "Remember when you came over for your bike stuff?" Or maybe she should ask him how he is and when he asks her, she'll say, "Fine, and pregnant."

She stares at his name until the letters don't make sense anymore, then slips her phone back into her pocket. It's not a baby. It's barely an idea. It's not even a fetus yet, just a lentil-size bunch of cells collecting somewhere under her belly button. It's just a little blue plus sign on a pregnancy test. That's it, that's all it is.

The schnauzer puts his paws on the edge of the bench and the man gives him a piece of his bagel.

It's like one of the Choose Your Own Adventure books she used to read as a kid—turn to page fifty-six for the cells to turn into a baby, turn to page thirty-four for the cells to disappear.

Grace can't keep herself from calling Jamie when she gets home.

"Hello?"

"Hey," she says. "How are you?" She plays with the corner of the *NOW* magazine she picked up on Bloor.

He pauses, like he's waiting for her to scream at him. "Fine," he says. "You?"

"Fine," she says and there's a window—a "fine and pregnant, six weeks along and peeing seven times a night"-sized window.

But she lets the window close and tells him there's a water bill.

He says he'll Interac the money over. "Is there any other mail?"

There is. It's nothing important, but she says yes, so that he'll have to come and pick it up and then she'll see him and there'll be another window, maybe a bigger window. Maybe she can tell him then—

"You can leave it in the mailbox," he says. "I'll bike by sometime this week."

And just like that, he's gone, and Grace feels like she's standing on the subway platform after the train disappears into the tunnel. The room rings with emptiness.

"Fuck!" she says, leaning back on the couch, staring at the pressed-tin ceiling.

She had just started getting used to waking up alone and spending Friday nights by herself or going out for beers after work. She'd just gotten used to filling her weekends and making supper again, though she's still not used to making food for one and always ends up with leftovers. She'd finally started to feel like things were going to be okay, her, alone, single again. And now?

She eats a peanut butter sandwich over the sink. She'd always assumed she'd have kids, in a vague, inconcrete way she never actually pinned down, and she and Jamie never talked about kids in any immediate sense. She feels stupid now—she's thirty-three. They should've sat down and talked about it, but then they never really talked about anything.

Grace calls Jenna, but she's in Philadelphia for work, so she tries her parents. Her mom's out, but her dad tells her about the early snowstorm they had. Even though it's the same as every other snowstorm story, Grace puts him on speakerphone and lets his voice fill the living room.

In the morning, Grace wakes up to the late-October light thin and persistent through the blinds. She knows nothing's changed, but she pees on a pregnancy test again and sits on the toilet, the timer on her phone set for three minutes.

Why did she sleep with him? How could she? It's not like she had wanted to get back together. And she had thrown out her pills when she got home from Newfoundland. She heard somewhere that it takes a while to get out of your system, but clearly not for everyone.

Her alarm goes off—a car horn blaring—and she turns the stick over. She stares at the plus sign rising in the tiny square, a star in a city window. She's still pregnant. Of course she is.

Grace sits at her desk and tries to write Amelia synopses, but the joy in the letters, even in the grumpy letters, is too much. She loved Gene and Gene absolutely adored her, and Grace is alone, and the letters are too much—all these plans to meet up in New York City, in Boston, references to the weekends they spent together, the gifts they gave each other—

She wants to stop, to take a break, and let Jeremy or Abigail read these love letters, write all these synopses so she can stare at the wall in the reading room, or Google abortion clinics from the reference desk. But Janice is on her to have them at least half done before the end of the semester, so she opens up another envelope.

Dear Gene,

It's the first day of summer, though it doesn't quite feel like it today. It's colder than I would've hoped, but the oaks and elms have filled out and are fully hiding the house from the road, and the last of the dogwood blossoms have fallen off (I will miss those beauties!). The pond in the back is filling with lily pads, and I had the neighboring kids over yesterday afternoon to play croquet, though to GP's dismay, we did not play by the rules, much preferring to whack the balls as hard as we could—more cricket than croquet. They're back there right now trying to catch frogs.

I'm hoping this'll be a real summer, one where I can drink lemonade and read books in the sun until I'm burnt to a crisp, and spend days at the beach, even if the ocean is too cold for a real swim. I want bonfires and clamming and cookouts and picnics and all the laziest, meandering flights.

There was one summer, before my dad's drinking ruined my parents' marriage and we moved out west, that is still the summer of my dreams—I spent it on the edge of the Kalamazoo River in Saugatuck. No electricity, no hot water, just campfires and hot dogs and pulling pranks on each other. I had a beau for the first time that summer—Ken. What a lovely guy. He's the one who taught me how to play the ukulele. We went on canoe trips with my friend Sarah and her boyfriend, Harry, and we swam in the river every single day.

I want this summer to feel like that summer. I want to pack sandwiches and go on adventures until the sun goes down. For the last few years, every summer has been nothing but work—lectures and hotel rooms (okay, that hasn't always been terrible—Baltimore with you was lovely), and more lectures and meetings. So many infernal meetings. Can't we all just agree to take summers off and get back to business in the fall? Though fall flying is marvelous— how about November? November to March, and then we can all just enjoy life for the rest of the time. Shall I pitch it to Teddy next time I see Eleanor? I think this could really have legs …

Okay, but really—let's find a weekend. Maybe the 12th? My birthday is the 24th, so I should be in Rye the weekend before—I think my mother's going to be in Marblehead, and maybe Pidge and the kids, we'll see. Let me know.

Love,

A.E.

Letter from Amelia Earhart to Gene Vidal, Grace types into a new Word document. *Recollections of blissful summers past and present.* She stares at the cursor on her screen blinking, blinking.

She hates that Jamie gets to go through his days, drinking coffee and eating whatever he wants—bacon, soft-cooked eggs, salami sandwiches—when she can't get out of bed until she's eaten a sleeve of plain saltines. He can take the streetcar to work without worrying about puking in a stranger's lap. He doesn't get stressed about dry-heaving in a staff meeting. He could keep plans to have sushi with Carolyn.

She feels like she should either be elated and committed to becoming a mom, or resolute in terminating the pregnancy, but she's not either. She's just sick and tired and mostly wishes she could rewind and not have sex with Jamie. She wishes she had just left that box full of inner tubes on the front porch and drunk the scotch by herself.

Grace tries to finish up the description, but she wants to drink lemonade and read books in the sun and have bonfires and cookouts and picnics and a lovely beau named Ken to canoe with. She opens up the document with the synopses she sent to Janice yesterday about Amelia's mother finally visiting her in Rye, about building a house in California, a benign, undated letter about the weather. It feels reductive to be condensing these letters to three sentences, four max, but she is too tired to question it or do any more than the bare minimum.

Just finish it already, she tells herself. The cursor blinks and blinks. Patrick comes out of Janice's office and waves. She can tell by the pause in his step that he's going to come over and chat, so she puts the letter away and opens her email window over top of the Word doc.

"How's Tuesday treating you, Grace?" he asks.

She nods. "Good," she lies. "You?"

She pulls out another letter after he leaves, determined to get through another synopsis before the end of the day.

15

It's the hormones, she knows it is, but she cries when her mom tells her she's sold her bin of My Little Ponies in the church rummage sale. She cries at the radio story about a choir in Scarborough. She cries when she burns her toast and when Janice admonishes her for being late for the third time this week. She almost cries at a staff meeting, and she can see Abigail staring hard at her, so she goes for a walk at lunch to clear her head. Everywhere she looks there are moms pushing strollers and kids on the backs of bikes and a long parade of toddlers in matching fluorescent green vests over their jackets, holding on to a skipping rope.

The greasy smell of the food trucks parked on St. George Street makes her gag, so she walk-runs to the Athletic Centre, where the smell of chlorine bleaches the smell of old oil.

She wants to let the cold water take her breath away, and let the nothingness fill her ears, the suspension of questions and panic and what-ifs. She wants the calm that settles into the rhythm of one-two-three-breathe, one-two-three-breathe, but she left her swimsuit at home. She wedges herself between two benches, her backpack as a pillow, and the swimmers' arms smacking against the surface of the water turns into a strange rhythmic lullaby. She sleeps like a rock sinking to the bottom of a lake and when she wakes up, she doesn't know where she is.

"I think I'm coming down with something," she tells Janice, back at the library, and Patrick sends her home with a bottle of Advil Cold and Sinus she's not allowed to take.

After supper, she types *Amelia Earhart* into her phone. The first news link is an article about a lunar crater they've named after her—the first crater anyone's found in a hundred years. The scientists were looking for lava tubes, Grace reads, not having any idea what a lava tube is, and found this two-hundred-kilometre hole instead.

She thinks it's a bit of a strange tribute to name this empty space after Amelia, though maybe it's fitting. It faces Earth, the Earhart, and the article says you can see it with a cheap telescope or even binoculars. Grace digs around in her closet and finds a pair of her grandfather's birding binoculars. She has never used them before, has never even taken them out of their case. They are small and compact, but heavier than they look, and Grace stands in the backyard, staring up at the sky. There is definitely a face in the moon and she wonders if the crater is the mouth or one of the eyes. She tries to glean more information about where it is from the article, but can't, so she goes back inside and put the binoculars back in her closet.

At the top of the article, they've included a photo of Amelia, her curls catching the light. It's not the best picture, and Grace wishes they had used one of her wearing goggles, or at least the heavy leather coat she is often wearing, instead of a wool skirt and what looks like a tweed jacket. One where she's holding on to a propeller, or sitting in the cockpit of the Vega, ready, would've been better.

In the photo, she's standing in front of the wing with an audience of white fedoras. Her hands look busy and her nose is wrinkled. She is squinting into the sun.

Grace looks at a small, open envelope, Amelia's letter unfolded next to her keyboard, the looping scrawl becoming as familiar as her mom's handwriting, or her Nan's.

Undated letter from Amelia Earhart to Gene Vidal, Grace starts, *exploring the weather patterns around Pennsylvania and a proposed October flight together.*

She stares at the screen, but all she can think about is this cluster of cells multiplying under her belly button. What the fuck is she going to do?

Amelia Earhart + pregnant, she types into a search bar. She's expecting nothing. There've been no letters about kids, no mention on her Wikipedia page. She scrolls down, and down, until the last link: *Amelia Earhart's secret 1924 pregnancy.*

Grace holds her breath and clicks.

There's a washed-out black-and-white photo of a man in a newsie cap and a tie, his arm slung around someone who was cut out of the photo. Lloyd Royer, it says underneath, a plane mechanic who worked at Kinner's hangar in California, where Amelia kept her first plane, a bright yellow biplane she named *Canary.*

It was 1924, or maybe 1923, the website isn't clear with the exact timing, but it says that Lloyd was Canadian. It says that Amelia's parents were divorcing, and Amelia left California abruptly, driving with her mom to Boston to meet up with her sister. Except they didn't drive straight west, they went north through Oregon and Washington, crossing the Canadian border, through B.C., then angled up to Alberta. They left in April, and arrived in Boston in August, staying in Banff in between. The website claims that the baby was born in Banff, that the baby was a girl, and that Amelia gave her up for adoption.

Grace knows it's just speculation, but the rumours about her and Gene being together is true. Maybe this is, too.

Dear Amelia,

There's a rumour you had a baby in 1924, here in Canada, and as stupid as it sounds, it makes me feel less alone thinking about the panic you must've felt when you realized you'd missed your period. How long did it take you to find out? One missed period? Two?

I picture Lloyd in grease-stained coveralls with hands that always smelled like gasoline, even though he's in a tie and suit jacket in this picture. Did you have a full-blown affair? A one-night stand? Did you have sex in the cockpit of your biplane? I imagine him as daring with a big laugh, and always ready for an impromptu flight.

Did Lloyd even know you were pregnant before you got in your car, luggage filling the trunk and piled in the back seat? Did you tell your mom while you were driving north through Washington, roadkill slugs in your wake? Did you tell her in the shadow of one of the Rocky Mountains, the snow refusing to leave despite the brilliant, shining sun?

Did you send Lloyd a letter from the road, penned at an inn or a motel, your mom already asleep, the car parked out back? Would he have tried to get you to marry him? Would he have tried to convince you to keep the baby? But then maybe you never told him. Maybe he never knew.

I wonder if your belly had stretch marks you had to explain away to Gene (or George). Did either of them ever know what happened during what this website calls your "missing year"? Other websites don't say anything about a baby, claiming you had surgery in Boston on your sinuses.

I don't know what to believe—if you were pregnant or not—but I want to rent a car and drive out west, letting the prairie skies overwhelm me. I want to stand on the edge of Lake Louise, stare at its impossible emerald-ness like you did.

—Grace

16

Grace gets a text from Jenna on Sunday morning. *Where are you???!!!!!!*

Brunch. Grace totally forgot. *Shit! Sorry! On my way*, she texts back, grabbing her jacket and a handful of crackers.

How could she have forgotten? She feels like an idiot.

Grace gulps in the damp, fall air and hopes she doesn't vomit on the way down to Dundas. She eats a cracker and wishes she had brought water. The trees are naked and look so ill-equipped for the cold. The storm sewers are clogged with wet leaves, a thick, brown mulch that makes her gag. Some houses still have Halloween decorations up— rain-soaked cobwebs clumped on bushes, plastic skeletons hanging from porches.

Grace spreads mint ChapStick under her nose and hopes the mint will override the smell of greasy bacon. It's a trick her dad said firefighters use when they're walking into a house or an apartment and they don't know what will be there—rotting food, rotting bodies. She shakes the thought out of her head.

Jenna's already got a table when Grace arrives and she's careful to breathe through her mouth to keep the fog of coffee from taking over. They've been coming here for so many years that "Want to go for brunch?" only means this place, and always means at ten, when it opens, because neither of them has the patience to wait in line.

Jenna stands behind the table in the corner and hugs Grace hello.

"I'm so sorry," Grace says into Jenna's shoulder. "I'm such an idiot. This week has been a total shit show and I left my planner at work, and I'm just so scattered—" She almost says it, blurts it out, but the server interrupts and tells them the specials.

Jenna waves off Grace's apologies after the server fills up their water glasses. "It's so fine. Really. Remember last year at the Firkin? That quiz night? I was like, two hours late."

Instead of getting coffee, Grace asks for orange juice and orders pancakes instead of the omelet she always gets. She waits for Jenna to say something, but she doesn't seem to notice.

"You made it through Halloween!" Jenna says, raising her coffee cup.

Grace and Jamie had met on Halloween. It was supposed to be a one-night stand. Jamie was dressed up as Little Red Riding Hood, with yellow yarn braids safety-pinned to his hoodie. Grace had dressed up with Jenna as pregnant Britney Spears and her backup dancer boyfriend, Kevin Federline. They played rock-paper-scissors and Grace got K-Fed, and used Jenna's mascara brush to make a thin 'stache above her top lip. Her hair was short then and she gelled it back and wore gold chains and a white Honest Ed's undershirt they stained with mustard.

When Grace woke up the next morning in Jamie's bed, her mascara moustache had rubbed off and so had Jamie's Red Riding Hood lipstick. He made coffee before she was up and though he's never copped to it, she's pretty sure he didn't remember her name. But he convinced her to go for brunch, offering her a shirt to wear overtop of her K-Fed tank top, and then invited her for Manhattans that night.

Every year since, they had thrown a Halloween party, parties that had become legendary. But this year Grace was too tired to mourn the Halloween parties. "I watched *The Office* and ate about a thousand mini chocolate bars," she says.

"And you're okay?"

Grace nods. She's not, but it's not why Jenna thinks.

"Okay, I need your opinion," Jenna says. "This sweater—I found it in Eric's mom's closet. I can't tell if it's awful or awesome."

"It's definitely something," Grace says. It's bright pink and fuzzy. "You look a bit like a Muppet."

"So, awful."

"No, not in a bad way."

"Oh, so a good Muppet."

"The best Muppet."

Jenna rolls her eyes. "Thanks."

Grace wants to ask her if she and Eric are still talking about having kids, if she can picture herself as a mom. She wants to ask her what she would do if she got pregnant with her ex's baby. But instead, she lets Jenna talk about Eric's current obsession with making homemade pasta, about trying to find a new family doctor, and about whether or not she's going home to Sudbury for Christmas.

"How's the library?" Jenna asks.

"Good," Grace says. "Fine. An undergrad dropped his phone on a cuneiform tablet this week."

"Oh, shit!"

"I know. It wasn't good." She shouldn't tell her, she knows she shouldn't, but she's holding on to too many secrets. "I'm working on a top-secret project. You can't tell anyone. Like, anyone. Not even Eric."

"Whoa. A top-secret library project?"

"Promise? You really can't say anything."

"I promise."

"Do you know Amelia Earhart?" Grace says.

"Of course. Everyone knows who Amelia Earhart is. Famous pilot, women's rights, all of that."

"Okay, I didn't know anything about her."

"She's a feminist icon," Jenna says. "Remember I did that project about her for my third-year Women's Studies class?"

"Vaguely?"

"Okay, so what about her?"

Grace lowers her voice. "My boss found a box of letters she wrote."

"Unpublished?"

"No one knows about them."

"Wow."

"And they're to her lover, this guy Gene."

"Wait, I thought she was gay."

"Nope—married, and having an affair."

"Holy shit!"

"Yah."

"So what are you doing with them?

Grace explains the synopses and the portal the web team is going build. "Janice thinks Purdue is going to freak out, and apparently the university's PR machine is going to turn it into a huge thing."

"Of course they are. Secret letters written by Amelia Earhart about an affair? Yah, that's a big fucking deal."

"Shhh!"

"Sorry, sorry."

Their food arrives and Jenna slips a piece of bacon onto Grace's plate.

"Oh, thanks," Grace says, even though bacon is on the verboten list, along with caffeine and sushi and wine. "I'll trade you." She sets half a pancake next to Jenna's home fries.

It's just bacon. But what if she wants to keep the baby? Grace takes a tiny bite. A tiny bite can't hurt.

"It's good. Super crispy today," Jenna says. "I can't believe she's not gay. I really thought she was."

Grace shakes her head and cuts another piece of bacon in case Jenna is watching her. But no, that's paranoid. Of course she isn't watching her. But she has another bite in case, the salt sharp and aggressive. She swallows it with a gulp of juice.

"Well, my work pales in comparison," Jenna laughs.

Grace tries to listen to her story about the account coordinator she just hired, but it feels like she's underwater. She can see Jenna talking, but everything is hazy and in slow motion.

"You okay?" Jenna asks.

"Fine. Yah. Sorry, just tired." Grace takes another sip of juice.

When Jenna gets up to use the bathroom, Grace slips the bacon under a pile of crumpled napkins and is relieved when the server takes her plate. She puts ChapStick on and tries to rub some under her nose without anyone seeing.

"This fall has been such garbage," Jenna says when she sits back down. "Let's go to Prince Edward Country. Drink wine, stay in an Airbnb, drink more wine."

Grace nods, intensely grateful for Jenna's friendship, her loyalty, her dependability. She wants to tell her about this collection of cells that won't let her drink coffee or eat bacon. The collection of cells that she might want, and might not want, to keep. The collection of cells that has taken over every single thought for the last week and a half.

But she doesn't. She hugs Jenna goodbye after the server brings their change and promises she'll look in her calendar and find a weekend they can go to Prince Edward Country. Maybe she will go. Maybe that's exactly what she'll need.

Dear Amelia,

You didn't want a baby because you had plans and dreams. A baby would've kept you from your life, I get that. But would a baby keep me from my life? I'm not even sure what my life is these days. Brunches with Jenna would be out, and drinks with Jeremy and Abigail on Friday nights, but I'm not sure I would really miss that. There's money to think about, of course, and sharing custody with Jamie, and I'm not sure I'd ever be able to date again, at least not for years, but I'm not sure I'll ever be ready to date again …

Fuck. I don't know. One moment I'm convinced I can do this, that I want to, and the next moment I'm terrified of the pressure of looking after a life, being responsible for creating a good, kind person in the world. When I write it out like that, it seems impossible. How does anyone do it?

Still, I'm getting older, and what if there is no right time? What if I never fall in love again? Or, if I do fall in love again, and it's too late and I can't get pregnant? What am I supposed to do when I don't know what the future looks like?

Instead of Googling whether or not abortions can permanently ruin your uterus, I found an article titled, "The Great Welsh Amelia Earhart Controversy." Turns out, there are two Welsh villages fighting over you. Pwll, the town where you opened the window of the the Friendship, is staking claim to you, but so is Burry Port, where you first stepped onto solid ground.

Pwll has an official government-issued plaque—bright blue and circular, written in Welsh first, then English— but Burry Port has three. One of them is a slab of black marble that looks startlingly like a gravestone. There's another at the base of a statue and still another carved into a piece of stone angled over the harbour.

I want to see the plaques, even the gravestone one, that trace the inlet from where Bill landed the plane to where you stood, gracious and disappointed that you hadn't been allowed to touch the controls, already plotting your solo flight in the red Vega.

I've read the article I don't know how many times—mostly because it keeps me from wondering if I should stay pregnant or not. The Great Welsh Controversy is all about all I can manage these days.

—*G*

P.S.: Did you ever wish you had kept your Canadian baby? Did you ever think about her, wonder where she was, if she had curly hair like yours, if she was drawn to every plane that flew overhead without ever knowing why?

17

Even though she tries to avoid them, every clock and every calendar follows Grace with the tick tock of days and multiplying cells.

Her bathing suit feels tight and her goggles start leaking two lengths in, but she swims hard, trying not to think about how tired she is, about the questions she needs to answer. One-two-three-breathe, one-two-three-breathe, the thump of her kick propelling her to the deep end. One-two-three-breathe, her arms pulling her to the shallow end. She swims so hard she has to gasp for air and a woman in a polka dot suit tells Grace she should move to the fast lane. Grace tries to smile and adjusts her goggles.

Jenna's been texting her all week, trying to figure out a weekend for a road trip to Prince Edward County, and Carolyn has been trying to schedule a sushi lunch, and her mom's been calling, but Grace let their texts pile up and her mom's calls go straight to voice mail. Last night, Grace finally called her mom back when she knew she'd be at bingo with Aunt Lorraine and made sure her message was perky and upbeat, so her mom wouldn't have any reason to worry. And this morning, in the reading room, she suggested ramen instead of sushi with Carolyn and finally texted Jenna back—*Sorry I've been so MIA. Phone's messed up. Yes to a wknd in PEC. Just need to figure out timing.*

Jenna came with her when she had an abortion in first year. She and the tall German guy from her art history class weren't exactly in a relationship and she never told him she was pregnant. It was necessary, that appointment on Bloor Street, where she and Jenna always got their STD checks. She's never regretted it. Not for a second.

Jenna had held Grace's hand in the waiting room, even tried to come into the exam room with her, but she wasn't allowed, so she sat in the waiting room with a bag full of Midol and terrible gossip magazines and licorice and fancy chocolate. It wasn't traumatic the way Grace had thought it might be, but it did feel bizarre to be handed a bunch of pamphlets and told to come back in four to six weeks unless she spiked a fever or started hemorrhaging. *That's it?* she kept thinking, waiting for Jenna to wave down a cab. *That's it.*

Jenna stayed with Grace for three days, setting up camp in her dorm room while Grace's body clenched and unclenched and she curled around cramps she had never known before then.

It was a blur, those few weeks. There are parts she remembers so vividly—the mint green of the gown she was wearing; the ice cubes floating in the water the kind nurse handed her after it was done; the thick, wet pads between her legs; the yellow plastic cup Jenna handed her when it was time for more pills; the shock of red pouring down the drain the first time she showered; her constant fear of bleeding through her pants when she finally did leave her room. But she can't string the moments together. She can't remember the cab ride there—maybe they took the subway? And she doesn't remember what she told her parents—they were still in Toronto then—or if she went to class, or handed in essays, or what she told her professors.

Grace could go back to the same clinic, the one on Bloor Street, across from a Polish bakery that makes the most delicious pastries. She can picture going with Jenna, rolling their eyes at the birth-control lecture the nurses will insist she take in the initial appointment, coupled with the burning shame they're so intent on passing on—how *could* she let this happen? She should know better. But then she *should've* known better this time.

She tries to think about something else, anything else—the letters she still has to get through, the mountain of cataloguing she has to do for Lucy, the birthday cake she said she'd order for Patrick, the Christmas gift she needs to find for her dad even though he always says he doesn't want anything. Eight more lengths, Grace tells herself, trying to count her strokes, but she loses track halfway down the pool.

She's late for work again and Janice calls her off the reference desk and sits her down in her office with the door closed.

"It's so unlike you," she says, then adds that she noticed a pen in the reading room after Grace's Wednesday shift, and she missed a synopses deadline last Friday.

"I'm sorry," Grace stumbles over her words. She feels the swell of tears behind her eyes. Fucking hormones.

"Is everything okay?" Janice asks.

Grace lets the tears fall and tells her about Jamie leaving as if it is new news, as if it's the reason she keeps sleeping through her alarm and doesn't watch what anyone has in the reading room. Janice hands her a tissue and pats her hand and tells her that it will get easier, that her heart will heal and she will find love again. Grace knows she should feel guilty for lying, and accepting the pep talk she needed a few months ago, but she takes it anyway and Janice puts her on retrievals for the rest of the day and gives her an extension on the next round of synopses.

Grace goes back to her desk and pulls out the shoebox, determined to get through three more letters before her retrieval shift.

Dear Gene,

No gossip columns about us, but I did read today that I had an affair with Charles Lindbergh—I thought you'd get a kick out of that one! Poor Mrs. Lindbergh must just loathe me. First they insist on calling me Lady Lindy, and now I'm having an affair with her husband. Do these "journalists" not have anything better to do than make up ridiculous stories? So far no one's gotten wind of us, though, and we can always say we're doing airline business. I don't really respond to questions that aren't about flying anymore. There's no point and I let GP's people handle it. What's the point in trying to correct all the nonsense? They just want to sell newspapers and don't really care how they do it.

It's why GP insisted I write those two books—so I could "control the narrative." And I get it. It was agonizing, having to sit there for days on end, bashing out conversations I could barely remember, adding shine and gloss to the most mundane things, but sales have been okay. Still, every interviewer asks the same damn questions— what was it like, growing up in Atchison? Was I scared on that Trepassey flight? (I didn't even fly the plane, for Pete's sake!) Did I think it was dangerous for women to be flying—that is the hardest one to smile through. I've written two entire books, and so many articles dispelling those myths. Every single lecture, every talk I do, all our airline work, and still they insist on asking.

Listen to me, all negative and cynical today. My mother still refuses to visit and I didn't sleep well last night. I still feel like a guest here at the Rye house, even though I've lived here for a few years already. There are just so many bedrooms, it's disorienting. I walked into one yesterday I swear I had never been in before. I did have a thought to get my sewing machine set up in one of them and turn an old parachute into some blouses the way I used to when I had my clothing line and maybe turn some leftover wing canvas into pants—sturdiest pants I've ever worn—but then I got a call from the airfield saying the conditions were ideal, so that was that!

*How'd that meeting with Frank Whats-his-name go this
week? I thought of ringing you at the office, but didn't
know if you'd be in. (Besides, letters are always nicer,
aren't they?)*

*That's all from me for the day. I think I'll go for a walk and
try to shake off this bad mood.*

Love,

A.E.

Grace stares at her screen, then back at the letter. It makes her feel
better that Amelia was having a bad day. She Googles Amelia's clothing
line, the screen tiled with photos of tailored jackets and collared shirts
and Amelia's easy black-and-white smile. The labels she used had her
handwriting, the bubbly scrawl Grace has come to know so well, with
a stitched red airplane passing through the last A in her first name, and
the first E of her last name.

Lucy walks past and Grace covers the envelope with a file folder
as nonchalantly as she can.

She stares at the blinking cursor on her screen and feels a swell
of confidence, of certainty in her chest. Amelia had a secret baby out of
wedlock in the twenties—surely she can have this baby. Amelia chose
to do impossible things weekly, and having a baby when you're single
isn't impossible—women do it all the time.

She realizes it is a baby, suddenly, not a collection of cells making
her puke by the cherry tree before work. Her baby.

She has no idea how she's going to tell Jamie, or her parents. She
has no idea how she's going to be a mom, or what "mom" even means,
or how she's going to afford any of it, but she's going to keep the baby.
She knows at least that much.

In between finding old medical textbooks for one historian and
pulling up the Fothergill collection for a grad student, Grace hides in

the basement and Googles *Amelia Earhart + Lake Louise + baby* on her phone.

There are no photos of her baby, of course, but there are photos of the green, green lake tucked between two mountains, evergreens standing sentry, and another of Amelia herself as a baby propped up on pillows and her almost bald head slightly angled toward the camera. She is dwarfed by a long white nightgown, its poofy sleeves ending in dimpled knuckles. Grace has never really been a baby person, never really played dolls or held the babies that come through the staff room with their mat-leave moms, but there's something about baby Amelia's skeptical eyes, her left ear sticking out more than the right that makes her want to scoop her up and bounce her until she hears her little baby-laugh.

> *Dear Amelia,*
>
> *I bought the pregnancy book Dr. Lavin recommended at a used bookstore on Bloor. There's a boring-looking pregnant woman on the cover, her hands framing her beach ball belly, smiling a secret, knowing smile. It's got lots of pregnancy facts, and information about the fetus, but it's written in this cutesy tone that involves painting nurseries pink or blue and getting foot massages from adoring husbands. It's making me even more nauseous than I already am.*
>
> *Still, there is a line drawing of a baby, just like the one floating somewhere under my belly button, attached to me through its umbilical cord. I keep staring at it, this human balloon. This week, the baby is a cherry.*
>
> *I want to know what eight weeks felt like for you. And what ten weeks was like. And twelve weeks. And thirty-eight weeks and thirty-nine weeks. I want to know what your labour was like.*

The rumours say you had a girl. The rumours say her name was Irene. My mom used to sing me a lullaby about a girl named Irene. Irene, good night, Irene good night. Good night Irene, good night Irene, I'll see you in my dreams. *Did you know that one? Did you sing it to yourself in Boston, wondering who your baby girl would end up being? Did you know her name was Irene when you and your mom got back in the car and headed east?*

—G

18

Grace tells Janice she has an eye doctor's appointment and leaves early, walking down to Jamie's work. She waits in the lobby and goes over what she is going to say—*Remember when you came over to get your bike stuff?* She picks up a *NOW* magazine and skims an article about terrible landlords in Parkdale, her eyes flicking up to the elevator doors every third word.

Eventually, the elevator opens and Viresh, Jamie's boss, walks out with Jamie. Jamie's gym bag is over his shoulder, his hair is longer since the night he picked up his bike gear. He's wearing a charcoal wool coat she has never seen before.

Grace's stomach fills with furious butterfly wings and she's afraid she'll vomit. All the brave words she's been rehearsing slide back down her throat and she is suddenly self-conscious and hating that her skirt feels tight across her widening hips. She lifts the *NOW* up a few inches like she's a spy in a terrible movie. He doesn't see her and keeps walking out toward the street.

She sits on the bench until he's long gone and decides on the walk home that she'll tell Jenna first, then her parents when she goes home for Christmas, then Jamie. He doesn't have to be the first person to know.

Grace still hasn't told anyone when her first ultrasound appointment rolls around and she lies on a hospital bed with her shirt pulled up and blue ultrasound goo covering her stomach, wishing she had told Jenna or Carolyn or even Patrick—someone, anyone.

"Here we go!" the technician says. She is young and perky and Grace doubts she has kids. This makes her feel even more alone.

The technician angles the monitor toward Grace, the ends of her braids tickling Grace's elbow. The screen is black and white and grey, and Grace's bladder is so full she's afraid she's going to pee on the bed. The technician moves the wand around and around through the gel and Grace stares at the screen. It's all grey fuzz and the swishing sound of blood and organs.

"There," the technician says.

Grace squints at the screen—a black kidney-bean-shaped pocket. "That's your uterus." The technician clicks some keys on the keyboard with her free hand. "And look, there's Baby."

A little velociraptor with a tiny seed-pearl spine, against a black-and-white moonscape. Its skull a bobbing lima bean.

It's impossible that this is a baby, her baby, inside of her.

"There's only one," the technician says.

Grace looks at her, confused.

"Not twins."

"Oh." She hadn't considered the possibility of twins.

The technician takes notes and measurements and Grace watches the baby wriggle in its tiny black pocket. It's bizarre to see something moving inside of her, something she can't feel.

"Want to see the heart?" the technician asks.

Grace nods and the technician points to a tiny flickering dot. She stares at the small flicker. It is impossible that it is a heart, a tiny, tiny heart, but it is. It's her baby's heart, fierce and steady. Its persistence frightens her.

"A hundred and forty-eight," the technician says. "A perfect heart rate." She moves the wand, and Grace wants her to move it back. She wants to see the heart again.

The technician prints off a photo on flimsy paper, and Grace walks into the late November afternoon, staring at her baby curled up like a little shrimp, unable to wrap her head around the fact that somehow she is growing organs and cartilage and bone, and a perfect, flickering heart.

Grace is too tired to walk home so she waits for the bus. It is unfathomable that this little being is inside of her right now, floating like an astronaut in space, bounding in slow motion, pushing off her ribs, suspended, heart flickering a steady hundred and forty-eight.

A bus slows, coasting through a slushy puddle, and she tucks the photo deep into her bag. She only has one copy. It can't get wet.

Her change clatters into the fare box and she makes a note, for the third time this week, to buy tokens. The bus lurches forward and she stumbles to a free seat. The man next to her is reading the business section of yesterday's newspaper, with Wu-Tang Clan pouring out of his headphones. In front of her a woman is standing, holding on to the pole, swaying from side to side, with a baby tucked inside her coat.

Grace can only see the baby's head and she wonders if she will tuck her baby in her coat next winter and sway on the bus with a huge diaper bag over her shoulder. What is in there? she wants to ask the mom. Diapers, obviously, but what else do you need to carry around? Blankets, or bibs, or toys? What could possibly take up so much room?

The baby grabs at the mom's earring and the mom catches Grace looking at her.

"Always with the earrings," she says. "I should know better."

Grace smiles. "I'm pregnant," she blurts out before the mom looks away.

"Boy or girl?" the woman asks, patting her baby's bum and hiking the diaper bag up higher on her shoulder.

"I don't know," Grace says. "I just had my first ultrasound."

"How far along?" the mom asks.

"Almost nine weeks." She puts her hand on her belly, like pregnant women do. It feels strange, but she leaves it there anyway.

"I knew I was having a boy before I peed on a stick with this one," the woman says against her baby's head. "We had to have a third because my husband wanted a girl. But it doesn't work like that, obviously, and now I have three boys under four."

Grace smiles and hopes the mom will ask to see the ultrasound picture, but instead the woman tells her that no one will give her a seat on transit. "I'm telling you right now. I was out to here," she says, her hand a foot away from her baby's back, "and nothing."

She tells Grace about her swollen feet, her heartburn, and the horror of labour. "Get the drugs," she says. "None of this natural-birth woman-warrior bullshit. Just get them. And whatever you do, don't let him look down there. It'll scar him for life."

The bus slows and the man with the Wu-Tang squeezes past Grace and gets off. The woman lowers her voice and tells Grace about her stitches and her post-birth hemorrhoids. Grace stares at the little whorl of hair on the baby's head and wishes she had told the Wu-Tang guy she was pregnant instead.

"You'll never sleep again," the woman tells Grace. "What's that song? It's the end of the world as you know it."

Grace forces a smile and, even though she still has three stops to go, rings the bell. She stands, steadying herself on the pole, then makes her way to the doors.

"Good luck," the woman calls as Grace get off the bus. Grace pushes on the door before the bus has fully stopped.

The light turns green and the bus pulls away, but Grace can't move—hemorrhoids and epidurals and episiotomies and forceps and stitches. Stitches—the thought makes her whole body seize. What is she doing? What the fuck does she think she's doing? And how is she ever going to do this alone?

She takes her mitt off and texts Jenna. *Can you come by tonight?*

Even though it's cold, she leaves her mitt off and holds her phone, waiting for it to buzz.

Everything ok? Jenna writes back.

Kind of.

Cryptic. K, let me see if I can reorg some work things.

Grace holds her phone, waiting—

The light changes again and Grace imagines Amelia standing on the edge of Lake Louise, her belly round against the opaque emerald water. She skirts the puddle at the edge of the sidewalk and puts her hand above her baby as she crosses Bathurst Street.

8? Jenna writes back as Grace turns up Palmerston.

Great.

Grace puts the gnocchi Jenna brings over in the fridge and Jenna opens a bottle of wine. Grace puts their bowls on the coffee table and Jenna hands her a glass of wine.

"I can't," Grace says.

Jenna raises an eyebrow.

Grace sits next to Jenna on the couch, tucking her feet under the cushion—the world's lightest anchor.

"I'm pregnant," Grace says.

"Wait, what?" Jenna's wineglass is suspended in midair.

Grace nods.

"Jamie?"

"Who else have I slept with in the last seven years?"

"That one time?"

"Yup."

"Seriously? That one night? Jesus. Those are some crazy odds."

"I know."

"You're some sort of fertility goddess or something. Fuck, sorry. I just—I'm a bit stunned. You're pregnant. Wow. That's awesome. Wait, it's awesome, right?"

"I think so. Yes," Grace says, letting a wave of relief wash over her. It's not a secret anymore.

"So when are you due?"

"June nineteenth."

"A Gemini." Jenna sips her wine. "So, you're how many weeks?"

"Nine tomorrow."

"Nine weeks! Whoa."

"I know."

"I think I'm in shock."

"Tell me about it."

"Wait, is that why you were all incommunicado about Prince Edward County? And why you bailed on dinner last week?"

"I'm sorry," Grace says.

"I was telling Eric something was up. He thought maybe you had met someone."

"Nope, just eating crackers in bed and trying not to barf at work."

"Oh, shit, you're nauseous?"

Grace nods. "I used to roll my eyes when people said they were nauseous, like how bad can it actually be, but it is so terrible. It's actually the worst."

"Ginger candies and saltines, and, shit, what did Eric's sister take? Papaya enzymes. And the skin on green apples. She swore by it. Have you tried the sailing bracelets, the ones with copper for seasickness?"

Grace shakes her head. All she's been doing is eating crackers in bed like her *What to Expect* book suggested. She should pick up ginger candies and papaya extract, or enzymes, or whatever, next time she's in Kensington Market.

"Did you think about having—" Jenna won't say it.

"An abortion?" Grace nods.

"And—"

"I decided not to this time."

Jenna stares at Grace's stomach. "You're pregnant. Holy shit." She wipes tears out of her eyes. "Shit."

"I know."

"You don't look pregnant."

"My boobs are bigger."

Jenna squints. "I really can't tell."

The waistbands of all Grace's pants are starting to feel tight, too.

"I was feeling pretty okay about it, especially after the ultrasound appointment, but—"

"But what?"

Grace tells her about the woman on the bus, the hemorrhoids and the stitches and the R.E.M. song.

"Oh, fuck her. What does she know?"

"But she's had three kids."

"Everyone's different. Every pregnancy is different and every birth is different. Eric's sister didn't need stitches at all, and no one I know has had hemorrhoids. And fuck, we never used to sleep in university. Like, never, remember? You'll be fine."

Grace isn't so sure, but it's a relief to hear it. "And what about my landlady?"

"What about her?"

"I'm afraid that when I tell her she'll kick me out."

"Oh, fuck that. Don't tell her. It's none of her business and she can't kick you out. It's a hundred percent illegal."

"So, I shouldn't tell her?"

"I wouldn't."

Grace tops up Jenna's glass and shows her the ultrasound—her tiny, floating astronaut.

"Holy crap."

"It's the size of a grape this week. Its heart is dividing into four chambers."

"That's crazy."

"I know."

"I can't believe you're pregnant."

"Weird, right?"

"Are you going to find out?" Jenna asks, holding the photo.

"Find out what?"

"Girl or boy?"

"Oh, I don't know."

They stare at the glossy, flimsy print and Jenna asks what Jamie thinks.

"I haven't told him yet," Grace says.

"Wait, what? He doesn't know? Grace!"

"I want to get to three months first," she says.

"Grace, he's the dad."

"There's still a pretty high chance I could miscarry," Grace says, but then she wishes she hadn't said it, as if even saying it could make it happen. She puts both palms on her belly, as if that'll keep the baby in.

"You said the heart rate was strong at the ultrasound, and being nauseous is a good thing. When my cousin miscarried, the baby's heart was definitely a concern from the beginning."

A hundred and forty-eight, the ultrasound technician said, a perfect heart rate. Grace wills the baby to stay put. You can't miscarry a baby by just saying the word, she tells herself. That's not how it works.

"Do your parents know?"

Grace shakes her head. "I'm going to tell them when I visit."

"At Christmas? You'll be four months then!"

"Fifteen weeks."

"But, shouldn't you tell them now? Before?"

"I want to tell them in person."

Jenna refills her glass. "So, you're pregnant."

Grace nods.

"Wow."

"Wow good, or wow bad?"

"Just wow."

Jenna drinks most of the bottle of wine and convinces Grace the baby will get used to the landlady's dog barking downstairs. "When they grow up with it, they don't hear it."

She doesn't want Jenna to leave, but she has a big pitch in the morning and still has to finish the deck.

"I love you," she says, hugging Grace goodbye on the front porch. "You've got this."

Grace isn't sure she does, but she hugs her back, grateful.

Congrats, mama, Jenna texts on the cab ride home.

Mama—her, Grace. It still seems surreal.

19

Grace's dad is waiting beside the luggage carousel. He looks so alone and out of place, standing there by himself, with more grey in his hair than there had been in June. He's a big guy, but he looks smaller today, older suddenly, a bit frail in his unzipped parka. He looks like a grandfather and Grace tries to picture him holding a tiny baby in his huge hands. She can't. She can't even picture herself holding a baby.

She's fifteen weeks along and the baby is the size of an apple according to the app on her phone, its skeleton just starting to harden, its ears migrating to the sides of its impossibly small head. Fifteen weeks—she's solidly in her second trimester, and though the nausea hasn't entirely let up, the threat of miscarriage has dropped significantly. Her body feels different in all of her clothes, but she still isn't really showing. She thought about calling Jamie a thousand times, but decided she wants her parents to know first, even though she has no idea how she's going to tell them.

Jenna thinks they'll be excited. "They're going to be grandparents! They'll be thrilled," she said when she dropped Grace off at the airport, but Grace isn't so sure.

"Gracie," her dad calls, waving. Now that Nan's gone, he's the only person who calls her Gracie.

141

She steps off the elevator and he hugs her tight, her face smushed into his shoulder.

"It's good to see you, sweetie."

His hood smells like wind and cold and Grace wishes into his shoulder that he were still in Toronto, not a four-hour plane ride away. When he finally lets go, he introduces her to a man in a bright red scarf, the owner of the Yorkton Canadian Tire, and his son, who is studying film in Toronto. Even though she'd rather talk to just him, her dad introduces her to the brother of a farmer a few miles down the grid road, Aunt Lorraine's neighbour and her twin daughters, and the woman who works the night shift at the Tim Hortons in Fort Qu'Appelle. In Toronto, everyone stares at their phones while waiting at the luggage carousel, but here it's like an early Christmas party. Grace smiles politely and shifts, trying to stretch out her back, wanting her bags to arrive already.

It's dark by the time they leave the terminal, and the air in the parking lot crackles like old window glass. She climbs into the cab of Pop's old truck and her dad asks about the flight. "On time and uneventful," Grace says and tells him about the video she watched about how potato chips are made—potatoes cleaned like they're at a carwash, then cut by enormous knives and roller-coastered into hot oil. She wonders what Amelia would think of her watching TV at thirty-five thousand feet.

Her dad turns onto the highway, snow piled high in the ditches. A radio tower blinks in the distance and diamond-shaped jumping-deer signs light up in the headlights. Grace forgot how paranoid everyone is about hitting deer around here. It's like the moose in Newfoundland. Her dad puts on his high beams and tells her about the snow they had last week, and the storm that might arrive on Boxing Day. There's a storm down in the Gulf, he tells her, and another coming up from Texas. She tries to listen, but the heat vents blow hot, dry air against her cheeks and make her eyelids heavy. Her eyes half close as his voice fills the cab.

When Nan got sick, then Pop almost immediately after, Grace's mom started talking about moving out to the farm. Grace didn't think she was serious at first. She was in second year and even though she went home only for the occasional Sunday supper, she couldn't imagine not having her childhood bedroom waiting in the suburbs, filled with Cabbage Patch Kids and high school binders she knew she'd never open again. And her dad was a city boy—he grew up downtown, and then spent twenty-six years as a firefighter in the west end. But her parents moved into the back bedroom on the farm, living with her grandparents and driving them to doctor's appointments and emergency hospital trips in the middle of blizzards. Nan and Pop didn't make it through the winter and Grace assumed her mom and dad would move back to the city after the funeral, but they stayed.

Grace thought her dad would hate it—the small-town gossip, the quiet of the farm, all the space—but he loves it, maybe even more than her mom does. They lease the land out to a farmer who grows alfalfa and wheat and her dad has taken over Nan's garden. He grows tomatoes the size of his hands, and peppers he pickles every August. One year, he mailed Grace purple potatoes he grew. No note, just potatoes in a bubble-wrap envelope.

"Perseus, there," her dad says, pointing to a cluster of stars over the steering wheel. "And Pleiades, can you see them? Those stars, the seven sisters, right over there."

There are so many stars, Grace can't tell which ones he's pointing to.

"There?" she asks.

"There." He points.

She still doesn't know which ones he means.

The moon hangs over the dark fields. It's almost full and so much brighter than Grace's city moon. She tells him about the crater named after Amelia, the one she can't see in Toronto.

"If you're going to be able to see it anywhere, it'll be here," he says.

"Do you still have Pop's old telescope?"

"Don't think so. You can ask your mom, but she might've sold it in the last rummage sale. *Reader's Digest* had an article about her, Amelia

Earhart, a while back," her dad says. "Apparently, she wasn't the best pilot. Passionate, it sounds like, but not the most technical."

"Really?"

"That's what the article said. Said that's probably why she crashed into the Pacific." He shakes his head. "What a way to go."

"Well, no one really knows what happened," Grace says, unable to bear thinking about Amelia's final flight, not when she's so alive and present in her letters to Gene. Grace wants to tell him about the box of envelopes, about Amelia's looping scrawl, but she's afraid if he mentions it to her mom, half of Saskatchewan will know about it, so she stares out the window and watches the radio towers blink red.

Her dad drives through Yorkton so he can show Grace the new aquatic centre. The building has a red, blue, and yellow façade that's lit by the parking lot lights.

"You'll love it," he says. "There are hot tubs and saunas and a steam room. Length swim at noon. We'll go tomorrow."

Grace nods and doesn't tell him that she didn't bring a suit. He told her to pack one a few days ago, but she purposefully left it at home. She's not showing yet, not really, but she's thicker these days and her breasts are bigger and she's afraid she'll run into one of her aunts or cousins who will be able to tell. The last thing she needs is the small-town rumour mill getting on Facebook.

Eventually they turn onto the grid road, snow crunching under the tires, the barn waiting at the end of the long driveway. Her grand-parents' house, now her mom and dad's, patient and grey and always bigger than Grace remembers. There is a string of Christmas lights tracing the peak of the front porch. Her dad pulls the truck beside the barn and plugs it in. Grace gets out and stands on the packed snow, under the sky full of stars—home, even though it's 2,500 kilometres from where she grew up.

The house still smells like it always does—pine needles and lemon floor cleaner. Grace's mom hugs her before the screen door has even closed.

"You're letting the heat out, Cheryl," her dad says.

She rolls her eyes and shuts the door. She looks exactly the same as she did when Grace was in high school—the same crinkly smile lines around her eyes, the same blue-striped housecoat. The only difference is her bob has gone from brown to silver.

"You look tired," her mom says, taking Grace's coat.

Grace is nervous she'll notice the cling of her sweater to her stomach.

"Too many Christmas parties before you left?" her mom asks.

Grace laughs to avoid lying.

Her dad carries her suitcase upstairs even though her mom yells for him not to.

"Like I'm going to be able to stop him," she says. "His back has been giving him grief all week." She shoos Grace into the kitchen and hands her a mug of hot chocolate.

"How are you, sweetie?" She sits next to her, the same places they've sat since Grace can remember, bananas ripening in the same basket, the blue-and-white napkins folded in threes, the cat and mouse salt-and-pepper shakers at the ready, Nan and Pop's chairs empty.

"Fine," Grace says.

Her mom presses her lips together. "Really?"

Grace thinks for a split second that she's asking about the baby, but realizes she means without Jamie—how Grace is doing without him.

"I'm good," she says. "I'm really fine."

Her mom pulls a plate of chicken potpie out of the oven and takes off the foil and tells Grace the itinerary for the week—finishing up the baking and decorating the tree tomorrow, Christmas Eve at Aunt Lorraine's, Christmas Day at Uncle Ernie's. "And Sheila wants to see you. And your cousin Casey was wondering if we can stop by."

Grace nods over her fork, trying to stay noncommittal. She's only here for five days.

Grace's dad puts three bowls of ice cream on the kitchen table.

"Rocky Road," he says. "Your favourite."

"Thank you," Grace says, grateful for all of the things that are the same as they've always been, even if Rocky Road stopped being her favourite flavour twenty years ago.

"And don't forget, we're going swimming tomorrow," he says.

"My neck's been funny today. Tight, you know?" Grace lies, rubbing her neck. "I might need to rain check?"

Disappointment flashes across his face, but he says, "Sure thing, boss."

She wavers, maybe she should just go, borrow a suit from her mom and share a lane with him and his retired farmer friends, take her chances on running into one of her cousins.

"There's some Advil by the sink and a hot pack on top of the microwave," he says.

"I'll heat it up," her mom says, standing.

And Grace wishes she had just told them the truth.

Like clockwork, her parents move to the living room at seven and turn on *Jeopardy!* Grace pretends to take Advil and joins them, the bag of warmed-up barley draped over her neck. They've put the tree up in the corner and pulled the ornament boxes from the basement. They always wait for Grace to decorate the tree.

During the commercials, her mom asks her a million questions—how's Jenna? How's Carolyn? How's the library? Has she thought about going back to school?

Grace tries to change the subject, but her mom won't let it go. Because neither of her parents went to university, they always insisted on Grace going. From kindergarten on they always asked her not what she was going to be when she grew up, but what she was going to take at university.

"What about teacher's college?" her mom asks. "You loved being a camp counsellor."

"But I like my job, Mom. I'm fine," Grace says, annoyed. "And

146

being a teacher and being a camp counsellor aren't the same thing."

"But you love kids. You'd be great. Wouldn't she, Russ?"

"Mom, I like the library." This happens every trip and, usually, Grace shifts the focus onto something Jamie's working on with the City.

"But if you went back to school, you could be a full librarian instead of a tech."

Grace hadn't ever thought of working at the library when she was doing her undergrad. She didn't even notice the people who worked there, guarding the elevator and asking for student cards, checking out books. She got a job as a library technician after she graduated and worked in the main library at first—night shifts mostly, where she would spend eight hours trying desperately not to fall asleep, or trying to figure out ways to look like she was awake when she was actually dozing off. The library was open twenty-four hours a day, but except for during exams, the only people who were in after midnight were couples trying to find an empty seminar room to have sex in, or graduate students easily identified by the bags under their eyes, hands trembling with midnight coffee. No one checked out books then, and no one had questions. Anyone who came into the library in the middle of the night knew where they were going.

After three years, Grace applied for a library assistant job at the Fisher. The hours were more regular, and the pay slightly better, and she figured the History of the Book and printmaking classes she took in third year might help in the interview. When she got the job, she wasn't expecting to love it, but she does—the hush and quiet of the stacks; the gauzy hum of the air circulator; that she can be invisible behind the reference desk; the solemnity of the researchers who sit hunched over five-hundred-year-old manuscripts in the reading room; the cracked, leather spines of old books; the lives of people, mostly dead, but some alive, contained in banker boxes. There's no way she'd be able to go back to the Fisher as a librarian if she did a master's, and now that she's worked with third-century B.C. Egyptian papyrus and centuries-old books, and the box of secret letters, she can't imagine working at any old library, filing normal boring books using the Dewey Decimal system or sticking call numbers straight onto spines. Plus, she's the most senior tech now and with the Amelia letters, she figures she might even be up for a raise before she goes on mat leave.

Grace is saved by the Daily Double, and by the next commercial break, her mom's moved on to the Christmas cards from their old Toronto neighbours. After a social media manager from Wyoming wins, her mom makes them watch *Merry Christmas, Mr. Bean* and her dad falls asleep in his chair. His mouth is slightly open, the skin around his eyes papery. Grace hates seeing him look so old.

"New pain meds," her mom whispers. "They make him tired."

They drink tea from Nan's old teapot, and Grace wishes her grandparents were still here, Nan's knitting needles whisper-clicking from her chair next to the fireplace, Pop piling presents under the tree, insisting they all go to church on Christmas Eve—"Not for God, but for the singing." It's been years, but it still feels strange not to have them around.

It's also strange not to have Jamie here. It's the first Christmas in six years he hasn't been with her in Saskatchewan. Grace can't help but wonder where he is—in the Florida timeshare with his mom and stepdad, visiting his brother in San Francisco, or out in Oakville at his dad's. Or maybe he's still working, walking south to his condo by the lake, slush falling from the sky. Grace doesn't know what's harder, imagining him having the best time, or the worst time.

And next Christmas—what will that look like? Will Grace have to go to his mom's place in Rosedale after Saskatchewan, and then a third Christmas at his dad's? She hasn't thought about how complicated holidays are going to be with three sets of grandparents.

Grace's mom brings out a plate of almond fingers.

Grace should tell them, wake her dad up and tell them in front of the undecorated tree. But instead, she reaches for another cookie and glances down at her stomach where the little apple is growing into an avocado. She'll tell them tomorrow.

20

In the morning, Grace can hear her dad putting coffee on in the kitchen. She's afraid of gagging at the smell, so she stays upstairs a little longer. It's still dark out, the sun slow to rise, the sky a dark, impatient blue. She hears her mom tiptoe past her room, and she finds one of her dad's old fire hall sweatshirts.

She pulls out her phone. She shouldn't have, but she took photos of a few letters before the library closed for the holidays.

Dear Gene,

I can usually let all the gossip and tall tales about me slide off my back, but the one that always gets under my skin is that I'm mean to Pidge and Mother—that I'm bossy and mean and stingy. I know that I can be bossy with both of them, but they can be like chickens running around with their heads cut off, all in a flap about god knows what.

Not to mention that Mother is terrible with money—she lost her entire inheritance, partly because of my dad drinking it away, and then she invested in a gypsum mine that went belly up, and that was the end of that. She came from money but has never been able to hang on to it, so yes, of course I help her out, but I also have to tell her what to spend it on or it'll be gone in a wink.

And Pidge, poor Pidge. She went to more schools than I did (and she actually graduated, where I could never quite stick around long enough). She's so well read and could do anything she wanted to, but she saddled herself to Al and is now stuck with the kids up in Medford (Deadford, ha ha). She's reliving my mother's life all over again, complete with the husband who goes through money like water. How could she not see that coming? I could all the way from Boston. So, of course I said something before they got hitched. How could I not? But that was because I'm a good sister, because I love her, not because I was being mean or vengeful.

Some days when she's complaining about how hard things are, I want to write her back that this is the bed she's made, but I don't. Instead, I send money, and send toys for the kids. I offer to host them here at Rye, but they never come. Ever. Mother goes to Marblehead with Pidge and the kids, but won't stop in for even a quick hello.

I feel like it all may have started around my Friendship *flight when reporters showed up in Medford and started hounding Mother and she insisted I wasn't flying across the Atlantic because I hadn't told her, and she was furious that she was the last to know. But if I had told her, all of the eastern seaboard would've known. Maybe she's holding a grudge, or maybe she's still angry that GP and I both have told her to stop talking to reporters. I don't know. Maybe it's always been like this.*

I must sign off. It's getting late and I need to prep for a flight tomorrow early morning.

Missing you,

A.E.

It's a strange consolation knowing Amelia's mother couldn't keep a secret either. Grace lies back and puts her hands on her stomach. Guilt washes over her—she'll be three and a half months along by the time she's back in the city. She could just call Jamie, just get it out of the way, but it feels too weird to do it from so far away. She'll wait, she has to. She'll tell her parents first—a practice run for telling Jamie.

I have something to tell you, Grace practises, walking down the stairs, grateful for her dad's oversized sweatshirt. Or maybe, *I have news.*

But she can't find the words over her dad's apple pancakes, or when she's clearing the table, or when she's washing her nan's old frying pan.

"How's your neck?" her dad asks.

Her neck? She forgot she lied last night. "A bit better," she says, massaging it with her hand. "Still not great." Her throat floods with shame. Her dad's been talking about going swimming together all fall.

Grace knows her mom wants her to stay, but the smell of coffee is turning her stomach, so she digs around in the mud room for a pair of mitts. "I'm going to go for a walk."

"We were going to decorate the tree," her mom says.

"We still can. I won't be long," Grace says. "I just want to see Aunt Lorraine's old place."

"It's minus thirty-five before the windchill," her dad calls out from the kitchen table. He scoffs at Grace's city-girl wool coat and insists she wear her mom's parka and snow pants.

"Don't forget a scarf," her mom calls after her.

Grace bundles up and steps outside. She has a pang of regret for not staying in and decorating the tree, but staying and not saying anything feels like lying, and she doesn't want to have to tell her parents after dry-heaving over the kitchen sink.

There are no smells outside—it's too cold—and the light is blinding off the snow. The wind pushes Grace down the driveway. Her eyes water and her eyelashes freeze, crunching every time she blinks. She has to breathe through her nan's scarf to keep the air from burning her lungs.

Aunt Lorraine's house is perched above the creek, a mirror image of Nan and Pop's house—the kitchen window on the right side of the door instead of the left, the upstairs bedroom windows stacked above, except all of the windows are broken and the front steps are piled high with snow. The screen door hangs off its hinges and Grace follows a set of tracks up to the steps—deer, coyotes, the light hop of birds.

In 2001, farming wasn't going well and Aunt Lorraine wanted to start fresh in town, so they sold the land and bought a brand-new house, with brand-new furniture, brand-new everything from Sears, packed up their two kids and moved to Melville. It's strange, to have left so much stuff behind, but Dad says it's a thing here, that there are abandoned houses all over the prairies full of furniture and cutlery and bedding. He says at this point, it would cost more to tear the house down than to leave it be.

It's just as cold inside as it is outside. The Formica table is dotted with bird shit and everything is covered in a light dusting of snow. It looks like a scene from Narnia. A barn swallow swoops inside. It circles the bulb at the bottom of the stairs like an enormous moth, then shoots up to the top floor.

In June, when Grace was here with Jamie, they were brave enough to climb the stairs—the summer light fell on the landing and there was a shard of sky where the ceiling opened up. She won't try the stairs today. She's afraid they will have rotted completely and she'll end up falling into the basement, where her dad'll find her hours from now, hypothermic and losing the baby.

Instead, she walks into the living room, where sun pours through the window. There's graffiti on the walls from years-ago high school kids, and their beer cans, bleached by years of sun and winter, are piled in the corners. There's snow by the stack of Uncle Richard's old *Reader's Digest*s and in the middle of the room there is a pile of deer pellets that look fresh. She tries to picture a deer standing here, next to the couch, its red plaid faded to a blurry pink.

Her toes start to tingle with cold and she stomps her boots, the snow shivering off the arm of the couch. She pictures a playpen in the corner, her parents across the creek, the screen door replaced, keeping out the birds and the deer. She imagines singing "Baby Beluga" in her cousin's old room, one of her nan's quilts spread on her bed in the room overlooking the backfield. There would be plenty of room, and she'd have help nearby. Jenna and Eric could visit in the summers and Jamie could stay in her other cousin's old room when he visits. She has no idea what she'd do for work, and the winters would be cold, but maybe she could grow to love it.

The bird comes shooting down the stairs and flies out the cracked glass in the kitchen window. Grace should ask her dad how much it would cost to make the house livable again. She should see if the Melville Library is hiring—

Her dad's already left for the pool when Grace gets back and her mom ropes her into making Hello Dollys, sharing all of the family gossip as she pours the cans of sweetened condensed milk on top of the nuts and chocolate chips. Grace makes a pot of tea after her mom puts the Hello Dollys into the oven and even though she's already made a batch of shortbread, her mom says she needs to make whipped shortbread, too.

"Did you see him for his birthday?" her mom asks, measuring a cup of icing sugar and dumping it into a mixing bowl.

"See who?" Grace asks. She stirs milk into her tea.

"Jamie."

"What? Of course not!"

"It was just last week. The nineteenth, isn't it?"

"Mom, he broke up with me, remember?"

"I just thought maybe you'd—"

"Mom! He left me. No notice. Up and gone. I'm not going to throw him a birthday party."

"I didn't mean throw him a birthday party," she says.

"Toronto's a big city, Mom. We don't run into each other."

Her mom pours another cup of icing sugar into the mixing bowl. "I left him a message," she says.

The room tightens. Grace stares at the circle of milky tea in the belly of her teaspoon. "You did what?"

"On his answering machine."

Grace looks up at her mom. "What?"

"I just said happy birthday."

Rage rushes through her limbs and it takes everything in her not to slam her mug on the table. "Jesus Christ, Mom! He's my ex-boyfriend. You're supposed to be on my side."

"I am on your side." She doesn't look up from the butter.

Grace rolls her eyes. Her daydream of moving into Aunt Lorraine's old house with the baby feels ridiculous. "Seriously, Mom? Elaine didn't call to wish me a happy birthday in August."

"It was just a message."

"Toronto isn't a small town, Mom," Grace says. "Stop meddling."

Her mom's eyes widen. She turns the beaters on, whipping the butter into the icing sugar.

Grace stares at the rim of her mug, furious. Her mom always loved Jamie—the first time they met she started calling him "the son I never had," but Jesus, that's when they were together. How could she call him now? And what did he think when he got the message? Did he think Grace reminded her it was his birthday?

Grace seethes over her tea, waiting for her mom to apologize. She doesn't, though. Instead, she drops spoonfuls of shortbread dough onto a cookie sheet, adding red sprinkles to the first batch and green to the second.

Grace texts Jenna from the living room and waits for the little bubbles indicating she's writing back. Nothing. She copies the text and sends it to Carolyn, even though she's skiing and probably won't get it till the end of the day. Grace turns on the TV and starts flicking through the channels, turning the volume up high enough so she can't hear the clatter of measuring cups in the sink.

I will not be like this, she tells her baby. *If someone leaves you, they will leave me, too. I will banish anyone who hurts you. I will not call them on their birthdays. I will stop loving them the minute they stop loving you.*

She pulls out her phone and flicks through her camera roll until she finds Amelia's looping script.

Dear Gene,

Thanks for the congratulatory telegram! It could not have arrived at a better time. My sinuses have been giving me grief ever since I landed, but it was truly a glorious trip. One of the very best (technically the best, if I do say so myself!).

When I stepped off the boat in Honolulu, they covered me in so many leis, it looked like I was only wearing flowers. So much smiling and photos, but I just wanted to know how much damage the salt had done to my plane. (She was fine. What a trouper, that one!)

I learned how to eat pineapple properly from an Olympic swimmer (who also happened to be the sheriff). How do you eat pineapple "properly," you might ask? I'll pop one in my suitcase next time I fly east!

It was exhausting, all of the meeting and greeting and smiling and handshaking when all I wanted to do was fly back across the Pacific, but that's the price for being able to do the flight. I shouldn't complain, though—I got to swim in the ocean (gosh, those beaches are something else!) and see a volcano and traipse through a jungle.

And when we got to the task at hand, of course the weather turned—this is what happens apparently when I try to do any sort of "big" flight. I have never seen rain like that before and it didn't help that we added five hundred gallons of gasoline. My ship was heavier than it's ever been, and the ground was too soft for takeoff because of the rain.

While the Army added an extension to the runway, dotting it with white flags, I managed to find a chair in the corner of the airport where everyone left me alone and napped (one of my special talents, as you know too well!).

I must admit, it was dispiriting to see the fire trucks, ambulances, and soldiers standing around with fire extinguishers while I tried to take off from that unpaved stretch of Hawaiian soil, Ernie, the mechanic, running in the mud alongside the plane. Poor guy. I could tell he was both terrified and hopeful. But I didn't even need the extra runway, my wings caught wind and before anyone knew it, I was six thousand feet above the fire trucks and ambulances and Ernie and Mantz. I sure showed them!

It was a long flight—eighteen hours—but I had the most memorable cup of hot chocolate of my life somewhere up in the stars. I flew through rainbows—actual rainbows—and used my landing lights to flash hellos to the ships below.

When I landed in Oakland, the boys made sure to get me in the hangar before the masses tore my ship apart and I don't know who ordered it, but there was a spread of food waiting and I managed to eat an entire roast chicken—a belated Christmas dinner, no pineapples in sight!

All of the planning and organizing took so long—over a year—but I can now say beyond a shadow of a doubt, it was worth it. And now I think I'll head to Mexico. I need some desert skies after all the lush green. Mexico, and then

New York. I'll meet you there. Let's stay at the Ritz instead of the St. Regis and get a room overlooking the park.

Love you (and hating these infernal sinuses!)

A.E.

Grace looks up the Ritz in New York. She looks up *Amelia + Hawaii* and sees the dotted line of her flight over the Pacific, and finds a photo of her laden with leis, and another of her standing next to her plane. It's not the Vega she flew from Harbour Grace, but it looks similar. Grace scrolls until she finds a plane-less photo. In it, Amelia is sitting at a table in a striped halter top that looks too contemporary for 1935. She's got a glass in front of her, and she's not looking at the camera. Instead, she's smiling at someone, something.

Jenna and Carolyn still haven't texted back, so Grace reads the letter again and tries to find the name of Amelia's Hawaii plane. Her phone is running out of battery, though, so she plugs it into an outlet in the corner of the room. She flicks around on the TV until she finds *National Lampoon's Christmas Vacation*. Chevy Chase is watching old movies in the attic when her mom brings a plate of shortbread into the living room.

"Have I missed the electrocuted dog scene?" she asks, perching on the arm of the couch.

"Cat," Grace says. "It's the cat that gets electrocuted." She takes a cookie with green sprinkles.

"Oh, right."

The cookie melts on Grace's tongue and tastes like every Christmas she can remember. Her mom offers Grace another—her version of an apology. Grace wants her to acknowledge that she shouldn't have called Jamie, that she's on her side, but she knows she won't. She never does.

I will apologize, Grace says to her baby. *I will say I'm sorry when I'm wrong. I will own my mistakes.*

Grace takes another cookie and makes room for her mom on the couch. She's only here for five days, four now, there's no point holding a grudge.

"Where's Dad?" Grace asks after Chevy Chase falls through the ceiling onto a bunk bed.

"He was going to pick up some milk after his swim, but if he stopped by the Tim's, he's probably yakking away with the CP crew." They're her dad's buddies now. In Toronto, it was firefighters, out here, it's the guys who work on the trains—engineers, loaders, inspectors, welders, signalmen.

He gets home just before Chevy Chase's brother kidnaps his boss. He joins them on the couch, and Grace can smell the chlorine from the pool and wishes she had gone with him instead of getting into an argument with her mom. The three of them sit in a row. The first Christmas it's been just the three of them since Grace met Jamie. And the last Christmas there'll only be three of them.

Grace slips her hand on her belly as discreetly as she can. She should tell them. She should say it now, but the FBI crashes through Griswolds' windows and she doesn't say anything.

She wills herself to say something as the credits roll.

"I'll get supper started," her mom says, standing.

Now, say it now. But she says nothing as she peels carrots, or sets the table, or over supper, where she pretends to sip her wine, clearing the table so she can dump the wine into the sink before either of them notices she didn't have any. After the dishes are done, her parents watch *Jeopardy!* and Grace knows better than to interrupt. She debates telling them tomorrow, but tomorrow's Christmas Eve and they're going to Aunt Lorraine's.

After *Jeopardy!*, Grace's mom insists they decorate the tree. They hang Nan's knitted bells and crocheted stockings and the ornaments Grace made in kindergarten—a silver-haired angel with a pom-pom nose, a clothespin Santa. The boxes empty and the tree fills.

Grace pulls out a felt reindeer Aunt Lorraine made with her birth date embroidered onto the back. Her baby will have its own ornaments to add to the boxes her mom keeps in the corner of the basement. Grace will have to start a box of Christmas ornaments in Toronto. She tries to imagine decorating the tree next year, with a six-month-old. She can't picture a six-month-old—do they crawl? Do they sit up? She has no idea.

The tree's so tall, her dad has to get the stepstool from the mud room to put the angel on top. Grace plugs the lights in and her dad stands back like he does every year and says, "Best one yet."

Grace stares at the felt reindeer. Now, she has to say it now.

"I'm pregnant," Grace says and immediately wants to take it back, wait till tomorrow, till Christmas, till Boxing Day, till she's back in Toronto.

"Pardon?" her mom asks.

"I'm pregnant," Grace says again.

A thick, heavy silence, as if the snow outside has moved inside and absorbed all the sound. Grace is still, so still, as if being still will keep her from his disappointment, her disapproval.

Grace pauses. "Fifteen weeks."

"What? Fifteen weeks?" Her mom's voice is pinched. Her dad stares at the tree.

"I—I only found last week," she lies. "I wanted to tell you when I was here."

The Christmas tree lights switch red, green, red, green like a broken stoplight. Grace stares at the felt reindeer.

"Well, Jamie must be thrilled," her mom says eventually.

"He doesn't know yet."

Silence.

"I told you, we don't really talk."

"Well you must've at some point," her mom says, her voice a sharp angle.

"I wanted to tell you guys first."

Neither of them says anything. The tree lights blink.

"And I wanted to be out of the first trimester."

"Well, you are out of your first trimester, Grace Marie."

"I'm going to call him when I get back to the city." She suddenly wishes she had told him first, told him weeks ago.

Grace's dad puts another log on the fire, then spends way too long poking the embers. Grace wills him to say something, anything. He doesn't. They weren't expecting this, Grace reminds herself. They were even less prepared than she was when she peed on that stick for the first time.

Grace's chest hurts. Her dad gets teary and he disappears into the kitchen. He comes back with a plate of cookies. Grace waits for her mom to tell him they're for Christmas, but she doesn't.

"Is that why you didn't want coffee?" her dad asks.

It's a relief to hear his voice. Grace nods.

"You couldn't stand it either when you were pregnant," he says to her mom.

She ignores him. "So," she says finally, "how are you feeling?" Her voice is still clipped.

"Okay," Grace says, taking a cookie. "Tired."

"Nausea?"

She nods.

"Vomiting?"

"It hasn't been so bad recently, but I was."

"That's a good sign," her mom says. "When are you due?"

"Mid-June," Grace tells her. "June nineteenth."

"That gives you and Jamie some time to find a new place."

"A what?"

"Your apartment won't fit the three of you."

"Mom—"

"Well, you're having a baby. You're going to get back together."

"Mom," Grace says.

"Grace."

"He left, Mom."

"This baby needs two parents."

A log in the fire falls down in a thud, the embers a tiny display of fireworks.

"We're going to co-parent," Grace says, hoping it's true. "We'll make it work."

Her mom's mouth is a thin line. "Grace Porter, you will need him. Tell her, Russ. Having a newborn alone is impossible."

He doesn't say anything.

"This baby will need two parents," her mom says. "You'll need the help."

Grace texts Jenna before she goes to sleep, pulling Nan's quilt up to her chin, wishing it still smelled like her.

Dad didn't say much and Mom was upset, she writes. She can hear them whispering, urgent parental whispers, but she can't make out what they're saying. *Ugh. Mom insists Jamie and I have to get back together. She says it's impossible to have a newborn alone.*

Grace sees the bubbles of Jenna writing back. She needs Jenna to tell her her mom's just worried, that she'll be okay without Jamie—

Can't talk. E's sister's here, Jenna writes.

Go! Say hi for me. Grace wishes she could text Carolyn about it, wishes she had told her before she left.

Will do, Jenna writes back.

Merry Christmas Eve Eve.

You, too.

Grace sends a heart emoji and waits for Jenna to send one back.

There's a knock on her door. "You up?" her dad whispers.

"Yup," Grace says, glancing at her phone. Still nothing.

"I found these in the barn," he says, opening the door. He hands

Grace a pair of binoculars. "It's not a telescope, but we might be able to see your crater. Full moon's out, so if it's visible, tonight's the night."

They pull on parkas and head outside, careful not to let the screen door slam. The wind howls down the grid road and every breath splinters in Grace's throat, her lungs. They stand next to the garden, taking turns with the binoculars. Venus gleams green over the barn and the moon is so bright it lights up the field.

"Canis Major," her dad says, pointing to a clump of stars above Aunt Lorraine's old house. "See, with the brightest star there. And that's Monoceros, next to it." He passes Grace the binoculars.

There's a face in the moon—a long nose, a curved mouth, and an eye that looks like it's winking.

"She's just worried, Gracie," he says.

"I know."

"She had a really hard time after you were born. She doesn't like to talk about it."

"Postpartum depression?"

"They didn't call it that then, but probably. It was hard, really hard, on her."

"I didn't know." Grace hands him the binoculars.

He raises them up to his eyes and points them at the moon. "You'll ask if you need anything?"

Grace nods.

"We can come out, or just your mom. We've got some savings, too." He hands her back the binoculars. "I'm going to sell your Pop's tractor in the spring. Make for a nice little RESP."

Grace's eyes burn and she swallows the knot of tears collecting in her throat. She wants to argue with him, tell him to keep the money, invest it, take her mom on a trip, but she knows he won't listen.

"Maybe your crater is the line near the bottom," he says.

"The smile?" she asks, looking through the binoculars again. There is a craggy edge, a dark grey shadow.

"Could be," he says.

"Could be," Grace echoes.

Grace wakes up the next morning to a knock on her bedroom door. She opens her eyes, but the window's in the wrong place, the bed is on the wrong wall, and then she remembers she's not in Toronto.

"You up, sweetie?" It's her mom.

"Kind of." Grace sits up.

"It's 9:30, sleepy head. Up and at 'em!" her mom says, coming into her room.

This is the first time Grace has slept in in as long as she can remember. She probably could've slept till noon.

"I brought gingerbread," her mom says, sitting on the edge of her bed, handing her a plate with three gingerbread stars.

Grace's annoyance dissipates. "Just like Nan used to," she says, biting the point off a star.

"And just like my granny used to. I figured if you were still queasy, the ginger would be good," her mom says.

"It is. Thanks," Grace says. "I'm actually feeling okay right now."

"Sick mom, healthy baby," her mom says.

"I just said I'm feeling okay," Grace says.

"I mean generally."

She's still getting used to the news, Grace reminds herself, and takes another cookie.

Her mom looks toward the window. "I just—I just really think you and Jamie should be together. For the baby's sake."

Her eyes are so certain, Grace wants to say yes, yes of course they will. "I don't know, Mom."

"Grace—"

"I just don't know." Her voice is louder than she intends.

"You have no idea how hard it's going to be."

Grace stares at the delicate painted roses that circle the plate. She wonders if postpartum depression is a thick, dark cloud that makes the ceilings too low, or a blinding light that obliterates everything else. "What was it like after I was born?" Grace asks.

"Well, it wasn't comfortable. Make sure you have tons of maternity pads, more than you think you'll need. I bled for a full month."

"I mean, more like, being a mom? Like, how you felt."

"It's so long ago now, but you were just so cute. Everyone said, even the nurses and they see thousands of babies. It was hot that summer, so you were just in a diaper, your big Huggies bum and your scrawny little newborn legs. You were like this little gnome, with thick, dark hair—you lost it all eventually and looked like a monk for a few months."

"Was it hard, though?" Grace debates saying the words "postpartum depression," but is afraid she'll scare her off completely.

Her mom furrows her brow. "Hard? I don't remember it being hard." She stands. "Kelly's coming by this morning," she says. "Just to pop in and say hi. And then Lorraine's tonight. I said we'd go over early."

"You can't tell them," Grace says.

"Of course I won't."

"If Aunt Lorraine gets on Facebook, everyone will know before Jamie."

"I'm not going to say anything," her mom insists.

Grace finishes the last cookie and hands the plate to her mom.

"Kelly will be here in fifteen," her mom says.

"I just have to get dressed."

"You know she's always on time."

"I said I'm getting up!" Grace says, back to being annoyed.

Dear Amelia,

I found a jpeg of one of your illustrated Christmas cards this morning. There's no date on it, but it's from some time in the thirties—after you married George, before your big flight.

There's a caricature of you flying one of those plane-helicopter hybrids. George is sitting next to you, looking grim next to your smile, and Santa stands underneath the plane, goofy and cheery, decked out in fur. It says, Happy Landings! *in a very art deco font. Your initials are under the exclamation mark.*

I didn't send any Christmas cards this year. It would've meant opening up last year's address list where Jamie's family and my family are tangled up in Excel boxes. I couldn't do it. It's strange to think that it's the baby's first Christmas, too (kind of).

I think Mom is starting to come around to the news, at least a bit. After breakfast, she gave me a sweater Nan knit for me when I was little. The little one's first Christmas gift, she said.

She didn't tell Aunt Lorraine last night, which seems like a miracle, and she wouldn't let Dad make coffee this morning. After we opened our stockings, she pulled out the family tree Nan made before she died. In case you're looking for names, she said. Turns out we are a family of Olives and Evelyns, Delberts, and Clarences ... I can't imagine naming this little apple Delbert, or Clarence, but Violet or Clara might be nice—

I asked Mom again about postpartum depression over lunch, but she seemed confused as to what I was asking about, and Dad gave me a silencing look from the other side of the table.

Did you have it? Does it work like that, even if you've given the baby up for adoption? I Googled it, but I couldn't bear to read about the potential for suicide, or wanting to kill your baby. Did Mom want to be dead? Did she imagine me dead? Was hers that bad?

It makes me so sad, not being able to talk, really talk, with her about important things, but what can I do about it?

—G

21

The night before she leaves, Grace packs and her mom sits on the bed with her. Her dad is bringing in firewood downstairs and Grace asks again what it was like when she was born. Her mom tells her about the crocheted blanket Grace came home from the hospital in, and about Nan coming to help for the first few weeks.

"But was it hard? Were you exhausted?" Grace asks, impatiently.

"It was tiring," her mom says without looking up.

Grace keeps folding shirts, hoping she'll continue.

"Your dad was working long hours at the station. There was no mat leave back then, and we had to pay the mortgage somehow, so he was working all the overtime he could get and you'd just cry and cry and I'd cry and your dad would come home to the two of us just sitting on the kitchen floor.

"You never took a bottle, which made it all even harder. I couldn't ever leave for more than a few hours. Though I can't remember now where I'd even go." She picks at a piece of thread on the quilt.

"Was there something that helped?" Grace asks, trying to hold on to everything her mom is saying.

Her mom stares at the quilt, then reaches for a T-shirt that she folds slowly.

"That helped? Your dad coming home," she says with a short laugh. "It's why you'll need Jamie. You will."

Grace folds a pair of jeans and puts them in her suitcase.

"You know what? I'll come," her mom says, her voice changed. "I'll come before your due date, and I can stay for as long as you want."

"Oh, okay," Grace says, wishing she would tell her more. It's not conclusive that postpartum depression is genetic, but she wants to know more. She needs to know more. "So, when did it get better?" Grace asks.

Her mom looks at her puzzled. "Better? I mean, it helped that you were really such a cute baby," she says, as if she hadn't just been talking about sitting on the kitchen floor sobbing.

"Mom, you said it was so hard and exhausting. When did it get easier?"

Her mom waves her hand. "It was so long ago," she says. "Here, let me fold that," she says, taking the sweatshirt from Grace.

Grace and her dad leave for the airport, gifts packed into her suitcase, the tiny sweater Nan had knit for her in her carry-on. They drive along Highway 10 through Fort Qu'Appelle. Last night's snow moves across the highway in thick ribbons, making the road look like it's moving sideways, instead of underneath the wheels, and gone.

"When was Mom okay?" Grace asks him, her hands on the heating vents.

"Took a few months."

"Was she suicidal?"

"No, no. It wasn't like that."

Her mom had cried when they left, putting her hand on Grace's stomach. "You be careful. No walking around when it's icy out," she said.

Grace hadn't even thought about that and she walks carefully to the car, then even more carefully from the parking lot to the terminal, suddenly terrified of falling.

"You're missing a doozy of a storm," her dad says while Grace checks in. "It's coming up through the Dakotas tonight."

Her suitcase rolls down the conveyor belt and disappears.

Her dad offers to get her a tea at Tim Hortons. "Maybe some Timbits?"

She shakes her head. "No thanks." And they walk slowly to the security gate. The airport is small and they're there too quickly.

"I'm sorry we didn't get to swim," Grace says.

He brushes it off and hugs her tight. "You take good care, for both of you," he says.

Usually it's a relief when her dad pulls up to the departures gate. Even during the good trips, Grace feels claustrophobic after a few days of hearing about everyone in town and visiting cousins nonstop and watching *Jeopardy!* every single night, but she just wants to drive with her dad back to the farm and wait for the Dakota storm and eat leftover turkey sandwiches at the kitchen table.

Her dad hugs her again with tears in his eyes, and the airport security guy, who can't be more than eighteen, tells Grace she's holding up the line. They can go around, she wants to say, but her dad lets go and turns to leave.

"Bye, Gracie," he calls. "Happy New Year."

She can't keep herself from crying as she unzips her boots and sets her phone in the grey plastic tray.

The plane pauses at the end of the runway like a gymnast before a tumbling routine, then the engines roar and they are thundering down the tarmac, and the ground tips away, blue replacing the salt-stained asphalt. Grace's ears pop, and the plane levels off, the earth buried by a thick blanket of clouds.

She pulls out the sour cream container her mom put in her carry-on—a stack of shortbreads and Hello Dollys. She made Grace promise to call her the moment she feels the baby kick. "I don't care if you're at work, just call me," she said. "It's truly the most incredible feeling."

Grace eats the shortbread and looks through photos from Christmas supper—her cousin's twins eating mashed potatoes with their hands, cranberry sauce smeared all over their high-chair trays, her whole family saying "Cheese" with paper crowns perched on their heads. She stares at a photo of the back field—all snow and sky—and begins to worry that that by telling her parents about the baby she's jinxed everything.

That's not how it works, she tells herself, and she's out of the first trimester, but she gets up, not caring that she has to wake the man on the aisle, and walks to the washroom, bumping wayward elbows and wide knees, terrified there'll be blood and she will have to say goodbye to this baby in a tiny washroom reeking of antiseptic and urine. She slides the lock in place and whispers a prayer to the bathroom ceiling.

There's nothing, no blood. No cramping either, she reminds herself, and she was nauseous this morning before getting out of bed. Her OB said she'd feel something, or see something, if she was miscarrying. She said Grace wouldn't be able to miss it.

Grace flushes the toilet, grateful and still nervous, and walks back to her seat slowly, as if small steps will keep this baby inside of her. She falls asleep, head at an awkward angle. When she wakes, her neck is pinched, and she misses the microwaved bag of barley from the farm as she watches the animated plane on the screen in front of her. It hovers over Thunder Bay. Grace checks her underwear in the bathroom again—nothing—and wishes she had packed her *What to Expect* book so she could read about this little apple hiccuping and somersaulting. She stares at the cloud castles outside the window. *Stay where you are*, she wills the baby. *Stay put. I will see you in June.*

22

The city is quiet, in that limbo between Christmas and New Year's when everyone is gone, or holed up at home. Every morning Grace wakes up and promises herself she's going to call Jamie, and every day she finds a reason not to.

The pool's open, and quiet. Her suit is tight now across her stomach and she wonders, walking across the deck, if anyone can tell there's a baby in there.

Grace's mom's calls every day to see how she is and asks if she's told Jamie yet, and Grace has to keep herself from hanging up on her. She should tell him, though. He needs to know. Grace pulls out her phone on the walk home from the pool, her ponytail freezing under her hat, and dials Jamie's number before she can talk herself out of it. He doesn't answer. She imagines him seeing her name come up on his screen and pressing "decline." She gets a sesame snap at the convenience store to stave off the post-swim hunger and calls again. No answer. She waits a few minutes, thinking he'll get the hint and call back.

He doesn't, though, so she tries him a third time when she's home, bathing suit hanging up in the shower, dripping rhythmically against the tub, her hair thawing. Jamie still doesn't answer and Grace wonders if maybe he did go away for the holidays.

Call me back, she texts him. *It's urgent.*

She eats the last of her mom's Hello Dollys and washes her breakfast dishes, then opens the mail that piled up when she was gone—Christmas cards from her aunts and uncles, one from her landlady, one from Jenna and Eric that includes an invite to a New Year's party at Eric's sister's house. She's flipping through Aunt Olive and Uncle Ernie's newsletter when her phone rings. Even though she's expecting it, it's still jarring to see Jamie's name on the screen.

"Hello?"

"What's up?" he says.

"Merry Christmas."

"You, too."

He's walking somewhere. Grace can hear it in the cadence of his breath, the traffic in the background.

"Everything okay?" he asks. "You said it's urgent."

Grace's stomach flips. She glances at the ultrasound on the fridge. She's not ready to say anything. She doesn't want to say anything. "I'm pregnant."

The whoosh of cars in slush.

"Pardon?" he asks.

She has to say it again, her heart beating in her throat. She has to say it three times and it's strange, sitting in what used to be their apartment, on what was originally his university roommate's couch, telling him about their baby.

The kettle hasn't even boiled by the time he rings the doorbell. He stands in the doorway staring at her and then her belly. She hangs his coat up and offers him tea—"Um, sure. I guess. Thanks."—and they sit on opposite sides of the couch, their mugs steaming on the coffee table.

"It's mine?" Jamie asks. "Are you sure?"

"Seriously?"

"It's been a while, I don't know—"

"It's yours."

"From that one time?"

Grace nods.

"Fuck." His face is wide and vulnerable, his hands on his knees like crumpled grocery bags. "Fuck."

Grace doesn't know what to say. She picks at the sleeve of the sweater her mom got her for Christmas.

"Have you thought about—" but like Jenna, he won't say it.

"I decided not to."

"You decided? Shouldn't this be a discussion?"

"About what I want to do with my body? Are you kidding me?"

"It's half mine, Grace."

Fury spews out of Grace. "It's my fucking body. I'm the one who's been nauseous for almost sixteen weeks. I'm going to be the one who has to birth this baby and feed it from my body. I'm going to be the one with stitches and hemorrhoids and you're all 'it's half mine'?"

"Wait, sixteen weeks?" he asks. "You're four months pregnant and you're only just telling me now?"

"Would you rather me not have told you at all?"

"You should've called me the minute you knew."

"I did."

"You did not."

"I did. You were pissy about a water bill, so I didn't say anything. And I went to your work weeks ago, but you were talking with Viresh."

"Jesus Christ, Grace! So interrupt me. Call me again. Email me, anything. This affects me, too, you know. This isn't just your life it's going to change."

She hates hearing him call the baby "it," like this avocado-sized baby is a thing, not a baby—her baby—with tiny parentheses rib bones and a perfect kidney bean skull.

"Look, the risk of miscarrying was twenty percent until I was in my second trimester," she says. "I didn't want to have to tell you unless it was a for-sure thing."

"And now it's a for-sure thing."

Grace nods.

"Jesus." He stands up. "Is that it?" He points to the moonscape ultrasound on the fridge.

She nods.

"Jesus fucking Christ."

He puts his coat on and leaves, shutting the door behind him.

The apartment rings with silence. She knew it wasn't going to go well, but this was worse than she'd imagined. She thought he'd cry, maybe. She didn't expect him to leave. She tries calling Jenna, but no answer. She finishes her tea. She puts his mug in the sink.

She tries Jenna again and wishes she had told Jamie earlier, or not told him at all. She's too tired to deal with him on top of everything else. She's going to have to tell work soon. And she's afraid Carolyn is going to be pissed she didn't tell her earlier.

She puts a load of laundry away and stares at her bedroom, wondering where a crib is going to fit. Maybe under the window? Maybe she could move the dresser? She rereads the Week Sixteen chapter in *What to Expect* and makes a grilled-cheese sandwich, then watches *The Office*, trying to keep herself from thinking about how she could've phrased things differently. She's on her third episode when the doorbell rings.

Jamie stands on the porch, the shoulders of his coat damp with melting snow.

"Can I come in?" he asks.

She nods.

"Okay, so we should make a shared calendar for appointments, and book a hospital tour," he says, sitting on the couch. He stares at the coffee table. "And you need vitamins, prenatals with additional iron and folic acid."

"Of course I have vitamins, Jamie. Jesus," Grace says. "And can you just slow down already? I'm fine. We're fine."

But he doesn't stop. He wants to be there for the birth. He'll find them a prenatal class. Grace avoids committing to anything and lets him talk. This is how he processes things—all the practical logistics. She watches the streetlights glow over his shoulder, snowflakes collecting

174

on top of them in small peaked hats.

"I'm exhausted," she says when she's tired of hearing him man-splain RESPs. "I need to nap."

"Of course, of course," he says, standing. "You need your rest."

She wants to tell him she's not breakable, just pregnant, but she wants him to leave, so she says nothing.

"Can you send me a picture of the ultrasound?" he asks, pulling his coat on.

She nods, but doesn't want to. She wants to rewind so this blurry moonscape can be hers, only hers, for a little while longer.

Grace is early for work when the library reopens after the break. She smiles as Abigail and Jeremy trade New Year's party stories but wishes they'd be done already so she can get back to Amelia's letters.

"What did you do?" Jeremy asks.

"Oh, it was pretty low-key," she says. Really, she went to bed at 9:00 p.m. and missed midnight entirely. She asks for the reading room shift and brings the shoebox with her.

Dear Gene,

It snowed this morning! There is something so magical and transformative about the first snow, don't you think? (Even if it does mean taking a break from flying!) Everything's so fresh and pristine. It makes me want to borrow the neighbour kids' sled and go belly whopping.

Some of my absolute favourite memories are sledding with Pidge and the boy who lived next door. My grandmother hated when we'd go. She insisted lying down on the sled was unladylike, but what was I supposed to do, sit up with my ankles crossed? I'm not sure she'd ever been sledding in her life, poor thing. I knew we'd be chastised the minute we got home, but the joy of it, the rush of it, always eclipsed her disapproval. Sometimes I wonder what it would've been like to grow up as a boy and not have to sneak around to do something as benign as sledding.

Off to find my mittens!

Love,

A.E.

Grace opens a Word document, wishing that the snow that fell last week hadn't already turned to slush. The forecast calls for snow today, but there was nothing when she left for work. She's just started the synopsis when her phone bings. A prof by the window glares at her and she mouths *Sorry* and turns the ringer off.

Happy New Year! Carolyn's texted.

Grace hasn't told her yet about the baby. Carolyn's always been adamant about not wanting kids, even tried to get a doctor to tie her tubes in her twenties. But Grace has to tell her, so she texts back before she can think herself out of it.

HOLY SHIT! Carolyn writes back, then calls immediately. Grace doesn't pick up.

I'm in the reading room. I'll call you after work, she texts back.

Carolyn's waiting for her on the steps of the library at five o'clock, bundled in a huge parka, snow in her hair. "Pregnant?" she yells.

"Shhh!" Grace says, pulling her hood up. "I haven't told work."

"Oh, shit. Sorry. Right."

They walk down the stairs together, snow whipping from the east.

"Oh my god! You're going to be a mom. A fucking mom!"

Grace half smiles and they walk down to Harbord. "It's so weird to think about," she says. "It still feels surreal."

"You're amazing," Carolyn says at the bus stop. "It's badass, being a single mom."

Some days it feels possible, other days, Grace feels her mom's warnings haunting her—that it's going to be too hard, that she's going to be sobbing on the kitchen floor, except no one will be coming home to take the baby from her.

"It's Jamie's?" Carolyn asks.

Grace nods, bracing herself for Carolyn's reaction.

"At least he comes from money," she says. "You can get all the fancy strollers and shit!"

Grace laughs.

"Okay, the minute you pop this thing out, I'll be on sushi duty."

Grace hates that she called the baby a "thing," but she lets it go.

The bus pulls up. "I've been too tired to walk home," Grace admits. "You heading west?"

"I've got some marking to do in my carrel." She gives Grace a quick hug. "'Kay, love you. Holler if you want to go for California rolls."

Patrick is the first person Grace tells at work. She was planning on waiting until after her next ultrasound before telling anyone in case there's something wrong with the baby, but he asks if she'll help him gather what he needs for his sabbatical and they spend days together in the stacks. Her nausea finally lets up, which is a relief because he starts bringing her a coffee every morning. It's so thoughtful, except she's avoiding caffeine, so she pretends to sip it and throws it out, nearly full. But after a week of throwing away coffees, she blurts it out in between the centuries-old leather-bound books in the northwest corner of the sub-basement. "I'm pregnant," she says, suddenly nervous he'll judge her for being a single mom, for being unmarried, all of the things the church would hate.

"Grace! Grace!" he says. He hugs her tighter than she expects. "What glorious news," he says, with tears in his eyes. "What glorious, glorious news."

His stepdaughter is pregnant, too, he tells Grace, just a few weeks further along. He starts picking up decaf coffees, and covering for her whenever it's her turn to clean out the staff fridge.

After she sees Abigail staring at her, trying to figure out what's different, Grace books a one-on-one with Janice.

"Congratulations," Janice says, and Grace knows she wants to ask who the father is, but she doesn't. Grace promises to have the letters finished in enough time for the portal.

"I'm meeting with the tech team this week," Janice says. "I'll loop you in, in case they have any questions for you."

23

At seventeen weeks, Grace starts to show and she buys a pair of maternity jeans so she doesn't have to keep undoing her top button. Her mom insists on weekly belly shots, even though she just looks chubby, not pregnant, not yet. Grace hates her mom's constant questions about how she's feeling, what colour crib sheets she's going to get, but at least she's stopped telling her Grace and Jamie should get back together.

Carolyn is teaching a new course and Jenna is travelling a lot for work, and when she's home, she's with Eric, or working late, and Grace lies in bed, not sleeping, never sleeping, and cycles through the what-ifs. What if the baby is born too early? What if the baby has an impossible-to-pronounce syndrome? What if the baby is born with its organs outside its body? There are too many what-ifs to sleep at night. There are too many what-ifs to do anything, really.

The only time she can tune out the what-ifs is when she's in the reading room, or in the sub-basement, with Amelia's letters. She rereads letters she's already read, and reads new ones—about her sister's birthday gift, about eating her first Californian orange, about Amelia landing in the desert in Mexico. She spends hours on each synopsis until Janice tells her they're getting too long and then she spends hours trying to trim them down.

How're you feeling? Jamie texts one evening. She's already in her pajamas, even though it's not even seven.

Ok, she writes back. *Not great*, she adds and presses send.

Before she's even finished another episode of *The Office*, Jamie rings the doorbell. He's holding two bottles of fancy sparkling waters. "Elderflower and lemongrass with ginger," he says. He pours her a glass and then he washes her supper dishes and takes the garbage out.

She ends up falling asleep on the couch, and he wakes her gently and helps her into bed.

"I'll slide the key under the door," he says.

It feels like a hazy dream that she wouldn't have believed if she hadn't woken up to the dishes in the drying rack and the sparkling waters in the fridge.

The next night, Jamie asks if he can bring over supper. It's not as weird as she thinks it'll be, and she gets him to Google gestational diabetes and assure her that everything's going to be okay. He starts coming over with supper, and more flavours of sparkling water. They eat on the couch like they used to, and he washes the dishes, and they sit on the couch some more, watching the last season of *The Office*.

One night, she rests her head on his shoulder, and the next night, she leans over and kisses him. It's gentle and tentative, and she tries not to think too much about it.

After three nights in a row of kissing on Grace's couch, Jamie invites her down to his condo.

It takes forever to get down there through the slush and the snow. No one offers Grace a seat on the streetcar, just like the woman on the bus had predicted, but the concierge says she can sit on the tufted leather bench while the voices of strangers waiting for the elevator bounce around the lobby. She can't believe this is Jamie's home now, a home with thousands of strangers.

She takes the elevator up to the twenty-ninth floor with a small white dog wearing a red sweater, and its owner. The walk from the elevator is long and impersonal, like a hotel, but even more beige. Jamie has left his door open, the smell of Bolognese wafts into the hall. He made it on one of their first official dates and Grace used to joke it was the reason she fell in love with him, but it wasn't entirely a joke. Jamie was the first guy she'd been with who could cook and who knew how to make fancy cocktails and which wine would pair with their meals at a restaurant.

He doesn't have very much furniture—an L-shaped leather couch that used to be in his dad's basement, and a huge TV. There are stools tucked under the counter in the kitchen and a desk she's never seen before is in the corner with a chair on wheels. That's it, nothing on the walls, no fruit bowl, no shoe rack, nothing.

They eat side by side on the stools, then sit on the couch and watch *The Great British Bake Off*. Grace has never seen it before, but it is light and lovely, without the cutthroat drama of U.S. reality shows. They eat ice cream as contestants bake biscotti and then elaborate cookie showstoppers. Grace is surprised that Jamie already knows the names of all the bakers and is rooting for the firefighter from South London. Who is this person sitting next to her who watches British baking shows? When they were together, he routinely mocked reality TV shows, and refused to watch anything that wasn't on HBO—*The Wire*, *The Sopranos*, *Six Feet Under*.

After the photographer from Cambridgeshire is crowned star baker, Grace is too tired to go home. She's pretty sure it's a bad idea, but she sleeps over. His new bed is a king, so big that when she wakes up in the middle of the night, she isn't sure he's still there.

In the morning, when Jamie opens the curtains, snowdrifts pile up on the narrow balcony and the lake stretches out like an ocean. It almost makes the lack of furniture seem intentional, like the lake takes up space where the coffee table would go.

Jamie makes coffee, but doesn't have any decaf so Grace drinks a cup of peppermint tea from a teabag she finds in the bottom of her backpack.

Grace tries not to think too much about Jamie, about her and Jamie, when she gets to work—if they should be together, what Jenna would say if she knew, or Carolyn. After she lets a grad student into the reading room, she pulls a creamy rectangular envelope out of Amelia's shoebox. The edge looks as if it was torn open in a hurry.

> Dear Gene,
>
> *I have been staring at this blank piece of paper for an hour now. My deadline for this* Cosmopolitan *article is looming and I have no idea what to write about. I always feel like I have a thousand ideas until it's actually time to sit down and write, and then poof, nothing.*
>
> *I wanted to write about equal rights and aviation, but my editor hated the pitch (okay, hate might be a bit strong) and now I'm back to the drawing board. The Q&A articles are the easiest and I'm hoping I can do one of those next. I did just get confirmation that my editor agreed to the most ridiculous title I've ever come up with for next month's issue*—Flying the Atlantic and Selling Sausages Have a Lot of Things in Common. *I sent it in as a joke, but they thought I was serious, and decided to keep it. Ha!*
>
> *Maybe I could write something about courage—flying and courage? Women and bravery? Something like that? I must stop dawdling. Please send all inspiration my way.*
>
> *Love,*
>
> *A.E.*

Cosmopolitan? Is she referring to *Cosmo*? Grace Googles it, and it's true. Amelia was the Aviation Editor. She texts Jenna, who responds only with a thumbs-up. Just a thumbs-up? It at least deserves the confetti emoji. She looks up 1920s and '30s *Cosmo* covers, with their art deco fonts. It takes her a while, but she eventually finds the article Amelia was having trouble writing: "Women and Courage"—a two-page spread. The text is too small to make out on the screen, but there's a head shot of Amelia, and a pile of clouds above the text. Grace opens a Word document but lets the cursor blink and blink. She closes it and instead stares at the delicate serifs on the C, at the silhouette of the plane shooting through the title. *Is courage the absence of fear, or is fear part of courage?* Amelia wrote as the subtitle. The question hangs above Amelia's smile, calm and serene. Grace doesn't know the answer.

24

Grace and Jamie quickly fall into a pattern—he comes over and makes supper while Grace naps on the couch. They watch *The Great British Bake Off* and Grace falls asleep before finding out who gets sent back home to their tiny little English village and Jamie describes the show-stopper bake while they brush their teeth. It's easy and simple, and though Grace isn't sure if he's only here because she's pregnant, she's so desperate for easy and simple that she doesn't question it.

One evening, Jamie surprises her with a Doppler machine and a bottle of ultrasound gel. "So we can hear the baby's heartbeat!" he says.

It's beige and medical-looking. "I hear it all the time with my OB."

"I know, but I've never heard it."

"Come to the next appointment, then," Grace says.

"Why don't we just try it?"

"It's not that easy. We're not doctors."

"Sure it is. I read about it online. Once you know where the baby's head is, it's pretty easy to locate the heart."

But Grace doesn't want Jamie moving the wand across her naked belly, the staticky swish-swish of her supper, the always-anxious moments before the steady lub-lub-lub. And what if they can't find it? Grace knows she'd panic. "I don't want my living room turning into an

OB office," she says, refusing.

"I've rented it till the end of June," Jamie says, and Grace can tell by the look on his face that he expects her to change her mind.

It sits on the coffee table all night, like an old wall-mounted telephone, and after he leaves for work the next morning, Grace slides it under the couch.

Now that Grace is really showing, her coworkers won't stop talking about pregnancy and all the horrific complications they've experienced—Janice's emergency C-section after thirty-eight hours of labour; Abigail's sister's prolapsed uterus, and her colicky baby; Janice's ruined pelvic floor. Grace avoids the staff room, and spends as much time as she can in the stacks or in the reading room, where no one's supposed to talk.

When she eventually gets the second trimester energy everyone promised would come, she stops being late for work and Janice starts worrying about her lifting boxes. I'm fine, she insists, but Janice pulls her from retrievals anyway.

"I'm setting you up in the second reading room," Janice says. "Lucy is working on a new acquisition. You can help her out, and work on the Amelia letters."

Lucy has received a truckload of banker's boxes from the family of a semi-famous poet, and Grace helps catalogue and archive Sylvie Wright's papers, then works on Amelia synopses at lunch. She's grateful to be in the reading room, and away from stories about babies being strangled by umbilical cords and Abigail rubbing her belly without asking. It even distracts her from thinking about the logistics of installing car seats into taxis and what to pack for the hospital, though nothing can eclipse the heartburn that is so terrible some days she can barely swallow.

There's no order to what is in each of the poet's boxes and Grace starts by gathering all of the materials from Sylvie's early years—school records, sepia childhood photographs in which everyone looks stiff and far too formal, and report cards written in spidery script. Every surface in the second reading room is covered with paper—manuscript pages, handwritten letters, and early editions. Occasionally Grace finds a stray nickel from the 1940s, or a button.

With the whoosh of the air circulator and the tower of old books above the manuscript-covered tables, it feels like being in church. Grace wants to ask Patrick if he ever feels like that, but it seems sacrilegious to compare a library to a church, even if it is to an ex-priest. He comes in every day, even though he's on sabbatical. If she were on sabbatical, Grace would stay at home in her PJs, but he's often the first one in, with lattes for her and Lucy, and sets up in the corner of the second reading room on the only table that's not covered in Sylvie's papers.

While they work, Patrick puts CBC on and Grace starts to know what time it is based on who is doing the interviewing—Anna Maria, Tom, Gill. None of them can stand the call-in show, though, so between twelve and one, they listen to the *This American Life*, or *Dear Sugars*, a podcast version of an advice column.

It's a relief to hear about other people's problems—their jealousy, their chronic loneliness, their infidelity—though Grace tries to tune out the ones about getting back together with your ex and single parenting.

One afternoon, after Lucy goes for lunch and Patrick puts on an episode about sibling rivalry and establishing boundaries, Grace pulls out the box of Amelia's letters.

Dear Gene,

I love it here at Purdue. These students are amazing (there are a thousand female students!). I've got the cutest little dorm room and sometimes I feel like I'm one of them, not a thirty-eight-year-old interloper.

I've decided that my thesis at every talk and every tea I'm expected to host is the importance of fun. When we're kids, fun is important and then all of a sudden, you grow up and you're not allowed to have any anymore. Well not you, not men, but for us girls and women. It's dreadful.

The part that kills me about being here is that no matter what these girls are taking, no matter how smart they are (and some are whip smart, just brilliant), they're still expected to get hitched, and settle down with a pile of brats instead of working after all of this. I can at least show them what it is to work and have an independent life, though sometimes I wish I wasn't married so my point would be even clearer.

But alas, my time here is wrapping up and I head back on the lecture circuit. I'm dreading it—all those boring old housewives after this last month with these amazing, energetic girls. I kind of just want to move here permanently. That's crazy, right? (Or is it?)

Love you!

A.E.

⚓

Dear Gene,

You know all of this nonsense with Myrtle Mantz is just her lashing out at anyone and anything, right? Can you imagine, me having an affair with Mantz? Don't get me wrong, he's a lovely guy and a heck of a pilot, but an affair? Please. Everyone knows he's been seeing Theresa for the last few months. I don't know why she's not the target of this mudslinging! I guess I should count myself lucky that this is the first time I've had a target on my back.

It's a nasty divorce and I haven't even been able to store my plane in his hangar for fear of lawyers and press and

sneaky photographs. It's all such a mess—and for what?
It's why marriage should be abolished already. What
nonsense!

Anyway, I've got to keep this short. There are a bunch of
ladies waiting for inspiration from yours truly.

A.E.

⊷

Dear Gene,

Did you hear about Wiley? He crashed that hybrid plane
he'd been building, the one with the pontoons, up near Point
Barrow. Will was with him, writing columns for the paper,
and they're gone. They're both gone. It was fog, apparently,
a soupy takeoff and the plane was nose-heavy. But I don't
get it—he was always the best one of us at flying blind. He
was always the one harping on me to trust the instruments.
He flew around the entire world only to be felled by some
fog up in Alaska. It doesn't seem right.

I know it happens. I do, but it's Wiley Post. And Will.
Will Rogers. I can't wrap my head around the fact that
they're gone. I haven't been able to sleep since. I keep
having dreams about taking off from Harbour Grace—the
fog, the gasoline dripping down my neck, the ice on my
wings, the tailspin I barely caught before landing myself
in the Atlantic. It's a recurring nightmare, except then I'm
awake and Wiley is still gone.

I've been avoiding spending any time at the airport. It's
just too strange being there without him, and Mae is beside
herself, of course. I'm of no help or consolation. I can't cry
around her, and I'm sure I come across as stiff and brusque,
which is not how I feel at all, but I'm afraid if I even open

189

my mouth, I'll start crying and won't be able to stop. I took over some flowers, but the house was full of flowers.

I know there are risks. Of course I do. I know that this could happen to any one of us when we hop in the cockpit, but there's also part of me that trusts it'll be fine, that we'll be fine. If we're prepared and know our ships and trust our instincts, we'll all be fine, back in the hangar in Burbank, razzing each other about something inconsequential.

What I need to do is go up for a spin. That's what Wiley would want. I know it. Maybe that's what I'll do this afternoon. Toss away all this lecture prep and go for a fly.

Missing you,

A.E.

Grace stares at the letter. Wiley Post and Will Rogers. Dead. She doesn't even know who they are but feels the burn of tears at the backs of her eyes.

She Googles them. Wiley Post—the first aviator to fly around the world. He developed pressure suits and discovered the jet stream. He stares at Grace from her phone, one eye covered in a white patch, his mouth set and serious. He stands in front of a plane, *Winnie Mae* written in all caps on the fuselage behind him. And Will Rogers—the name sounds familiar. He was an actor, a vaudeville performer, a newspaper columnist. He has a wide smile, and ears that stick out from his cropped thirties haircut. He looks like he's on the verge of laughing in every single photo.

"You okay?" Patrick asks from the table in the corner.

Grace looks up from her phone. "Oh, yah. I'm okay."

"You don't look okay."

"No, I'm fine. I'm good. I just—"

"I'm going to stretch my legs. Want to join me?" Patrick asks.

She should stay here with her work laptop and write synopses for these letters, but she stands. "Yah. Sure," she says, slipping her phone into her back pocket, Will still about to burst out laughing. "Let me just put this box away."

25

After a week of suppers and sleepovers, Grace calls Jenna to tell her about Jamie. She doesn't pick up, and texts back that she's sitting on the runway, on her way to Chicago for work.

Grace doesn't want to text her the news, but not telling her feels like she's lying, so she writes *J and I are back together*, and presses send.

There are bubbles of Jenna writing back, and then they disappear. Then more bubbles, then nothing. Fuck. Grace feels the defensiveness rising every time the bubbles disappear. Who is she to judge? She's pregnant. It's his baby—

Wow! Jenna finally writes back.

Wow good or wow bad? Grace writes back, bracing herself for a fight.

Good! Jenna writes back. *Wow good! If you're happy, I'm happy.*

Grace feels the adrenaline dissipate. *I'm happy. We're happy!* she writes back, even though writing we feels strange and a bit forced.

Do you two want to come for dinner next Friday? I'm back from Chicago on Thursday. Could also do Saturday, too. LMK.

Jamie meets Grace at her place and they walk down to the streetcar together, holding hands at the stop, and it's like they're in a time

193

machine, except Grace is carrying their baby and Jamie spends the streetcar ride researching the best crib mattress and trying to convince her to try out the rented Doppler.

"Grace, I checked," Jenna says as they all settle into the living room. "You can totally have wine. Think about all those pregnant women in Paris, fuck, anywhere in Europe. Do you think they don't drink for nine months?"

"Ten," Jamie says.

"Pardon?"

"Ten months—forty weeks," he explains. "Four weeks to a month."

"Right. Forty weeks."

Grace knows every pregnant woman in France drinks, but she can't. She can't drink, or eat sushi, or oysters, though she never really ate oysters. No bacon, no medium-rare steak or deli meat or runny eggs. Her OB said she was borderline anemic so she's been making as much red meat as she can stand—meatloaf mostly, Nan's recipe but with grass-fed ground beef and organic ketchup. She can feel herself turning into one of *those* pregnant women, the insufferable ones she and Jenna used to make fun of—organic this and green juice that (pasteurized, of course), but she gets it now. It's the one thing she can control in an overwhelming sea of impossible-to-control variables.

"I'm okay, thanks," Grace says.

"Well, you know what's best," Jenna says.

Grace takes a sip of her sparkling water. God, she's tired of sparkling water. She asks Jamie to get her bag and shakes out two TUMS, a pink one and a yellow one, their chalky sweetness reassuring and familiar.

Eric's wineglass is filled with sparkling water.

"He's doing a booze-free month," Jenna explains.

Grace raises her glass to cheers him.

"You can't cheers water!" Jenna yells. "Seven years of bad sex!"

Grace avoids looking at Jamie. Eric's face turns red.

"What is sex like when you're pregnant?" Jenna whisper-asks

while Eric and Jamie set the table.

Grace shrugs.

"Wait, you're not sleeping together?"

Grace shakes her head. She's pretty sure Jamie wants to, but she just can't. Her body feels so strange, like it doesn't belong to her.

That night, Grace stares at the ceiling, unable to sleep. Jamie's next to her, sprawled out on his back and taking up too much space. But then she thinks of her mom's nameless postpartum depression and reminds herself she's grateful he's here. She'll need someone to pass the baby off to. She'll need someone else to change diapers and rock the baby to sleep, and besides, if she's with Jamie, they can split rent and utilities.

But she still wants to nudge him awake and tell him to go to his empty lake condo so she can wake up alone, and quiet. She just wants the quiet. She slips out of bed and opens her laptop on the couch, angling the screen away from the bedroom door.

Her dad has sent an email with photos of the snow that almost reaches the top of the first-floor windows and BabyCentre sent an eighteen-week update. The baby is the size of a bell pepper, it says. She clicks the link, but the illustration is creepy. *Amelia Earhart*, she types into the browser to get away from the 3-D fetus. There are the usual links—her Wikipedia page, articles on history.com and the Smithsonian about her disappearance, but under a PBS article is an eBay link.

It takes Grace to an Amelia-branded tweed train travel case. It's boxy and rectangular with a sturdy handle on top. Grace reads the caption, learning that Amelia started selling branded luggage in the thirties, a brand that lasted into the sixties, apparently, twenty years after she disappeared. Grace finds another, a pale blue case, more like a bowling bag or purse than a suitcase, and debates putting a bid in.

She keeps clicking until she finally finds a red one, bright lipstick red, lined in taupe silk. *Overnight Travel Bag*, it's called. And she imagines Amelia at a desk with a ruler and a pencil sketching out its corners, its clasps, even if there was no way she did. She chooses the Buy Now option and types in her credit card information.

"What were you doing last night?" Jamie asks in the morning. He's already showered and is dressed for work and she's still in bed.

"Nothing," Grace says, sitting up. "Just surfing the internet."

He hands her a mug of tea. "Your wallet was on the couch."

Grace's face flushes. "I was thinking about buying some baby stuff."

"Don't get baby stuff, we're going to get so much stuff at the shower."

"Wait, what shower?"

"My mom wants to have one for us."

Grace blows across her tea. "I don't want a baby shower."

"Can we talk about this later?" he asks. "I'm going to be late."

"Fine," she says, relieved they aren't talking about Amelia's suitcase.

"Have a good day." He kisses her forehead goodbye.

She hates feeling like a child so she pulls him back and kisses him properly. "'Kay, bye. Sorry about my dragon breath."

His key thunks the deadbolt locked, then slides out, metal on metal. Grace closes her eyes, hand on her belly. She imagines the suitcase flying across the U.S., all the way from Oregon to Toronto.

Grace is pulling meatloaf out of the oven the following week when she hears Jamie's key fumbling in the door. She wishes he'd knock, or ring the doorbell. It's still officially her apartment.

"What's this?" he asks, carrying a large package with airmail stickers all over the brown paper. He leaves it on the floor and hangs up his coat.

Grace knows exactly what's in the package. She wants to tear the paper open, but she busies herself with the meatloaf, and rearranges the ultrasounds stuck with magnets on the fridge. When Jamie takes the recycling downstairs, Grace opens the box. The suitcase is as red as

KittyVintage promised, and slightly scuffed on one corner.

"What is it?" Jamie asks when he's back upstairs. He folds the brown paper and tucks it into the blue bin under the sink.

"I found it on eBay," Grace says.

"An old suitcase?"

"Not just any old suitcase—" Grace starts.

"We're having a baby and you're spending money on old suitcases you can't even travel with?"

"Seriously?" Grace shoots back.

"I'm just saying, we're going to have a lot of expenses and we should probably not be spending money on—" he waves his hand toward the suitcase.

"It's my fucking money and I do not need a lecture on budgeting," Grace says, louder than she means to.

Jamie's lips are a tight line, but he says nothing.

Grace presses her index finger into the metal nameplate until her finger holds a backward *AMELIA*. It's her money. It's her suitcase. Who is he to tell her otherwise? Grace helps herself to meatloaf and thinks he might leave, but he doesn't. He gets himself a plate of meatloaf and sits next to her on the couch. They eat in silence, passing the ketchup back and forth without speaking.

She has to share her body, her apartment. She wants this one thing, one thing for herself. Is that so much to ask?

"You're right, it's your money," Jamie says while they brush their teeth. "I'm sorry."

Grace spits into the sink and rinses her brush, vindicated.

"It's just there are going to be a lot of things we'll need," he continues.

"For fuck's sake, Jamie, it's a suitcase."

"I just think—"

"Jesus, let it go already."

In the morning, Jamie brings her tea and her prenatal vitamin as an apology and she waits until he leaves for work before pulling out the suitcase. The silk lining is soft and cool, the silver buckles shiny and polished. Grace feels like crying. There's a tag on the inside, with Amelia's loopy signature and a plane heading up to the top corner. She doesn't care that she should've saved the money and put it toward a stroller or the cord blood bank, this suitcase is beautiful, and it's hers. Grace pulls out the tiny sweater Nan knit for her, the one her mom gave her at Christmas, and folds it inside the beige silk interior.

She won't be flying anywhere anytime soon, but, she decides, the suitcase can be her hospital bag.

26

Jamie meets Grace in the lobby of the hospital for her twenty-week appointment. Jamie reaches for her hand while the ultrasound tech spreads blue gel on her belly. They've been back together for three and a half weeks and she's still getting used to his fingers interlaced with hers. They watch their baby hiccup and suck its thumb, its finger bones translucent, its vertebrae like a string of the tiniest pearls. Jamie has never seen the baby and is mesmerized by the heartbeat, his eyes filling with tears as he stares at the screen.

The next day he shows up with all of the ingredients to make Bolognese. They watch Bread Week while they eat and Jamie pauses it after the technical challenge and gets down on one knee.

Grace looks at the tiny blue velvet box, then looks up at him.

A year ago, even eight months ago, this would've been ideal—a set of three diamonds, splitting rent, both of them under one roof—it's all right there. She can hear the joy in her mom's voice.

"Jamie—"

Saying yes would be so easy. It'd be safe, and convenient. "I—" Grace looks up from the ring. He's so earnest, trying so desperately to do the right thing. "It's a beautiful ring."

"It was my grandma's."

"Your granny's?"

He nods.

"But she was so mean."

"It's a family heirloom."

"But she was a dick. Like, a complete asshole to everyone."

But when she sees the look on his face, she feels like the asshole.

"The last few weeks have been so good," he says. "And our baby—"

"Jamie—Jamie, I can't," Grace says. She doesn't even know what she's saying, but she realizes with a clarity that's startling that she deserves a chance at love—love like the love between Amelia and Gene, not a marriage of convenience.

He looks down at the ring. "Grace—"

"You couldn't tell me when you were unhappy," Grace says slowly. He stares at the ring. She looks at him, looking at the ring. "You spent months wanting out, remember? And didn't mention it. You wouldn't go to therapy."

"I'll go now," he says, still on one knee, their pasta bowls dirty on the coffee table. "To therapy. To counselling."

"Jamie, you fell out of love with me."

"But that was before."

"Before I got knocked up and now you're back in love with me?"

"I'm serious. We should be together," he says. "I love you."

"I wish I could say yes, I do." She knows she can't be with Jamie. "But this isn't enough."

"What do you mean enough? It's been fine, we've been fine."

"Fine?" she says. "Jamie, we don't talk about anything, not really, and is fine really good enough?"

"Wait, are we breaking up?" There's an edge of panic in Jamie's voice.

Grace pauses. "I don't know."

"But you're pregnant."

"I think we're trying to hold on to something that's gone. It is, you know it, too. I don't think we should be together-together."

"You can't be serious," Jamie says. "Grace—"

She puts her hand on her belly without thinking. "We're going to be okay, and we'll be really great co-parents."

He stands and shoves the ring box in his pocket. He puts on his coat without saying anything.

"Jamie," Grace says.

But he won't look at her.

After he leaves, Grace doesn't bother washing the dishes and puts the rest of the pasta sauce in the freezer. She goes to bed, sad, and relieved she didn't mention anything to her mom. She thinks about Amelia, married to George, rich, bossy George, when she had loved Gene. Grace opens her laptop and finds a photo of them together. Gene is sitting in the harness of a parachute next to Amelia. They are beaming. They are both exploding with joy.

Dear Amelia,

Did you regret marrying George? So many people have called it a "marriage of convenience," but was it? Did you love him? Or did you wish you had said no again the sixth time he proposed? Did you wish you had put off George another few times and waited until Gene got divorced? You and Gene always look so happy together, and your letters are so full of love. Did you wish you had married him instead?

I don't regret saying no, but the evenings are especially lonely now and the days drag on and on. I miss the ease of sitting on the couch, and can't bring myself to find out who won The Great British Bake Off. *He won't answer my calls or texts or emails. I call and text and email anyway, explaining over and over again why we don't work, how we can co-parent, how we can both love the baby without having to be in love. He won't respond, though. Of course he won't.*

Really, I'm just so glad I didn't tell my mom—she'd lose her mind if she ever found out I said no to his asshole grandmother's ring. She'd never forgive me for breaking things off.

—G

27

By mid-February, while the baby does somersaults and kicks her ribs, Grace finds a letter from Amelia that solidifies her decision—

Dear Gene,

It's been a while, but it happened again this morning—I got another proposal in the mail. For a while I was averaging about eight a week, but it's tapered off. Today's proposal was from a chap named Ken (my first beau's name, though it's certainly not him from the photo he sent. Can you imagine if it was, though? Wouldn't that be something!) No, this gent has a plane—a Curtiss Robin, apparently—and promised me unlimited access to it.

Sometimes I wonder if these men are really serious. Sometimes I like to daydream what it would be like to show up at the return address and accept. Wouldn't that be a riot? I'm sure their sweethearts would be none too pleased, or their wives they promise they are divorced from.

I want to write each one of them back and tell them that I'm not sure I'm suited to marriage at all. Did I tell you about the letter I wrote GP? I might've. Skip ahead if I'm repeating myself. It was right before we tied the proverbial knot and I had to make sure he knew exactly how I felt. It maybe wasn't the kindest gesture, articulating my reluctance to marry literally the day of our wedding, but I had to. I made him promise that we'd never interfere with each other's work or play (and yes, this is considered play—the best kind of play, wouldn't you say?). I'm so tired of the archaic woman-as-chattel definition of marriage. I'm not sure it's what GP would've wanted, but I wouldn't have been able to go through with it otherwise. I'm sure Nina feels the same way (not that I believe everything the papers say—I of all people know the lies they spread).

How did you decide to marry Nina? Did you make a grand proposal, all champagne and oysters? I don't know why I'm even asking. This is strange. Please don't respond. Or do. I don't know. I do, I do want to know. I'm curious.

Love,

A.E.

Grace writes up a synopsis for Janice and decides she's fine, the baby's fine, and Jamie'll find his way to fine at some point.

Jamie texts her at the end of the week and asks if he can come over. Grace assumes he wants to discuss the co-parenting article she sent him, but he stands in her living room without taking his coat off and holds out a large manila envelope.

"What is this?"

"A custody agreement."

She stares at him. "What? The baby's not here yet."

"My lawyer said it was a good idea, you know, with you and me not being together."

"You got a lawyer?" Grace's heart pounds in her throat. "Are you

204

fucking kidding me?"

"Well, it's my mom's lawyer."

"Jesus Christ, Jamie."

"It's to protect both of us. And the baby."

"The baby is the size of a grapefruit and you'd like to fight over who gets which weekends with him or her?"

"It's not a fight, Grace."

"I'm not signing a custody agreement."

"Grace—"

"Do you know anything about babies? Do you know how often they breastfeed? You can't just have the baby every other weekend. It's a baby. A fucking baby."

"It's not like that. Not right away."

The thought of ever being away from her baby makes the air in the room disappear. "I'm not signing it," she says, her arms tingling with rage.

"I'll just leave it here," he says, putting it on the coffee table. "Just take a look through it."

She throws it across the room after he leaves. There is no way she is signing away her baby.

"But won't it protect you, too?" Jenna asks when Grace tells her over the phone.

Fury flashes through Grace. How could she understand? Jenna has a perfect husband and a perfect house. She'll never have to worry about custody agreements.

"Imagine you were pregnant and you had to sign a legally binding document to be separated from your baby—your *baby*—for days on end. Fuck, no."

Jenna says nothing and Grace wishes her tone hadn't been so sharp. Guilt replaces her anger. "I'm sorry. It's all just so fucked up. It makes me crazy, thinking about it."

"It'll be okay," Jenna says. "And if you need a lawyer, Eric's brother-in-law's cousin does family law."

"Thanks," Grace says.

Carolyn says the same thing—that it'll protect her, protect the baby, but Grace refuses to sign the document. "Fuck that," she tells her belly. "Fuck that shit."

Grace channels her rage into work, ploughing through synopses— Amelia debating whether to accept an invitation to speak in Marquette, terrible weather on a flight through Nebraska, some instrument she was excited about that Mantz was adding to his plane.

Have you thought about the agreement? Jamie texts and Grace deletes it without responding.

Carolyn asks to meet her for lunch, but she doesn't respond to that text, either.

It's her baby. Why doesn't anyone get that?

I'm sorry, Jenna texts. *This would all be really hard.*

Hard? Hard is an understatement, she wants to wail, but Patrick is working in the corner and Lucy is organizing the poet's grant rejections next to her.

I don't want to sign it, Grace writes back. *It feels like I'm giving up my rights to my baby.*

Don't sign it then.

Maybe after the baby's here.

Jenna sends back a thumbs-up. *Let me know if you want the name of that family lawyer.*

Yah, send it. Might as well have someone on hand.

She calls the lawyer, but she charges $900 an hour. There's no way Grace will be able to pay for one hour, let alone all the hours it would take to go through the agreement, and then amend it and go back and forth with Jamie and his mother's lawyer. She stands in her living room and stares at the manila envelope.

Can we just hold off, just for now? Grace texts Jamie, then plays a card she knows he won't be able to resist. *This is all making me super anxious, and my blood pressure is spiking.*

She sees the bubbles of him writing back, but then nothing.

We'll sign an agreement at some point, okay?

More bubbles, but still nothing.

Can we revisit when the baby's a year?

Six months, he writes back.

Six months—it makes her want to vomit, but she figures she can put him off again then.

Okay, she writes back. *Thank you.*

More writing back bubbles, and she waits on the couch with her phone in her hand. But nothing. She makes some tea, but still nothing.

I'm emailing you three articles about things to avoid in co-parenting situations, he writes back eventually. *And I'm sending over a list of days for hospital visits.*

She promises to check her work schedule and find a time that works, then kicks the custody agreement under the couch with the Doppler machine, relieved she doesn't have to think about officially sharing the baby until at least after Christmas.

28

There has never been so much of her—the hard blue-white swell of her stomach that roils with somersaulting elbows and knees. She is beautiful or revolting, depending on the moment and the lighting and how her clothes hang or cling to her strange body. She doesn't have any stretch marks yet, but she keeps waiting for her skin to split. She's twenty-seven weeks along, still months to go, but her back aches in that textbook way pregnant women's backs ache and she has to carry TUMS with her wherever she goes for the heartburn that makes it impossible to swallow.

Grace sits on the steps of the library in her coat, even though she can't zip it up anymore. She eats leftover meatloaf for lunch, watching a man scare the pigeons from the sidewalk like he's conducting an orchestra of dirty wings, disproving clucks, and the scuttle of bony red feet.

She spent all of February terrorized by the thought of slipping and falling. The sidewalks were a skating rink; leaving the house was terrifying. She even called in sick just so she wouldn't have to brave them. But Janice sent her an email, worried about the number of days she was missing, so she started carrying a yogurt container filled with salt so that even if the walk out was terrifying, the walk back was safe.

But it's been a mild March so far, and rain has replaced the snow.

Her mom finally got a cellphone and texts her multiple times a day, sending photos of her dad's seedlings and asking for pictures of Grace's belly. Profile shots, she's demanded. Just this week, she discovered emojis and now Grace gets cryptic messages—yellow smiley faces, an arrow, a confetti cannon, and a question mark that Grace thinks means *How are you?*

Grace tries to take a picture of her belly with the cherry trees in the background. They're weeks away from blooming, but the promise of buds is there. The stripes on her shirt make her stomach look even wider than it is. It's not the greatest shot—a bit tilted and blurry, and her coat is in the way, but her mom won't care.

She has to get back to Lucy's poet's boxes, but as she goes to stand, her belly tightens into a hard, compact ball—a Braxton-Hicks contraction, which were terrifying at first, but now happen regularly. Her OB says they're a reminder to slow down and hydrate, so she takes a sip of water and tries to breathe.

"They're just your uterus getting ready for the big day," Dr. Lee said, and Grace pictured her uterus dressed up in a wedding dress, a veil flowing out behind it. It's easier picturing her uterus as a bride than it is thinking about giving birth. The only births she's seen are movie births—all stirrups and two screaming pushes and a swaddled cherub placed in the arms of a tired, but glowing mother, the father hovering, proud and beaming. But in real life there is blood, a placenta, a cream-cheesy coating called vernix, the potential for the baby to be strangled by the umbilical cord …

Grace has been reading all the birthing books she can find at the main library. The really technical ones, with chapters about vernix and breech births, others that are written in a revolting cutesy tone, one on hypno-birthing, and a super hippie have-your-baby-in-a-field-of-wildflowers book where babies' heads appear out of seventies bushes.

Her mom insists she just "popped right out," which after looking at those birthing books seems entirely unlikely, but her mom insists

Nan and Aunt Lorraine had quick births, too. But easy births seem impossible, and every time Grace sees a woman with a baby, or even a toddler, she wants to stop her and ask a thousand questions—what was labour really like? How did you know you were having contractions? Did you get an epidural? Was that needle worse than labour? Can you really "ride the wave" of a contraction? Did you think you couldn't do it? Did you tear? Did you heal? What does crowning really feel like? Were you scared? Were you terrified? Did you have postpartum depression? Did you want to kill yourself? Did you want to kill your baby?

"They're going looking for her," Janice hisses in the reading room.

The history professor looks up from his desk in the corner.

"Pardon?" Grace asks. She puts down the pencils she was sharpening.

"Amelia Earhart. They're going to try to find her, well, evidence of her, I guess."

"Who is?"

"A researcher. He's taking an expedition to the tiny island at the end of April. I sent you the link," she says. "We've got to get these letters done so we can get them out. I want them online before the researcher is back so we can capitalize on the attention. It's all over the *National Geographic* site and we could get all those clicks."

The baby loops and then jabs the inside of Grace's right ribs.

"Feisty little one," Janice says, recognizing the hand Grace puts on her ribcage.

"Never stops moving."

"Are there any letters about her final flight?"

"Not so far, but I can check," Grace says.

"Let me know by end of day," Janice says, pushing her glasses up on top of her head.

"Okay."

After Janice leaves, Grace opens the email. It's a link to an article about a guy named Stan Powell who believes Amelia and her navigator,

Fred, landed on an island in the Pacific—Gardner Island, now called Nikumaroro. He believes they crashed there after leaving New Guinea while they searched for Howland Island. He's sure they spent a week radioing for help before the tide swallowed the plane. Someone found a humerus bone there in the forties, though it was assumed to be a man's and then went missing before anyone could use modern forensics. A few years ago, a search party found a woman's shoe, a piece of fuselage, and shards of a jar of freckle cream.

The expedition is still weeks away, but Grace feels protective, and defensive. *Let her be*, she wants to tell this Stan Powell guy. *Leave her alone.*

Grace goes back to her desk and looks through the box of letters until she finds one about Amelia's final flight.

Dear Gene,

I'm going to do it. I'm going to fly the whole waistline of the world. Mantz has agreed to be my technical advisor and Fred has offered to be my navigator and Teddy is letting me land on Howland Island, a tiny little speck in the Pacific to refuel. Can you see if he'll build me a runway? (Though don't mention it to anyone. Don't think it would poll well these days.) The official line can be that it's related to some military air bases in the area.

Did you ever meet Fred? Great Pan Am pilot, and he can do celestial navigation, though rumor has it he was fired because of the drink. My inclination is not to believe rumors, but if you hear of anything substantial, let me know. I'm not sure I can stomach another flight with an alcoholic.

Anyway, I figure easing into my forties with a grand adventure behind me might make getting old a little easier——? I don't know. I do know that the Electra is a

*beaut. Silver and slick and Mantz is going to put in all sorts
of doodads—a fuel minimizer, wind de-icers, three fuel
tanks in each wing and six more in the fuselage. It's going
to be a flying laboratory by the time we're done with it!
GP has started raising money for the trip and has to figure
out clearances and visas—he'll be running around to every
embassy in D.C.—and then we'll have to buy gas and ship
it to each port. It's a mess of a project, to be honest, and it
seems impossible that it'll all work out, but then, it will,
won't it?*

*I do worry a bit about the long stretches over the ocean
without pontoons. I couldn't sleep last night because I
couldn't stop thinking about it. But would they do me
any good in the long run, just bobbing up and down in
the Pacific? Landings would be tricky, and getting into a
port for refueling would be hard. I hated the* Friendship's
*unwieldy clown feet, but then—I don't know. What do you
think?*

*To be honest, some days I think this whole idea is
ridiculous, other mornings I wake up and am certain it's the
best idea I've ever had. What do you think? Really. Tell me
honestly.*

Love,

A.E.

*P.S.: Just heard from Mantz. He's set up a blind-flying
trainer in his hangar. He says I need to log at least 100
hours. What have I gotten myself into?!*

*P.P.S.: GP wants me to do the last stretch of the flight
solo. Says it's better for my "brand," but I really think I
need a navigator with me. Tell me I'm right. (I got credit
for flying the* Friendship *across the pond and I didn't touch*

213

a single instrument, so I'm pretty sure my "brand" will be just fine.)

Grace has been avoiding Amelia's final flight, preferring to think of her weekends with Gene, her summers in Rye, the Thermos of Cochrane Hotel tomato soup instead. But she pulls up a website with a map of the flight—a cross-country skip from California to Florida, then all the way around the world until New Guinea, the flight that doesn't have a final destination—a dotted line that trails off into the Pacific. She remembers what her dad said about Amelia not being the most technical pilot.

The dotted line is unnerving, so she closes the link and finds a video of Amelia and the Electra poised against the hulking backdrop of Californian mountains. The video is from her last photo shoot in Burbank, just days before she set off around the equator. Grace watches Amelia climb up the wing, her back round, her knees bent. The wind tangles her curls.

The film cuts to the hangar, and she's walking with her navigator, according to the caption. His too-big shirt puckers around his suspenders like a parachute. Fred looks back at the camera, but Amelia doesn't. She walks under the wing of the plane and keeps walking until the camera can't distinguish between her and the far wall, her shirt and pants disappearing into the darkness, her hands white and still swinging.

Janice insists Grace get on daycare lists, especially the one near the library. It seems insane—the baby is only as big as an eggplant—and Grace expects the daycare administrator will laugh at her calling when her due date isn't until June, but the woman who answers doesn't hesitate. From twelve to eighteen months, it costs $106 a day, she tells her. Grace gasps aloud over the phone—it's more than she pays in rent every month—but she doesn't have a choice, so she gives the woman her information and she tells Grace to call back when she knows the baby's name.

There's no way she'll be able to cover daycare costs on her library salary, so she texts Jamie. It's been six weeks since she turned down his proposal, five weeks since she refused his custody agreement.

He comes over after work and they don't hug hello. It's awkward, but he's asks how she's doing, and she asks how he's doing, and she's grateful they've always been good at sorting out the practical things. Grace makes a pot of tea and Jamie sits on the couch and opens up his laptop to an Excel spreadsheet.

The numbers make Grace cry. "How are diapers so fucking expensive? This is impossible."

"It's going to be fine," Jamie says—this is what happens when you come from money, you can be measured and calm and not panic. He punches in numbers and comes out with an amount he'll contribute each month. Grace stares at the number. She can't remember what his salary is, and maybe he's gotten a raise since the last time they did their taxes together, but it seems like a lot.

The baby kicks, its elbow, or knee, under her ribcage. Grace puts a hand on her stomach, waiting to feel it again. "I swear, this baby is going to dislocate one of my ribs one of these days," she says. Her belly undulates, the stripes on her shirt an unpredictable current.

"That is insane," Jamie says, reaching out his hand. "Can I?"

It's both intimate and entirely not, holding his hand against her belly.

The baby kicks again. "You feel that?" Grace asks.

He shakes his head. They sit in silence, waiting, Grace's belly's a Ouija board.

Nothing. Nothing. And then the baby kicks straight up into Jamie's palm.

"Holy shit!" he says and starts to laugh.

"Right?" Grace says. "It's fun now, a little less so at four in the morning." Though she doesn't ever really mind it then, either. She loves feeling her strong baby. She loves the undeniability of its presence. She loves knowing how safe the baby is inside her belly, the safest the baby will ever be.

"I meant to tell you, I've got a pediatrician lined up," he says before he leaves, zipping his laptop into its case.

"Okay." She feels stupid for not thinking of that.

"My brother went to school with her. She's just over on Roncy."

"Okay."

He pulls his shoes on. "My mom had postpartum depression," she blurts out.

"Okay." He nods slowly.

"And I'm afraid I'm going to have it."

"All right. Is it genetic?"

"They're not sure."

"Okay, well, I can keep an eye out. Maybe Jenna, too."

"Okay, thanks," she says.

"You'll have your follow-up with your OB when the baby's six weeks, and maybe mention it to your family doctor so she can be on the lookout, too?"

"Yah, okay. Good idea."

"It's going to be okay, Grace."

She doesn't know if he means the postpartum depression, or the money, or the co-parenting, but she nods, grateful for his steadfastness.

He squeezes her shoulder. "And you be good to your mama," he says to her belly.

Mama—it's still surreal. The baby sticks a foot under Grace's rib and she has to gently push it back.

I can do this, right? Grace texts Jenna while she sorts through Sylvie's first manuscript drafts in the second reading room.

Your body's built for this, she writes back.

No, no, I mean co-parenting.

Oh, yah, totally.

It's not crazy?

It's not conventional, but it's not crazy. Jenna adds a smiley face.

And it'll be good. Eventually you'll get a break every other weekend, or whatever you and Jamie decide.

Janice always complains about never getting a break from her kids, but it's so hard to fathom wanting to be away from this kid, this baby—the size of a cauliflower this week. Her baby does a lazy somersault and Grace puts both hands on her stomach.

She finishes ordering Sylvie's first manuscripts, her notes scrawled in blue ink above the typewritten text, and after Lucy and Patrick leave for lunch, she pulls out two of Amelia's envelopes.

> *Dear Gene,*
>
> *I keep reading about how dull I am. How preoccupied and distant and aloof I am. Am I really, though? If there's a mob wanting to grab my arms, I retreat, but I try to be warm and generous. I'm tired. I'm so tired, but I always try to smile and give as much as I can.*
>
> *I know it's just gossip and a way to sell papers, but it's hurtful. You'd be aloof too if you gave 150 lectures in a single year, I want to tell the reporters.*
>
> *Forgive me, I'm just tired and in a terrible mood.*
>
> *Tell me about Philly. I was thinking of you last Wednesday.*
>
> *I'm going to head to bed and hope this fog lifts in the morning.*
>
> *Love,*
>
> *A.E.*

The corner of the paper is crinkled, the ink slightly smeared as if water had been spilled on it. Grace includes a note about that in the synopsis. The next letter looks like it's been torn off a pad of paper.

Dear Gene,

*Don't be alarmed, and don't panic if you read anything—
yes, I'm at the hospital, but it's just my sinuses acting up
again. Dr. Goldstein is a gem, and I'm trusting he'll be
able to sort it out. I need these headaches gone!*

*And NO, don't come to visit. There's nothing to see and I'm
trapped in a hospital bed and am no fun at all.*

*As soon as I'm cleared, I'm heading east and will meet
you in Chicago (or maybe even Cleveland if you can get
away a few days earlier? Arlene has offered to host us for a
weekend!).*

A.E.

29

Grace lies back on the crinkly paper, her twenty-nine-week stomach eclipsing the far wall. Her OB is running late and though that would usually make Grace annoyed, she doesn't mind. Lying here, staring at the ceiling tiles feels like a mini-break from hauling this enormous belly around the city, trying to keep strangers from touching it.

Jenna was supposed to come, but wrote early in the morning to say she got booked into a last-minute meeting and now Grace wishes she had asked Jamie if he was free.

"Grace!" Dr. Lee says, letting the door slam behind her. "We're here to do an ultrasound today."

Grace can't tell if it's a question or not, so she nods. At first, she thought Dr. Lee was too direct, too abrupt, but she's grown to like her. Grace can imagine her telling her to push or breathe. She can imagine listening to her in the chaos of labour.

"And you're well? Heartburn okay? You're still taking an over-the-counter antacid?"

"Yup."

"Baby's kicking, moving?"

"Lots."

"You're still carrying small."

Grace feels so big it seems impossible that it's considered small. "I've been eating as many avocados as I can." Janice keeps telling her she's too small for twenty-nine weeks and it's messing with her head.

"I'm not worried. You've got a long torso, and every woman carries differently," Dr. Lee assures her. She takes Grace's blood pressure and adds a note to her chart. "Lean back, shirt up. Let's see how Baby's doing."

She squirts gel onto Grace's stomach and angles the screen so she can see it. It used to take some searching, the wand against her full bladder, but the baby is easy to find now, taking up all the space.

"And there's Baby," Dr. Lee says.

Thin arm bones, and a delicate little ribcage, a huge head, a nose that Grace thinks looks like her dad's.

She used to hear moms say, "I would give my life for my kids," and always thought it was hyperbole, the thing moms were supposed to say to prove their love for their kids no matter how many times they yelled at them to hurry up, or to eat their supper, but she gets it now. It's not hyperbole. It's not even so much a thought as a fact, a visceral reality. She would rather her baby exist than her. She would actually do anything for this small creature—it's the strangest, most overwhelming feeling.

"Baby's measuring well." Dr. Lee leans back and looks at her chart. "And you don't want to know the sex, right?"

Grace nods. She decided early on to let it be a surprise in the delivery room—what difference did it make if it was a girl or a boy? But with the ultrasound goo still on her stomach, she wants to know. She's suddenly desperate to know.

"Can I still find out?" Grace asks.

"Of course!"

Grace hesitates.

"How about I write it down and put it in an envelope and if you want, you can open it, okay?" Dr. Lee says.

"Okay."

The doctor licks the envelope closed and puts a question mark on the front.

Grace was going to invite Jenna and Jamie over and open the envelope with them, but she can't bear to wait and the minute she gets home, she tears it open. *Girl*, it says, with a heart next to it.

"Hello, little one, little girl," Grace says, her hands on her belly. She's no longer an abstract mass that kicks and somersaults and has the hiccups every day at 2:00 p.m. and 10:00 p.m., but a girl, a little girl, her little girl.

"I love you so much," she says aloud. A little girl with shoulders and elbows and knee caps—she already loves them. She loves her spine, her legs, her tiny ears, her heart tucked just below hers, though she's terrified she'll have an eating disorder, that she'll be bullied by mean girls in Grade 4, or when she's twenty-seven. She's terrified she'll be hurt by men, that she won't be able to teach her how to wear eyeliner, that she will forbid her from wearing short shorts and that she will anyway. That she will lie to her, that she will hate her body, the body Grace already loves so fiercely.

How do you teach someone to be independent and generous and not give a shit about the stuff that doesn't matter? Grace wonders. How do you teach someone to be careful and fearless, grounded and still be a dreamer?

Jamie stands at the door holding two plastic bags, the handles thin and digging into the insides of his knuckles. "I saw the delivery guy as I was coming in," he says.

"Oh, thanks!" Grace says. She tried telling him the baby is a girl over text, but deleted it and invited him over instead. She had to tell him in person.

"It's a lot of food!" Jamie says.

"I'm starving." Grace is always hungry, even though the baby has made her stomach half the size it usually is. "I have cheques somewhere, or I could just Interac you the money—"

He waves her off and she gets plates and Jamie opens the aluminum foil containers and it's like every other time they've eaten Thai food.

"Who's on the fridge?" he asks, spooning coconut rice onto his plate.

"Um, your baby," Grace says. There's the first ultrasound where she was just a little kidney bean, one from when she was an avocado, and yesterday's where she's head-down already, thank god.

"No, not the ultrasounds, the kid. Is it your nan?"

It's Amelia when she was eleven. She's wearing a huge bow in her hair that Grace is sure she hated and she can feel how itchy the collar of her dress was. "My mom sent it," she lies.

"You look like her," he says.

That's impossible, there's no way she does, but her chest warms at the thought of it. Grace looks at Amelia's wide eyes, her half smile, and wonders what her little girl will look like at five, at eight, at ten—

"How are you feeling?" Jamie asks.

"Okay," Grace says. "Tired, but okay. I saw the doctor this week and she said I should start taking liquid iron, but the baby's growing well, everything's good."

"Amazing," he says.

Will she have Jamie's copper-penny eyes, his dark hair with the intense cowlick that gives him the craziest bedhead? Or maybe she'll look like Nan, or maybe Dad, or maybe Jamie's brother, Connor? It's bizarre to think that she will contain all these people somehow, like a mirrored elevator, the hints of relatives Grace didn't know—the Violet her Nan was named after, the Delbert so high up the family tree there aren't any photos of him.

Grace spoons some green curry onto her plate and makes room for the mango salad. "So, you know how I didn't want to know if it was a boy or a girl?" she starts. "At the last appointment the doctor let it slip." She doesn't tell him that she asked. She doesn't say anything about the

Post-It note she tucked into Amelia's suitcase in the bedroom.

"And?"

"Do you want to know?"

"I've always wanted to know!"

"It's a girl!"

His face splits into a huge grin. "A girl! I knew it!"

"You did not."

"I did! I told Connor I thought it was a girl. A girl!"

"A girl."

"Watch out, my mom is going to lose her shit. She wanted Connor to be a girl so badly she didn't cut his hair until he was, like, eight."

"I thought she just liked his ringlets."

The baby kicks.

"By the way, my mom's throwing us a baby shower," he says.

"What?"

"At the Granite Club."

"I said I didn't want a baby shower."

"You know my mom."

"Have you ever been to a baby shower? They're horrible." And she knows that one thrown by his mom would be all of the worst parts about a baby shower amplified—all the stupid games, and the sitting around opening presents and having to ooh and ahh over onesies and receiving blankets. "I'm not going."

"Come on, it's one afternoon."

"I'm exhausted all the time. The last thing I want to do is spend a Saturday with all of your mom's friends at the Granite Club."

"Okay, what if it's just at her house?"

"I don't want a baby shower." There's no way she's going to buy a maternity dress she'll never wear again and be on display for his mom and her WASPy friends.

"Please, Grace?"

Grace digs her heels in. She spent seven years feeling uncomfortable and inadequate next to his mom. She'll have to share the baby with

223

Elaine for the rest of her life, but she doesn't have to do this.

"Is this really the hill you want to die on?" Jamie asks.

"There's no hill, and I'm not dying. I'm just not going to a baby shower I don't want. You can go. She's your baby, too."

"Fine," Jamie says, and Grace can tell he expects she'll change her mind.

Her landlady's dog barks downstairs.

"Well, we should probably think about names," he says.

"I guess," she says, relieved to move on. "I'm just getting used to it being a her."

"Can we agree not to do a boy's name, like Charlie, or Frankie?"

"Charlie?"

"Like, short for Charlotte."

"I've literally never thought of naming any baby Charlie, boy or girl."

"And not one of those new ones."

"New ones?"

"Like McKenna or Madison."

They keep going like this, promising not to name the baby after the mean girls in Grade 4, or Jamie's ex-girlfriends, or the very Scottish relatives on his dad's side.

Jamie washes the dishes while Grace puts the leftovers into Tupperware and for a split second, she can picture them here with their little girl, not together, but together, parenting, doing laundry, washing supper dishes, blending up food for her and putting it in ice cube trays.

The next morning, Jamie sends an email with a link to a Google doc with potential names. It's twenty-seven names long and Grace is supposed to add to the list and highlight her favourites in green. He's highlighted his top picks in yellow—June, Clara, and Mia. They're good names, but they're not *her* name. She doesn't know what it is yet.

Grace likes Isla, and Emily, but naming someone something that will define who they are, something they'll carry with them their whole lives, is so daunting.

"Violet," she says, Nan's name. She presses her hands on her belly, waiting for a kick. Nothing.

"Amelia," she tries.

Still nothing.

30

Spring arrives and the mornings are dark, the evenings full of light and promise. The first crocuses make Grace cry, and then the daffodils' yellow trumpets, and then the bright red tulips that shoot up through last year's leaves, insistent and confident. Everything seems so tender, the pale green so vulnerable Grace can barely stand it.

On one exceptionally warm evening, the ice cream truck starts cruising down the street, its tinny song more a plaintive Polish folk tune than the jolly one of most ice cream trucks. Jamie and Grace used to line up behind the neighbourhood kids and get chocolate vanilla twists, the cones always stale, the ice cream always melting too fast. Grace wants to run after the minor-keyed tune and catch the truck before it hits Harbord Street, but she read a BlogTO post about listeria and ice cream trucks so she lets its sad song disappear up the street.

Grace's bathing suit barely fits, but she goes to the pool at lunch anyway. She's far enough along that she can't justify spending a fortune on a maternity bathing suit. Instead, she pulls out the bikini she took to Saint Kitts four years ago. She feels exposed and naked, walking across the pool deck with her belly button leading the way, but in the water, her huge round belly is weightless. Even her legs are light, and she feels like a planet and an astronaut combined. She breaststrokes to the deep end, with David Bowie's "Space Oddity" in Chris Hadfield's voice in her head. Sometimes she forgets that the baby can only hear her voice, her heartbeat, not whatever is in her head.

Jamie's mom has been leaving Grace voice mails about the shower that she deletes without listening to. Jenna thinks she's crazy, not giving in, and she knows Jamie is waiting for her to change her mind, but she's holding the line. She refuses to be bullied into a shower she never asked for.

When Grace is halfway back to the shallow end, the baby kicks—a swift thump to the inside of her right ribs. Her whole belly seizes. It's too deep to stand, so she paddles over to the wall and hangs on, trying to breathe. She pictures her uterus bride, holding tight to her baby girl like a girdle, a corset, Spanx.

Let go let go let go—

A short whistle from the lifeguard chair.

"You okay, ma'am?" the redheaded lifeguard calls down from the chair. The rest of the guards stand, their flutter boards raised in the air.

"I'm fine," Grace insists.

"Do you need help getting out of the pool?"

"I'm totally fine." She really wishes everyone would sit down. "I'm not in labour, I promise."

The lifeguards put their flutter boards down, but the redhead keeps her eye on Grace and people keep passing her, staring. Her OB says swimming's good for her, for the baby, she wants to tell them.

But what if she did go into labour here, in the pool? It would probably be better than if she was at home. Here there are people trained in first aid, though probably none of them have delivered a baby. She's scared of going into labour alone—will she know it's labour? And who will she call first? Jenna probably, then Jamie. Will they both come over? Will they meet her at the hospital? How will she know when it's time to go to the hospital?

Grace inches along the edge of the pool toward the shallow end like a scared five-year-old failing her red badge. She hates the unpredictability of labour so much it almost makes her want to beg for a C-section, a date she can choose, and a specific time. At least then she'd know when it was happening. At least then it wouldn't catch her by surprise.

Even though it was just a Braxton-Hicks contraction, Grace starts packing for the hospital, following the list her OB gave her at her last appointment: adult diapers, maternity pads, granola bars, a baby nail file. Grace packs a pair of jogging pants, along with a hoodie and an old, stretched-out sports bra. She puts in a toothbrush and a travel-size tube of toothpaste, then adds extra hair elastics, Advil, and extra-strength Tylenol.

There's still room in Amelia's red suitcase, so Grace adds the blanket her mom knit, then the copy of *Goodnight Moon* from Patrick. Even though she's still got ten weeks to go, she leaves the suitcase by the front door. "Ready," she says to her belly. "We're ready."

She's almost finished with Amelia's letters and has been going through the last few more slowly, and rereading her favourites—the ones about Newfoundland, the one about the scarf Gene bought her, the one about Wiley. Janice brings someone from the digital preservation team on board to build the page in the portal. The web person asks Grace for a sample letter and Grace gives her the one about Myrtle Mantz, but then wants it back as soon as she hands it over.

Janice loops in Special Collections, and the comms team, too, and they ask for synopses, and scans of some of the most dramatic letters. But what do they mean by "dramatic"? Grace gives them a scan of the Wiley letter, but they want something else, *something more Amelia-focused*, they write, so she sends them the letter about Amelia deciding to fly around the world.

Perf, the head of comms writes back, then asks her to transcribe it for them.

She doesn't want to. She doesn't like all these people reading the letters, her letters, people who don't know anything about Amelia, but she doesn't have a choice.

31

Grace shoehorns herself into the table by the window, her belly pressed against the edge. She's sweating from the walk down, the back of her maternity T-shirt damp. She can't imagine how uncomfortable she's going to be in June.

"Do you think the chocolate poop diapers are out already?" Grace asks Jenna, hugging her over the table.

"The what?" Jenna asks.

"At the shower."

"Oh my god, I forgot that's today! I still can't believe you didn't go."

Janice convinced Grace to do a registry, though, so she wouldn't get a thousand pink onesies that the baby would grow out of before she could put her in them. "People want to spend money on babies," she insisted. So Grace and Jamie had sat in Grace's apartment with a spreadsheet on Jamie's laptop and found thermometers and breast-feeding pillows that looked like TV dinner trays and spit-up cloths with flying dogs on them. They picked a high chair, and a set of crib sheets and a baby monitor, a diaper pail and a humidifier, and a set of hooded bath towels.

"Eric went on the registry yesterday and said the only thing left was a Sophie giraffe," Jenna says.

"Holy shit! Everything was gone?"

Jenna nods.

"What is up with that giraffe? Ever since Jamie and I did the registry, I see them everywhere. Wait, tell me you guys didn't buy it." She can tell from Jenna's face that they did. "Okay, I take it back, I love the giraffe. Still, you were not supposed to get anything from that stupid list."

"It's fine."

"Okay, then brunch is on me."

"Oh, fuck no. Now you're just being nuts."

"Okay then, thank you." Grace pulls out her bottle of TUMS and shakes out two. "You're too good to me. To us."

The server brings Jenna a coffee and tea for Grace. She tells Jenna about the portal and the comms strategy, and the search team that is going to the South Pacific. She tells her about the Google Alert she set up on her phone to get any new news about Amelia. Grace pauses to take a sip of her tea and Jenna fiddles with her spoon.

"You okay?" Grace asks.

"I need to tell you something," she says, her voice quiet.

Grace puts her tea down. "Okay."

"I know I've been totally absent lately—"

"No, no, you've just been busy," Grace says.

Jenna doesn't look up from the table. "Eric and I can't get pregnant."

Grace's throat tightens. "What?"

"We've been trying for a while—"

"Since when?"

"Last spring."

"A year ago? Wait. What?"

"When we realized it was maybe a thing, you were dealing with Jamie moving out and I just … You didn't need that on top of everything you were going through."

"I guess, but still, that's huge." Grace feels stung. How could her best friend be going through something so huge and not say anything?

"Well, it didn't work, anyway, and we just did a bunch of tests and it turns out Eric's sperm has low motility." She starts to cry.

"Oh, Jenna. Fuck, I'm so sorry." Grace reaches across the table. Jenna lets her hold her hands, but doesn't squeeze back.

"And then you got pregnant, just like that, and you didn't even want to be."

Grace wishes she could hide her huge belly. "Fuck. Fuck. I'm so sorry. I'm so, so sorry."

"It's not your fault. I'm just—I'm so jealous. I want to be pregnant. And I don't want to be jealous. God, I hate being jealous." Jenna wipes her eyes with the backs of her hands. "Fuck. I told Eric I wasn't going to cry."

"Jenna—I don't even know what to say. I had no idea," Grace says. "God, I would've been so much more sensitive." She's been texting Jenna about every ache and pain and round of acid reflux for months, complaining about the exhaustion, about being kept awake by the little girl's dance routines, all the OB appointments, forcing her to feel the baby kick—

"I'm happy for you. Really. It's just hard sometimes."

The server interrupts, carrying their plates on one arm, a pot of coffee in the other. They rearrange the table, making room for the side of ketchup, Jenna's extra bacon, the salt and pepper shakers.

"Is there something you can do?" Grace asks after the server leaves.

"We're going to start with IUIs for a few months."

Grace feels like an idiot for not knowing what an IUI is.

Jenna tells her about tracking her cycle and basal temperature and cervical fluid on an app. "And then they take Eric's sperm and clean it and who knows what else and then they turkey-baster it up into my uterus."

"That's the medical term?"

Jenna smiles. "Okay, a catheter. We'll do that for a while, maybe three or four cycles, and then if that doesn't work, I'll start Clomid, which apparently will turn me into a fertility goddess. Or at least make me fat and crazy hormonal and make all the eggs. And if that doesn't work, then IVF." She starts crying again.

"It's going to work," Grace says, then wishes she hadn't.

"Maybe," Jenna says, and her voice breaks Grace's heart. She attacks her omelet with the side of her fork. "Eric feels like shit and I've been totally hassling him. That's why he hasn't been drinking and I've been making him eat clams and nutritional yeast. And he started seeing a Chinese medicine doctor and has been drinking all these teas to balance his liver and kidneys. I know it's not his fault, but I just, I can't help it sometimes. I just wish it were fine. I wish it were just—"

"Easier," Grace fills in.

"Yah. Easier."

Grace is flooded with guilt. "Let me know what I can do," she says, cutting into her pancakes. "I can come with you to appointments if you want. You just say the word."

"I don't think a super pregnant woman at a fertility clinic is the best thing."

"Fuck, of course not. I'm sorry."

They eat in silence, and the server tops up Jenna's coffee without asking.

"What if we can't get pregnant?" Jenna says, her cutlery suspended above her plate. "What if it never happens?"

"Don't go there yet," Grace says.

"I know, but what if?"

"You have to give it some time."

"Okay, can we talk about something else?" Jenna asks, crumpling her napkin. "I feel like all I ever talk about these days is sperm and cervical fluid."

Grace stares at her plate, but the only things she can think of are Amelia and the baby. Shit. Shit. "Do you listen to the *Dear Sugars* podcast?" she asks.

Jenna shakes her head.

"Okay, you're going to love it. It's an advice column, essentially, but also so much more than that. The hosts are super lovely. Their voices are so soothing, but also commanding. And they get letters about, well about everything—estranged parents, fucked-up teenagers, divorce, grief, cheating, everything." Grace doesn't mention the episode she just listened to about infertility and surrogacy.

"So, other people's suffering," Jenna says, smiling.

"Kind of, but more of a reminder that everyone's having a hard time, and that we're also all okay, or at least going to be okay."

Grace insists on paying the bill and Jenna offers her a ride home.

"Could you drop me off at the pool?" Grace asks. She tries not to notice the fertility clinic pamphlets in the back seat.

"Here," Jenna says, handing Grace her phone. "Can you subscribe me to that podcast? I feel like I want to listen to other people having a shitty time."

"Totally," Grace says, opening the podcast app.

After Jenna pulls in next to the pool, Grace leans awkwardly over the gear shift to hug Jenna goodbye. "I love you," Grace says.

"I love you, too," Jenna says. "Nothing changes that."

It's Grace's turn to cry.

"Don't you dare start," Jenna says.

Grace hauls herself out of the car and waves until Jenna's taillights disappear down Harbord. She's too tired to swim for very long, but the weightlessness is a relief. She floats on her back in the deep end, her belly a white half-moon above the turquoise surface, while injured triathletes tread water around her.

She cycles through every time she called Jenna to whine about how ugly maternity clothes were, or complain about her boobs being sore, or how she hated having to sleep on her back. She feels like such an ass. But she didn't know. How could she? But then she thinks about how Jenna knew more about pregnancy than Grace did. She already knew all the midwifery clinics and had a list of doulas and opinions about cloth versus disposable diapers. Grace should've known something was up. She should've figured it out.

In the showers after her swim, an elderly woman, naked except for an orange flowered bathing cap, stops Grace. "You look radiant, dear," she says.

Grace smiles, trying not to feel awkward about her enormous belly covered in shampoo bubbles. She lets the hot water blast against her eyelids, her cheeks, grateful that she's pregnant even if she didn't mean to be, and that there are good, kind strangers in the world she's bringing this little girl into, especially naked elderly ladies in hilarious bathing caps. She rinses the shampoo out of her hair and squeezes the conditioner into her palm.

And then she realizes she hasn't felt the baby kick recently—not over brunch, not even when she had a glass of grapefruit juice, not while she was swimming and the baby usually does flutter kicks against the right side of her ribs when she's in the pool. She stands under the hot water, her bathing suit hanging off the faucet, and pushes on her side where the baby's feet, or maybe her knees, usually press back.

Nothing.

She presses again, but again, nothing.

Grace wracks her brain for her last kick, her last set of hiccups, her last somersault, but can't remember the last one.

"C'mon, little one, come on." Grace pushes at her belly. "Let's go, baby girl. Where's my soccer player?"

Still nothing.

Dr. Lee said that if the baby was ever still that Grace should try drinking something sugary, so she gets changed as fast as she can, realizing only after she pulls her shirt on that she forgot to wash the conditioner out of her hair.

She fumbles for change, and counts out enough to get a Coke from the vending machine.

One sip, nothing.

The sweet makes Grace's teeth ache. She gulps back half the can. Still nothing.

She takes her bag and the rest of the can to the pool gallery and lies on the bleachers, hands on her belly. She pushes on her stomach and wills the baby to move. "Come on, baby girl. Come on."

The swim team is on the deck, their trackpants in small, navy-blue puddles. The lane ropes carve the pool into eight long stripes as the swimmers stand on the blocks and whip their arms in circles and snap their bathing caps over their hair.

Kick, Grace tells the baby, *kick*.

She closes her eyes the way she did when she first felt the baby move. She was lying in bed on a Saturday, trying to have a nap and there it was, a tiny curl, the size of a nickel. She couldn't believe it at first and waited till she felt two, three, four more. She called her mom, half-laughing, half-crying, and her mom cried and made her lie there until she felt it again with her on the phone.

Grace can hear her own heart thudding in her ears, still plugged with pool water. It's too loud, too persistent. She doesn't care about her heart. The only heart in her body that matters is her baby's. She wants to call 911, but they wouldn't do anything. She takes her phone out and looks up the number for the maternity clinic at Mount Sinai. Her OB works there some weekends. Dr. Lee would tell her to calm down, to breathe, then squirt pale blue gel on her belly and press the wand against her tight skin.

The swimmers dive in, splash, pause, splash, pause, splash and the baby kicks. Just once.

"Baby girl!" Grace says, pushing back.

The baby presses back into Grace's palm and tears stream down her cheeks.

"My girl, there you are. I love you. Don't you dare do that again."

"She was probably just sleeping," Dr. Lee says at Grace's emergency appointment on Monday morning. She listens to the baby's heart-

237

beat—a perfect 156—and hooks Grace up to the ultrasound so she can see her. She's sucking her thumb, curled up and content. Grace watches her baby's heart beat inside her tiny ribcage until the doctor has to see another patient.

When Grace gets home she pulls out the Doppler machine Jamie rented and lies on the couch, smearing pale blue gel, the colour of the swimming pool, all over her stomach. She presses the wand against her skin—the swish of gel and her lunch, until her baby's swooshing heartbeat fills the living room. She wishes Jamie had splurged and got the kind that counted the heart rate for her, but instead, Grace sets her phone timer and counts—152, 143, 148—faster than her own, but steady, steady.

Dear Amelia,

I can't stop listening to her perfect little heart. Yesterday, I even fell asleep on the couch listening to it. I wish you could hear it, the whoosh, like waves falling on top of each other.

Was the blue of the ocean always beautiful from the cockpit perch of your Electra, or was it ever menacing? Was it ever lonely up there in the cockpit, or did you feel like your most essential self, reading the wind and the altitude and trying to avoid the wall of monsoon rain that apparently stripped the paint off your wings?

When you landed each day, was it nice to finally talk to Fred, instead of passing notes back and forth along a fishing line from the cabin to the cockpit? Would your ears ring from the roar of the engines? Would you send telegrams to George? Did you miss Gene? I can't imagine what you saw, who you talked to, what you ate each night—

The search team that's going after you at the end of the

month thinks you landed on Nikumaroro—an atoll in the middle of nowhere. I didn't know what an atoll was and had to look it up. Atoll—a ring-shaped coral reef that encircles a lagoon.

It's poetic, this ring of coral, its unreal blue where a volcano used to be but sunk down underneath the water, leaving behind a lapis-lazuli centre. And on the far side of the reef, the Pacific stretching out past where your eyes could make sense of. There were clams, turtles, coconut crabs, and apparently a campfire on the southeast curve of the ring.

Did you know that it was called Gardner Island then? Did it matter to you what it was called?

—G

32

The baby kicks Grace awake before the sun's even up, her squished bladder full to bursting. It's barely light out, but at least the robins are already singing. Her uterus seizes in a Braxton-Hicks contraction. Water, she needs water. She hauls herself out of bed and drinks one glass, then another. She tries to go back to sleep, but she can't, so she makes toast and tea and brings it into bed and types out a note to Jenna. *Thinking about you. xoxo.* Today's the day of her first IUI treatment. Grace adds confetti cannon emojis, then takes them out and presses send.

She opens up her laptop, balancing it on her belly—Jamie's sent another reminder about the baby name Google doc, and a list of thank-yous they need to write for shower gifts. She leaves his emails unanswered and clicks on the baby vegetable-size link—the baby is a cabbage this week. Her brain is beginning to fold into its thousands of folds and her fingernails are starting to grow. *Nine weeks to go!* exclaims the banner at the top of the page. Nine. She's going to be a mother in nine weeks, maybe less, and she has no idea how to change a diaper, or get a baby to latch, or fold a swaddle. The baby kicks again. In nine weeks she's going to have to share her with Jamie, with her mom, with the world. She doesn't want to. She wants it to just be the two of them still, the two of them forever.

She gets to work early, before Lucy and Patrick, even before Janice. She has one letter left in the soft cardboard box. She starts reading it at her desk, but is afraid she'll be interrupted, so she takes it up to the mezzanine. A swell of vertigo rises as she steps out of the elevator. It is dizzying up on the fourth floor, perched over the reading room, but she steadies herself and sits awkwardly in front of the medieval medical texts. The baby turns lazily as she pulls the last letter out of the box. It's smaller than some of the other envelopes, the flap torn and jagged. The letter itself is even smaller than the envelope.

Dear Gene,

I'm missing my little red bus today. Don't get me wrong, my 5C is great. Lighter, and her revised tail surface is great, but it's no 5B. Have you seen a more elegant bird? I dare say I haven't. It was the gold that did me in—that line of subtle sparkle that isn't ostentatious, or flashy, just classy and delicate. And the red—that deep red—like an overripe sour cherry. She was my first monoplane, and I loved that beautifully cantilevered single piece of spruce. How could I not be absolutely besotted? I'll never forget her silhouette once we got to Newfoundland—her curves against the scrubby trees and sheer rock faces. She was really something else.

She was so elegant on the outside but all business in the cockpit—nothing extra, nothing frilly. A bit rudimentary, maybe, but if I close my eyes, I can still see every single instrument. That wooden rudder, the angle of the two side windows. I know it better than I know the back of my hand. (What a silly phrase. I don't know the backs of my hand. Do you? Does anyone?)

*When I first got her, I crashed—nosed over, ruined her
fuselage. I got it replaced and reinforced, but I still feel like
such a dolt. It was such an avoidable crack-up, though I
guess better into a tree in New Jersey than over the Atlantic.*

*I only had her for three years. It felt like a lifetime. I
wish I hadn't sold her off. What a heel. Though I needed
something to fly, and she had done her service, three times
over, really—she took me across the pond, and then across
to Cali, down to Mexico, and back.*

*Sometimes I think I should stop in at the Franklin Institute
when I'm in Philly to see her, but I never do. It'd be too
hard to see her on display, not in a field, covered in mud
and god knows what else. I hope people see her and are
inspired to fly, but I couldn't bear seeing her grounded.*

She was my first great love. Don't laugh, she really was.

I must bid you adieu so I can get this in the next post.

Love,

A.E.

Grace looks up the Vega and stares at a black-and-white photo of Amelia in Londonderry in her flight suit, sitting on the wheel coverings, a
photographer in the frame, taking pictures. She looks happy. She looks
rested, though there's no way she would be, having flown overnight
across the Atlantic from Harbour Grace.

Grace reads the letter again, then refolds it, sliding it back in its
envelope. This is it, the last letter. It feels unfathomable that she's read
them all, that she's done, but she is. She still has to get the last round of
synopses approved, but this is it. She pulls all of the envelopes out of the
box, careful to keep them in order, and stares at them—Gene's name
scrawled across each one, the envelopes torn open sometimes along the
flap, sometimes along the side. What would Gene think of her reading

them, of the whole world reading them? She picks up the empty box but hears something rattling. A safety pin, rusted and old. Maybe one of the safety pins Amelia used to pin maps to her pants while she flew. Maybe. Just maybe.

Grace opens and closes it. She should leave it in the box. She should tell Janice about it. It should be catalogued. But she stands and slides the pin into her back pocket. She puts the letters back in the box and carries them down to the scanner to make internal copies before she has to hand them over to the digital preservation team.

Grace's Google Alert bings to tell her the search team is heading out to the South Pacific at the end of the week. Grace looks up a map of Amelia's final flight—a zigzagging line across the equator. Oakland to Miami to Puerto Rico to Venezuela to Suriname to Brazil. Then after Brazil, a long skip across the ocean to Senegal, Mali, Chad, Sudan, Ethiopia, Pakistan, India, Myanmar, Thailand, Singapore, Indonesia. Did she bother changing time zones, Grace wonders, still in bed, or did time stop mattering at a certain point?

She finds new videos, from Miami, from Venezuela, from Dakar. YouTube is filled with grainy, soundless clips captioned haphazardly with inconsistent caps and dates and claims that may or may not be true. Grace lies in bed with her laptop on top of her long pregnancy pillow, and watches one claiming to be the last video ever seen of Amelia. "Last Takeoff," it's called, and looks like it was filmed somewhere hot and mountainous—maybe New Guinea, but it doesn't say. In it, Amelia and Fred stand beside each other in short sleeves, maybe getting their picture taken, maybe listening to someone beyond the frame. The two of them climb up the wing, almost running. Fred offers Amelia a hand she doesn't need, and they both duck into the cockpit.

The plane starts to taxi and the Electra barely gets off the ground, the wings wobbling as the wheels clear the runway.

Amelia only had seven thousand miles to go when she and Fred disappeared. They had already flown twenty-two thousand miles and only had three stops left—Howland Island, Honolulu, and Oakland, and she'd done the Honolulu-Oakland flight before—that's when she had the best hot chocolate of her life, flew through rainbows, and ate an entire roast chicken after she landed. Grace wonders if she was already planning on that roast chicken again for her celebratory meal.

Grace wants to stay in bed all day, staring at the tiny dot of Howland Island, the island with the runway Roosevelt had built that Amelia and Fred couldn't find no matter how hard they searched, but the baby presses against her bladder and Janice has called an all-staff meeting to announce the letters and reveal the portal. Grace gets up and pees, then gets dressed, careful to slip the safety pin into the pocket of her maternity jeans, and heads out, the sidewalks dusted pale green with pollen.

Abigail rubs Grace's stomach before Grace can move out of the way. "Look at you!" she crows. "How're you feeling?"

"Nervous," Grace replies, and then realizes she's talking about the pregnancy, not the announcement.

"It's not long now!" she says, and Grace wishes she could move and stand next to Lucy.

Janice calls the meeting to order more formally than usual, and Grace notices the chief librarian is standing by the door, arms folded across her chest. Janice is bursting as she claps her hands together. Janice tells the staff about finding the letters during the shelf read, the synopses, the portal.

"Grace, here, has done an exceptional job with them," she says.

Grace feels the back of her neck get warm, her cheeks flushing.

"And we've got full support from the university to get these up and out." Janice explains about the timeline, the rush with the expedition on its way to Nikumaroro. "We're going to capitalize on the timing."

"You were working on this?" Abigail hisses, swatting Grace's elbow. "I thought you were cataloguing with Lucy."

The head of the digital archiving team walks everyone through the portal, the Myrtle Mantz letter repeated over and over again, a stand-in for all the other letters. It's strange to see Amelia's handwriting blown up on the screen and Grace wants to look away. She presses the head of the safety pin into her thumb until it leaves an imprint.

The head of comms talks next about press releases and media strategy, and the chief librarian thanks Janice and Grace, and the rest of the team. "This will put the Fisher on the map," she says, and everyone claps.

Grace pastes a smile on her face, and it takes everything she has not to run out of the library. The project has doubled, tripled, quadrupled in size over the course of the meeting, and the letters have moved further and further away from Grace—to the digital humanities team, the digital preservation team, the heads of donor and alumni engagement. She wants to grab the box back and take it back to her desk, unfolding the letters one at a time, lifting the torn envelope flaps, watching Amelia's scrawl loop over and over again.

After the meeting, Patrick gives her a nod and a wink from across the room and she wonders if he's known all along.

"Congrats!" Jeremy says. "That's what you've been working on, all secretive."

Abigail smiles stiffly and Grace can tell she's upset, either that Janice hadn't chosen her for the project, or that Grace hadn't told her, but Grace doesn't have it in her to do anything about it.

Eventually, everyone goes back to work. Grace debates asking Janice if she can just go home, but she's in her office with the head of digital preservation, so she follows Lucy into the second reading room.

Grace's ankles are swollen from standing through the meeting, so she sits with her feet up on a chair. She tries to focus on Sylvie's poems written on the backs of grocery lists, but she can't stop thinking about Amelia and that zigzagging line across the equator, the line that just ends somewhere over the South Pacific. When Lucy goes for lunch, Grace pulls out her phone and angles herself near the windows so no one can see her from the door. Patrick's engrossed in a manuscript and doesn't notice, or at least doesn't say anything.

When Amelia and Fred took off from Lae, New Guinea, with Howland Island as their next stop, there was a boat, the *Itasca*—a picket ship, floating just off the coast of the island—amplifying radio waves, ready, waiting to hear from Amelia. But Amelia and Fred left behind radio equipment with shorter wavelength frequencies. Their radio antenna was broken and they had fifty gallons of fuel less than they'd planned. Fred was counting on using celestial navigation, but the clouds took over and buried the stars. And they couldn't find the island, or the *Itasca*, even when they dropped down to one thousand feet.

Were they still passing notes to each other from behind the fuel tanks to the cockpit? Were they yelling to each other? Were they both in the cockpit, searching desperately for the smoke from the boat?

Maybe the boat was on naval time and Amelia and Fred on Greenwich Mean Time. Maybe the maps were wrong. Maybe the instrument panel was broken and they didn't know.

"We are running north and south," Amelia said, the last words the *Itasca* caught, but that was it. That was all.

And, Grace supposes, there are only so many circles you can fly before the fuel starts running out.

And there are only so many circles you can fly before the promised island with its brand-new runway refuses to appear.

And there are only so many circles you can fly before you go into a tailspin and make a crash landing on Nikumaroro, with its coral beach and undrinkable water, the Pacific half-devouring the plane—

"Grace?"

She looks up. Lucy's standing in the doorway.

"You okay?"

She nods. "Yah, sorry. I just—" She waves her phone.

"Everything okay?"

She forces a smile. "Yup."

"Have you had lunch yet?"

Grace shakes her head.

"You need to eat! Go," Lucy says. "Get some fresh air."

Grace gets a cheese sandwich from the coffee shop at the Athletic Centre and sits in the bleachers over the pool. The bread is dry and hard to swallow, and the mayonnaise makes the cheese slippery. She picks at the sandwich, and looks for pictures of the *Itasca*—a huge grey behemoth with its tall, pixelated mast and ropes and portholes, the centre of it built up like a birthday cake. The U.S. got rid of it after it couldn't find Fred and Amelia and the UK renamed it the HMS *Gorleston*. Gorleston—a tiny East Anglian town on the coast known for its school for deaf and blind children.

The baby presses her heel against Grace's ribs and Grace imagines her waking up, stretching, yawning. Grace stares at the intense blue of the pool, and her body starts echoing with the baby's tiny hiccups, a rapid-fire Morse code. It's two o'clock, it must be.

She has to go back to work, but Grace looks up the origins of *Itasca*—a suburb of Chicago, a national park, a lake—the headwater of the Mississippi River. It's a made-up word—the "itas" from the Latin *veritas*, truth, and "ca" from *caput*, head. Even if the boat had failed her, she thinks Amelia would like that—the made-up-ness of its name.

Dear Amelia,

The atoll was almost four hundred miles from the Itasca. *It doesn't sound far, but that'd be from here to somewhere between Montreal and Quebec City. Far enough away that you couldn't see it, which was probably easier than if you could. What would you have done if you could? Would you have made a raft and chanced it? Would you have swum, your long legs kicking, carrying Fred on his back like the lifeguards you used to see training on Californian beaches?*

Would it have made a difference if the Electra had been Vega red or Friendship *orange instead of muted silver? Something other than the colour of clouds?*

*Did the heat on Nikumaroro remind you of Kansas?
Probably not as dry. Did the ocean remind you of
Newfoundland, or was it too hot, too blue, to be even
remotely similar? Did you wish you had insisted on
pontoons for the Electra? Did any of it feel like an
adventure, or was being stuck on a desert island too awful
to bear?*

*They say you shucked Nikumaroro clams the way you
shucked oysters in Boston during your Denison House
summers. Someone, years ago, found your opened shells,
pink and waiting for rain.*

*I'm sure it's impossible to imagine, but in 1939, the Brits
claimed the atoll and put in paved coral roads and a parade
ground. There were wells, and twenty-six kids playing tag
under the coconut palms, making sailboats out of clam
shells and a post office. Imagine sending Gene a postcard.
It's laughable, I'm sure, or maybe too hard to think about.
Never mind. It's probably best not to think about that.*

*The water ran out in the sixties and a year after everyone
left, the post office was shuttered. I wonder if it's still there,
or if the rats and the coconut crabs took it over, turning it
into whatever they needed it to be.*

—G

33

When Grace gets home, her Google Alert sends her a pdf of the brochure for the mission that left for Nikumaroro. Turns out it's not just scientists, or historians, or experts. Anyone could've gone—anyone with nine thousand dollars, not including airfare. Grace is shocked that anyone can go and dig around on the atoll. It seems so tacky, having a bunch of rich people, who in the photos are all white, and sunburned, dressed in khaki shorts and sensible running shoes, with Tilley hats and enormous cameras around their necks, doing the work scientific teams should be doing.

There's a map of the trip—a teardrop angling northeast from Fiji, sailing first to an island called Rotuna, followed by a one-thousand-mile sail to Nikumaroro, the atoll they call "Niku." Grace can't imagine being stuck on a boat for twenty days, especially after the nausea of her first trimester, but if she were on the boat, she'd skip the lectures about coral reefs, island ecology, and the cultural heritage of Polynesians and spend the days in the pool. She wonders if it's an actual lap pool, or a kidney-shaped floating pool like in suburban backyards.

They're going to spend six days on the atoll, breaking into groups to dive around the coral, dig up the colonial village, and poke around the "7 site"—a bunch of bushes shaped in the number seven where a woman's shoe was found a few year ago.

Shouldn't archaeological digs be something that scientists do, not white-haired retirees named Dorothy and George? Shouldn't people be trained for this?

What's even worse is the brochure offers activities like any other cruise would—"snorkeling and swimming and kayaking," as if it's a fucking Disney cruise. How can there be downtime when they're doing an archaeological search? How could anyone go for a dip, or take out a kayak, when there could be Fred's femur bone, or a piece of fuselage to be found? It all seems so fucked up.

Grace shuts her computer down and turns the ringer off on her phone. She stares at the crib box at the end of her bed, the pale wood poles, the plastic bags of silver hardware. She needs someone else to hold up the pieces while she screws them together, but she doesn't want Jamie to come over and she can't ask Jenna.

She tries to put it together herself, but eventually gives up and crawls into bed. She wills herself to sleep, but the blue ring of Nikumaroro burns on the backs of her eyelids. She wouldn't ever be able to afford the trip, and even if she could handle the seasickness and the boring old people, there's no way she could do it with a baby. Still, she wants to walk on the hot coral roads and swim around the reef and stand on the edge of the atoll, looking out at the Pacific, picturing Hawaiian leis and imagining what roast chicken would taste like in Oakland, the Golden Gate Bridge perched in the distance.

Dear Amelia,

There's a rumour you made forty-seven calls, forty-seven agonizing radio calls with your plane smashed against the coral, broken, and Fred broken—"out of his head," a Texan housewife declared, his voice competing with yours for air space. A fifteen-year-old girl from Florida heard you talking about being terrified about the rising water. A woman in Toronto heard you say, "We can't hold on much longer." You would have known the battery would die, and that the gas would eventually run out. Did losing the radio frighten you more than the lack of rain?

I picture the radio cradled in your hands, your voice, breaking, but trying so desperately to be even, direct, clear, despite your cracked lips, your bleeding lips, thirsty.

I can't bear to think of your fear, your desperation—

I can't bear to think about those radio calls. It seems impossible that they didn't go and scoop you up, like they would in a movie, in the penultimate scene before you stepped back onto American soil, waving, tired around the eyes, with a change of clothes someone would've brought for you, the wind lifting your scarf over your shoulder, captured for the front of every newspaper.

Why didn't they find you? Why couldn't they find you?

—G

34

Grace doesn't sleep well all weekend, kept awake by half dreams about the Electra, about the forty-seven radio calls, about the shells, pink and so desperate. She still needs to put the crib together. She should go through the piles of stuff Jamie dropped off from the shower, but everything feels too heavy—her arms, her legs, everything.

She takes her toast outside and her landlady's dog barks at a man delivering flyers. She sends her mom a picture of the plate balancing on her belly, the sun a burst of light behind the eclipse of her stomach.

Radiant, her mom writes back, even though there are crumbs on Grace's shirt and it doesn't quite reach her pajama pants anymore. *How are you feeling?*

Good, she lies. *Big. Unwieldy*. That's not a lie. She feels like the *Itasca*—huge and unmoored, drifting, and terrified that she will die in childbirth and her baby will be an orphan, or that her baby will die in childbirth and orphan her—is there a word for that, a baby-less mother?

Her mom sends back a clock emoji and a bomb emoji and Grace wishes she hadn't discovered emojis.

I still have eight weeks to go, she writes back.

Her mom sends her a photo of her flight itinerary. She's arriving on the twelfth of June. Grace found a B&B on Euclid, an eight-minute walk from her apartment—close enough, without being too close.

Your dad will fly out as soon as the baby's here and we'll book our return flights from Toronto.

Grace's phone bings again—another Google Alert, this time with a CNN article titled "Amelia Earhart: Found!"

Grace's hearts starts racing. How? How could they already find her? They're still supposed to be on the boat sailing to the atoll.

It's not the expedition, though, it's a link to a newly discovered photo of Amelia, or at least that's what the article claims. There's a person sitting on a dock with her—or his, it's impossible to tell—back to the camera, head turned over the right shoulder.

Grace holds her breath and squints. Could it really be her?

There are a lot of people standing around and one guy has Fred's sharp hairline. The article insists the smeary blur on the right-hand side of the photo is the Electra being pulled by a Japanese ship.

Grace gets her laptop so she can see the photo on a bigger screen and looks for Fred's sticking-out ears, a scarf tied around Amelia's neck. The article says the photo was taken by a spy who was executed. It says the photo was taken on Jaluit Island, a tiny ring of land in the middle of the Pacific Ocean. It says Amelia and Fred were spies and the Japanese took them to Saipan as prisoners of war. It says the torso measurements of the person sitting on the dock and Amelia's are the same. It says the teeth and hairline of the man are Fred's. It says it's her because the person in the photo is wearing pants.

Grace types *Jaluit* into Google Maps, but the blue of the Pacific is overwhelming, so she opens a new screen and tries to find the sound of Amelia's laugh instead. There are video clips of her voice, but she can't find her laugh anywhere. There must be a radio reel, or a film clip, someone has digitized. It must be somewhere.

She's halfway through a video of Amelia's tickertape parade in New York City—the air filled with confetti and excitement—when Google sends her another alert, a new clip from the History Channel with the former FBI executive assistant director—a wide-set bald man who looks like a rugby player in a ridiculous leather bomber jacket. He says he found the Jaluit photo in a top-secret file in the National Archives in D.C. It was misfiled, he claims. He found it in 2012.

If it really was her, why would he have kept it a secret for years? It's bullshit, Grace thinks. It has to be. And then he shows his cards—there's a documentary airing this week called *Missing Evidence* and the History Channel is trying to drum up viewers.

Grace closes her laptop and takes a load of laundry downstairs, balancing the plastic handle on her hip and trying to keep her pants from falling down with her other hand. She makes another pot of tea and eats another avocado mashed onto toast. She watches a video of how to swaddle a newborn on her phone. She rinses her plate. She looks at the name spreadsheet. She folds a pile of crib sheets.

She looks at the Jaluit photo again. She stares at it, hard.

She watches the clip a second time and before she even knows what she's doing, she's falling down the rabbit hole she's avoided since July when Janice handed her the shoebox of letters and Grace first read that Amelia had disappeared. There are black-and-white maybe-photos of Amelia, paragraphs of text in all caps, in Comic Sans, underlined insistence, arrows pointing to this corner of her mouth, this island in the Pacific, this window of the Electra—

She crashed into Nikumaroro and radioed for help, shucking clams, praying for rain, and eventually dug a grave for Fred.

She died in the ocean off Howland Island, her plane sinking into the Pacific, so fast and so deep, not even Roosevelt's extensive search could find them.

She and Fred were U.S. spies, the Electra fitted with cameras, sanctioned by Roosevelt to take aerial photographs of the Japanese in the Marshall Islands.

She issued a distress signal near the Japanese islands so U.S. Navy surveillance planes could fly over and do pre-war recon.

She was pregnant with twins and "off her game."

She was eaten by coconut crabs.

She was executed in Saipan, her Electra buried in an airfield.

She was captured by the Japanese navy and nicknamed Tokyo Rose, one of the hosts of a propaganda radio show that was supposed to make American sailors homesick.

She lived in a palace in Tokyo as the emperor's mistress.

She was held by the Japanese in an internment camp in China and sent a telegram to George in 1945—"Camp liberated—all well—volumes to tell—love to mother."

She was sent back to America after the war and renamed Irene Craigmile Bolam, disappearing into a New Jersey suburb, into anonymity and sameness. Irene—the same name as her Lake Louise baby.

Grace tries to picture Amelia as Betty Draper's neighbour, but it's laughable to think of her in a nightgown that matched the bedsheets, wearing a slash of midday lipstick and crinolines instead of her flight suit, her goggles.

She could grow out her barbershop curls and wear dresses and aprons, but she could never get away from her freckles, her cheekbones, her easy limbs. There's no way she wouldn't be recognized, but there's a whole website filled with photos of Irene's face transposed onto Amelia's face, insisting on the truth.

The truth, capitalized.

The truth, underlined.

The truth, italicized.

Grace can't stop scrolling.

It can't be true, none of this can be true, except Amelia was friends with Eleanor Roosevelt. And it was 1937, with the Second World War looming. The Electra was outfitted with all kinds of tracking equipment—would cameras have been such a stretch?

Was she a POW? Was she a radio host? Was she a suburban housewife in hiding in New Jersey?

Grace leaves her laptop in her bedroom and lies on the couch, pressing the wand of the Doppler against her skin. The On button has a reassuring green glow. Whoosh and whoosh, her stomach gurgling.

She adds more gel and moves the wand around until she finds her baby girl's heart. Steady and even, fast but not too fast. Her metronome, her rhythm. Grace starts counting: one-two-three-four-five-six-seven-eight-nine. She gets to a hundred and starts back at one. She counts her baby's heartbeats until she can breathe again.

The Jaluit photo isn't her. Of course it isn't. She gets an NPR update about it, and then one by the *New York Times*. It was taken two years before Amelia's last flight and published in a Japanese travelogue about the islands of the South Pacific. The Japanese history blogger who debunked it said it only took him half an hour of looking in Japan's national library. Why didn't that smarmy FBI director double-check? she wonders. Why didn't the entire production team that made the History Channel documentary pause for a split second to see if it was real?

Grace can't stand men like the FBI director, like Stan, the guy leading the expedition, who lay claim to Amelia in a way she would despise. They want her as theirs and denounce each other publicly, discrediting each other's finding to any reporter who will listen, claiming her last days as their own.

But how can those last days matter as much as all the days before? How can those final moments eclipse all the years she spent flying and laughing and pinning maps to her trousers, and designing parachute silk blouses, and teaching Syrian refugees English, and driving her mom across the country in her bright yellow car, and taking photographs of oil geysers, and maybe having a baby in Banff, and making soldiers blancmange in Toronto, and worrying about her sister, and longing for long, lazy summers, and opening oysters on the beach, and loving Gene, and trout-fishing in Newfoundland, and breaking altitude records.

Grace gets the safety pin from her dresser and clicks it open, pressing the pointed end into her thumb. She closes all the tabs of the crazy websites with their fake science and terrible Photoshopping and wishes she could erase the Jaluit photo from her mind, and the photo of Amelia's face transposed onto some poor New Jersey housewife, the Japanese POW camp in Saipan—all grey stone and black bars, the sky ferocious white.

Dear Amelia,

Your letters went live today—the press release went out first thing, and I keep checking the library's Twitter feed. Every time I open it, there are a hundred more, two hundred more retweets. Janice just sent an email—she's worried the website is going to crash with all the traffic. The Globe and Mail *did a piece on them on the weekend, quoting history scholars and aviation experts, though I couldn't get through it. They mentioned you being in Newfoundland, but didn't include anything about your Vega, or how you'd pin maps to your pants, or how you taught English at the Denison House. Though the piece alluded to your feminism, your "modern take on marriage," it was all focused on Gene and George, and the scandal of your affair. Out of everything you accomplished, everything in those beautiful letters you wrote, and all they seem to care about is that you were having an affair.*

Today is also the day Stan and his team of scientists and rich retirees land on Nikumaroro and I bet they've already started digging around for you and Fred. There are divers who are searching along the coral reefs, old rich people taking photos of the beach, avoiding coconut crabs, biding their time until they can go kayaking.

I called in sick—I couldn't handle going in, not with everyone reading all of your letters, and not while the four forensic dogs—border collies named Piper, Berkeley, Marcy, and Kayle—search the atoll. They have to wear booties to protect their paws from the hot coral, and thermal vests to keep them cool. Apparently, there's a backup dog, a

Jack Russell terrier named Asha.

There's a pile of rocks they think might be Fred's grave. A grave you would've dug, rocks you would've piled, and it makes me cry, just thinking about it. Digging a grave with your hands, and Fred, gone, with his brand-new wife at home, a widow now, his navigation school that would never be—

They're planning on digging up Fred's bones, dismantling the rocks you piled carefully, the dull clink of stone on stone while you tried to ignore the sound of scuttling crabs.

I hate the thought of you alone on the island, with those shells upturned, pink and hopeful, even as your hope was waning. The thought of your grief overwhelms me.

—G

35

Grace gets an email from the web team with stats from the portal—the letter about deciding to fly around the world is the most popular, followed by the one about the Hawaii-California flight. But what about the trout-fishing one in Trepassey? Grace wants to ask. Or the one about Wiley, or the brown silk scarf?

The Fisher made the New York Times, Carolyn texts. *Did you know about these Amelia Earhart letters??!!! She's such a badass!*

Grace doesn't pick up when Jenna calls, but she texts right after. *Oh my god, you're famous. Your letters are everywhere! Even my mom knows about them!*

Grace turns her phone off and lies on the couch, her belly roiling with the baby's elbows and knees. She hates that people are reading Amelia's letters to Gene. She hates that the retirees are combing through the sand, the coral, the vegetation, looking for Amelia. She's more than just her love affair with Gene. She's more than just potential fragments on an atoll.

Even though it's getting dark, Grace walks across Harbord and down Spadina to Amelia's hospital—the architecture building near College. The diggers are gone, but the fence is still up and she can't get close.

"Fuck," Grace says to the old brick spires, startling a man walking past her on the sidewalk.

She's too tired to walk the whole way back, so she flags a cab and stares out the window, wishing she could avoid talking about her due date, the size of her belly, the cab driver's daughter whose baby was stillborn.

As soon as she's home, Grace brings the Doppler into bed and presses the wand against her belly. The baby's heartbeat is just to the left of her belly button. It is reassuring to hear the swishing lub-lub-lub after the cab driver's awful story.

Grace counts for a minute, two minutes, three minutes, waiting for this strange underwater lullaby to calm her down, but she can't stop thinking about the Amelia stranded on an atoll with a broken plane with the tide coming in and the Amelia who is being written about in donor letters and alumni emails. Grace opens up her laptop and clicks on the folder labelled *A*. It's not the same, reading the loop and scrawl of her handwriting off a screen, but it's at least something—

> *I have no idea when, or how we'd make it happen, but we should find a little two-seater and go somewhere for a few days, a week. If anyone asks, we can say it's airline business, and I'm sure we could stay at Carl's ranch in Colorado without it being a big to-do. Wouldn't that be fun? Flying, just the two of us together. Let's do an open-air cockpit so we can really feel the wind. Closed cockpits are such a thing now, and don't get me wrong, I'm grateful—my cold cream consumption has gone significantly down and it's a relief not to have permanent circles around my eyes, but I love the screaming wind.*

She opens the letter from Trepassey—

> *I didn't ever do any fishing in the ocean—the fog was too thick, and I spent so much time on the plane being batted*

around by the wind that the last thing I wanted to do was
hop in a boat and bob all over that long, narrow bit of the
Atlantic. But if you walked inland a bit, there were these
amazing streams just teeming with trout. It was impossible
not to catch one.

The baby kicks and Grace scrolls through her phone to the pictures from last summer in Newfoundland—the row of jellybean houses, the curtain of the closed Trepassey museum fluttering out an open window, the long green stretch of the Harbour Grace runway. She opens the letter about her Vega.

Have you seen a more elegant bird? I dare say I haven't.
It was the gold that did me in—that line of subtle sparkle
that isn't ostentatious, or flashy, just classy and delicate.
And the red—that deep red—like an overripe sour cherry.
She was my first monoplane, and I loved that beautifully
cantilevered single piece of spruce. How could I not be
absolutely besotted? I'll never forget her silhouette once we
got to Newfoundland—her curves against the scrubby trees
and sheer rock faces. She was really something else.

Grace pulls up the video of Amelia taking off from Newfoundland in her beloved Vega. Two minutes and six seconds with the grey skies and the Harbour Grace airstrip. In the video, Amelia signs documents and smiles, and walks, and smiles again. She looks up at the sky, squinting into the wind. She takes off, up and over Lady Lake, onward to the ocean. Grace stares at the screen, but can't remember the smell of the grass, the ocean, the smoke from the lobby at Hotel Harbour Grace. She scrolls through the Newfoundland photos on her phone and finds one of the clover dotting Amelia's airfield, the commemorative plaque on the rock, but they seem so distant, so remote, like photos someone else took.

Grace watches the video again, and then again—the wind tugging at Amelia's collar, the spin of the Vega's propeller, but Grace can't stop herself from wondering if the forensic dogs are looking through the underbrush right now. She wonders if a Tilley-hat-wearing retiree is turning over an opened shell—

She types *Amelia Earhart + Vega* and the screen fills with red wings, and silver propellers angled in front of exposed motors. There are teardrop-shaped covers over the wheels—wheel pants, the website calls them, like aerodynamic booties for the tires. It says the single wing is forty-one feet wide.

Grace clicks on the second photo and her computer jumps to the Smithsonian National Air and Space Museum page where there's a virtual reality tour of the cockpit. She zooms in and out on dials that mean nothing to her, dials that meant everything to Amelia. Grace spins the camera around and looks at the cabin—an empty cylinder except for a tiny rectangular window under the wing. Grace moves the camera around to the rudder that seems too rudimentary to actually be part of an airplane.

Grace moves the camera back to the control panel and marvels at the needles, the numbers, the bisected window that would've been filled with clouds and eventually the green edge of Northern Ireland, until her laptop dies. She plugs it in, makes a pot of tea, and returns to the Vega's cockpit. She doesn't sleep; she can't. If she can't have the letters back, if she can't stop the retirees from digging around Nikumaroro, she'll hold tight to the plane, Amelia's most beloved plane, her first love, her "elegant bird," the plane she flew from Newfoundland, from that stretch of scrubby grass in Harbour Grace, salt thick in the air, the blade of propellor spinning into a circle.

36

Grace sits on the tarmac, the CN Tower perched over Lake Ontario. It's only fitting that her flight's delayed, though at least there's no fog. The flight attendant said they're waiting for some equipment, but no one can say when it's supposed to be here. Grace checks her phone. They were supposed to leave a half hour ago.

She checks Google, expecting to find another article about the letters, or an update about the Niku search, but nothing so far. She told Janice she had appointments all day and texted Jenna late last night, hoping she'd turned her ringer off. She didn't tell Jamie she was going—she knows he would've forbidden it. Her mom's been calling every day, but she won't know Grace isn't in Toronto as long as Grace sends her a text every now and then when she has Wi-Fi.

She didn't even know if she was allowed to fly at thirty-three weeks, but it turns out she has until thirty-six weeks, when the baby is the size of a honeydew melon. Still, she bought travel health insurance and paid for the top package, just in case.

She didn't pack much, just a backpack with her passport, a cardigan, and her wallet, a bottle of TUMS, some pens and paper, and Amelia's safety pin. She checked, and then double-checked that safety pins are allowed on planes—they are, along with knitting needles—and she took a screenshot of the page in case anyone tells her otherwise. There was no traffic on the way to the airport, just bike commuters in fluorescent vests and joggers in orange and turquoise shoes. The sky was a thick peach-pink, the sun a glowing red sphere that looked like a planet in a sci-fi movie.

When she arrived at the airport, it was 1:00 a.m. in the South Pacific and the Niku crew was probably sleeping on an anchored boat just off the coral coastline.

Grace was afraid she wouldn't be allowed to board without a doctor's note, so she wore her backpack on her front and draped the scarf Jenna gave her for her birthday last year over top, ready to defend herself. But no one said anything when she checked in and the flight attendant at the gate didn't even glance at her stomach.

Grace's phone lights up. Her heart pumps, but it's just a text from Jamie.

I've got the stroller. I'll drop it by after work, k?

Her return flight doesn't land till 11:00 p.m. *Maybe tomorrow? You out tonight?*

Trying to wrap up a work project, Grace lies. *Don't know when I'll be done at the library. Tomorrow after 6?*

K. You should see this thing. It's like NASA designed it.

She sends a thumbs-up emoji, then sends her mom a screenshot of an article about babies recognizing voices in utero. That'll do until she lands and finds Wi-Fi again, she figures. She Googles Amelia, but there are no updates, no scraps of fuselage, no shoes, no dismantled stones from Fred's grave.

When does your flight get in tonight? Jenna texts. *I'll pick you up.*

11, Grace texts back, grateful Jenna didn't try to talk her out of it. *I'll just take a cab.*

Don't you dare. I'll be there. Be safe. Text me when the plane lands.

I will. xoxo

Out the window, Grace watches the pilot pacing the tarmac. Eventually he climbs back up into the cockpit, where he chats with a flight attendant over a clipboard. Grace checks her email—more portal updates, a congratulations from the Dean, another note from the comms team with a spreadsheet of impressions. She doesn't open any of them, but opens the email from her dad. It's an article from the *Toronto Star* with excerpt from Amelia's letters. *Did you know about this?* he writes. *Is this why you were talking about her over Christmas???*

The flight attendant comes on the PA and apologizes for the delay. "We'll be up soon," he promises.

Dear Amelia,

I've been plastered to the window ever since the plane took off—tiny baseball diamonds, and miniature tennis courts, the perfect oval of a racetrack, golf courses with sand traps that look like scattered beans. I love seeing the world as you saw it—the swirl of an off-ramp, the fishbones of an empty parking lot, the tiny, open eyes of backyard pools.

They just pushed the drink cart down the aisle. They didn't have any hot chocolate, so I had a tomato juice in your honour. It's always so much thicker than I remember, more soup than juice and so salty.

I'm trying really hard not to think about everyone clicking on your letters to Gene, and gossiping about your affair instead of actually reading what you wrote. I'm desperate to block out the snorkelling seniors and sunburnt "researchers," their ship moored off the ring of the atoll, dinghies bobbing, and the dogs—where are the dogs? Every time I glance out the window, I have to try really hard not to think about what Niku looked like from the cockpit of your Electra—the too-intense blue, the dizzying angle of coral, the Pacific rushing too fast, too fast.

I'm terrified of losing you to this stupid search, to all of the articles about you cheating on George. I'm afraid that

*you'll disappear in all this noise—the you that didn't
care that women weren't supposed to fly across oceans, the
you that walked the same Toronto sidewalks that I walk,
the you that believed in love, true love. If I could fly to
Niku and search for you myself I would, but instead, the
closest thing I have is your beloved Vega. I need to see the
wing you climbed up, the propellor that spun into a blur.
I need to be near the plane that rolled down that stretch
of Newfoundland grass, gathering speed, the plane that
nearly fell into the ocean, the plane you righted through
your sheer will to live so hugely, so fully. I need to be close
to something that was an extension of you.*

—G

*P.S.: I just looked out the window again and the miniature
Monopoly houses and freeways have been replaced with
soft, green mountains—the Appalachians, I think. There
are no roads, no cars, just thick, dense green.*

37

Grace knew it would take a while to get from the airport into the city, but she didn't know it would take this long. With sixteen stops left, she closes her eyes against the midday sun. It's already 12:40.

Behind her, a sprawl of teenage boys talk about cellphone plans and which team is going to make it through to the NBA finals. Grace rests the side of her head on the subway window and lets the Virginia suburbs shudder past. She clicks the safety pin open and closed, open and closed.

Tysons Corner.

East Falls Church.

Clarendon.

Court House.

She's too wired to fully let herself sleep and, besides, it's too cold. She's glad she brought a cardigan—the A/C is jacked and she's freezing.

She was expecting the customs officer, who was straight out of a G.I. Joe cartoon, to tell her that visiting a museum and flying home all in one day was suspect and turn her away, but he squinted at her passport and at her face, at her passport again and up at her face, and waved her through. Before catching a shuttle bus to the subway station, she stopped at a snack stand, where there were chocolate bars she'd only ever read about—Almond Joy, Baby Ruth, Milky Way, Mounds, PayDay. She couldn't make a decision, so she bought all of them.

"How far along?" the woman behind the register asked.

Grace froze for a moment before realizing that she didn't have to hide her pregnancy anymore. "Thirty-three weeks," she said.

"You are close, my dear. This is a good place to have a baby. Your baby will be lucky."

Grace nodded and didn't correct her.

"You make sure you drink lots of water. It's hot out there," the woman said, handing Grace a bottle. She waved her off when Grace tried to pay for it and pointed Grace to the shuttle bus fare desk and made sure she had exact change for the train. Grace had to keep herself from crying at her kindness as she half-ran the length of the terminal, chocolate bars bouncing in her backpack.

The subway ducks underground and the lights in the tunnel flicker through the scuffed window. She is tired, so tired, heartburn searing the back of her throat. She's already taken her daily quota of TUMS.

The subway pauses, and the conductor comes over the intercom, saying he's waiting for the train in front to clear the station. *Go*, Grace wills the train in front of them, refusing to let the panic of being stuck underground in a city eight hundred kilometres from home take hold. She doesn't even know if she's still in Virginia, or in D.C. yet.

Her belly tightens into a hard Braxton-Hicks ball—she shouldn't have had tomato juice and eaten chips on the plane. She wants to drink more water, but has no idea how long this subway ride will take, or how long they'll be stuck in the tunnel. She tries to breathe and will her uterus to relax. She left the house six hours ago and she's still on the subway, and this whole trip is starting to feel foolish, dangerous even, and way too overwhelming for her pregnant body. Why didn't she just pay the extra money to at least land at the airport in the city? Why did she have to come in the first place?

But then she remembers the retirees turning over Amelia's carefully balanced stones, and the team of dogs with their protective booties scouring the coral, the stats on the portal climbing, the letters excerpted in the *Guardian*, and the *New York Times*. She forces herself to breathe.

The train rolls into the next station. *Foggy Bottom.*

Farragut West.

Federal Triangle.

It's 1:24. Two more stops.

"L'Enfant Plaza," the conductor drawls—the baby plaza. Grace can't tell if it's funny or prescient. She stands and her belly parts the packed commuters as she leaves the full train and follows the sea of people down the platform. She hadn't realized she was so deep underground—it takes two long escalator rides to bring her back up to the surface.

She's hit with a wall of unforgiving southern heat and is grateful for the bottle of water from the woman at the airport snack stand. The sidewalks are busy with people folding and unfolding maps and pointing to gleaming white buildings. Everyone here looks like a tourist—multipocketed khaki shorts, smart walking shoes, backpacks, fanny packs, visors and ball caps. Though, she doesn't look much different with her backpack and her running shoes.

Grace passes a stand with twirling racks of postcards and piles of oversized T-shirts. There's a popcorn vendor on the corner, but the lineup of people wearing official-looking lanyards around their necks is too long. Next to the popcorn cart is a young man selling water bottles from a cooler on wheels, yelling, "Ice-cold water, one dollar," on a loop.

Grace glances at the map on her phone and follows the curving sidewalk until the Smithsonian National Air and Space Museum looms across six lanes of traffic. The building is huge, all concrete and windows. It is so much bigger than she thought it'd be. Security is strict, and Grace's backpack goes through the scanner while she gets patted down.

"How far along?" the security guard asks.

"Thirty-three weeks," Grace says.

"What? No way. Look at this," the guard calls to the woman

273

working the scanner. "She's thirty-three weeks. Remember how big I was at thirty-three?"

Grace wants to ask her if she knew when she was going into labour. What it was like, if she fell in love with her baby right away, if breastfeeding was hard, if she tore, if she healed, but she hands Grace her bag and a family files in behind her, surrendering their wallets and phones.

The museum is packed—with school groups wearing matching T-shirts, and kids playing tag and moms yelling at them to stop, and men with large cameras around their necks, and teenagers in camo pants. Above the loud mess of people, there are planes suspended from the ceiling—airmail planes from the twenties, First World War planes, Second World War planes, fighter jets, missiles, even spaceships—

Grace stumbles over to the information desk.

"Are you looking for anything in particular?" the docent asks. He's an older man, probably a former pilot, his white hair parted with military precision.

"Amelia Earhart," Grace says, her voice catching. "Her Vega."

"It's up there," he says pointing to the second floor, right above them. "Take the escalator before the gift shop."

Grace clutches her map and heads toward the escalator, but all of a sudden, it's too much. She's nervous and not ready, not yet. She ducks into the Early Flight gallery. Translucent wings stretched over delicate wood frames hang overhead. Grace stands in front of a plaque she doesn't bother reading and takes a deep breath. Then another.

She's in the way, forcing kids and elderly men with walkers to go around her, so she ducks out as fast as she ducked in and takes the escalator up to the second floor.

She bursts into tears when she sees it—it's red, so red, and its wings stretch wider than she anticipated. The photos and blurry VHS tapes did it no justice. The silver propeller is an elegant *accent aigu*—and the gold stripe that is impossible to see in black-and-white sparkles the entire length of the fuselage, darting in a swooping sideways V on the wheel pants.

It's beautiful, this plane, Amelia's first love, which she managed, somehow, to land in a cow field in Ireland, even with the leaky fuel tank and iced-over wings.

Grace had expected the wings would be sharp and angular, but they're not. They're soft and rounded, smoothed over like a piece of beach glass. The plane looks so heavy in person—impossible that it would ever fly, let alone make it all the way across the Atlantic. The wings are barricaded by Plexiglas and it's surrounded by info boards and artifacts—a cotton flying smock, commemorative coins, a trophy, and a trophy box George had built for Amelia.

She circles the plane again, checking for evidence of the fire on the cowling, but there's no trace of it. She feels unsteady, like the ground beneath her is moving, so she finds a small bench near the tail of the plane. There's a screen with an ancient cartoon of Mickey Mouse flying an airplane playing on a loop. She furtively eats a PayDay bar and then an Almond Joy while her baby kicks her ribs.

From the bench, the gold stripe seems thicker, and more sparkly. And she hadn't noticed the slight octagonal curve of the fuselage around the motor. There are tiny lightbulbs under each wing, tiny beacons, though they probably would've been impossible to see from the ground. Grace clicks the safety pin open and closed and tucks it back in her pocket.

She circles the plane again. On the far side of the tail is a case with one of Amelia's flying jackets—Grace can feel the coolness of the leather, the slight scratch of the tweed, the always-stiff buttons—and a pair of Amelia's flying goggles, though they're missing a lens. There's also a blown-up photo of her in a thick crowd, followed by a model of her Electra, and a map of the Pacific. The islands and atolls are tiny green dots.

But no. The atoll doesn't matter. The Niku search doesn't matter. The portal and the articles about her "scandalous" affair don't matter.

Amelia is so much more than her relationship with Gene. So much more than her disappearance. Grace can picture her ducking under these red and rounded wings, the black block letters spelling out *NR-79521*. She can see her hands touching her face, nervous, and excited, the tomato soup from the Cochrane Hotel waiting for her in the cockpit.

Grace stands next to the sparkling gold stripe, exactly where Amelia stood while the wind whipped through her curls and yanked at her collar, the air salty, with Lady Lake on one side, the Atlantic on the other. The gold swoops over the wheel coverings, the same wheels that carried Amelia down that stretch of clover-dotted grass, propeller a circular blur, wings wobbling slightly, a moment of hesitation before they caught the wind and carried her over the hotel, over the harbour, east and east, until her plane was a tiny speck against the cloud-filled sky.

ACKNOWLEDGEMENTS

I'm grateful for financial support from the Ontario Arts Council through their Recommender Grants for Writers program, and the publishers who recommended my work, and to Access Copyright Foundation for funding my research trip to Newfoundland.

I'm indebted to Purdue University Archives and Special Collections, and Jean L. Backus's collection, *Letters From Amelia*, for access to Amelia Earhart's letters, which inspired my own.

My heartfelt thanks:

To Jay Millar and Hazel Millar for seeing what this book could be, and believing in it from its original incarnation. It has been a joy and a privilege to work with both of you and it is a delight and an honour to call you my friends.

To my brilliant editor, Meg Storey, for her invaluable insight and care, and generous feedback. Developing this world with you was nothing short of thrilling.

To the brilliant team at Book*hug—Tree Abraham, Shannon Whibbs, Melanie Little, and everyone else who brought this book to life.

To Kelvin Kong for helping find this manuscript a home.

To Stacey May Fowles, Amy Jones, Jon McGregor, and Anne Michaels for the generous readings and enthusiastic support.

To David Eso, Jeanette Lynes, and Goose Lane Editions, Jim Johnstone, *Grain* magazine, *filling Station* magazine, Jon McGregor and *The Letters Page*, Conan Tobias and *Taddle Creek*, Aaron Schneider and Amy Mitchell at *The Temz Review*, and *The Varsity* for publishing early letters to Amelia.

To Rhys Brisbin for sending me Amelia news for the last 18+ years, and everyone else who has sent me Amelia headlines.

To Mom for instilling a deep love of reading, and for always being my biggest cheerleader.

To Dad for answering all of my plane questions and taking me to air force bases and every Toronto air show as a kid.

To Papa Doug for his flight logs and stories about his days of flying, and Nana Ruth for always believing that my words would find their way into the world. I miss you every day.

To gracious and generous Newfoundlanders: Beth Follett and Stan Dragland for the extraordinary St. John's home base; Angela Antle and Mark Quinn for the wine, chanterelles, Trepassey stories, and Newfoundland connections; Larry Dohey and the team at The Rooms; Erin Noel for all the Newfoundland tips, especially the swimming hole on the way to Trepassey.

To John Shoesmith at the Thomas Fisher Rare Book Library at the University of Toronto for the extensive tour and answering all of my rare book library questions.

To Shannon Litzenberger for the long-ago residency in Saskatchewan, and to Lynn and Dave Litzenberger, and Anne Winitsky for being such generous hosts.

To the kind docent at the Smithsonian National Air and Space Museum who didn't flinch at my tears.

To Mrs. Patterson and Mrs. Salgo at Martingrove Collegiate who fostered my love of reading and writing.

To my dear early readers: Emily Arvay for her insight on the epistolary form, and years and years of cross-country letters; Esther de Bruijn, whose encouragement and insight rang so clear and true; and Corinna Barsan for her edits and careful reading.

To my beloved writing group, the Semi-Retired Hens: Samantha Garner, Teri Vlassopoulos, and Julia Zarankin, who have transformed my world and make everything I write so much better. I am so excited for all of our current and future projects.

To my brilliant un-book club: Michelle Arbuckle, Hazel Millar, Carey Toane, Vikki Vansickle, and Jacqueline Whyte Appleby. Thank you for being so much more than a book club.

To Kate Holden for the park visits and weekly pandemic childcare (and the days we ditched work and talked instead).

To my dear friends: Jamie Banting and Patrice Hall, Katherine Boyes, Matt Brubacher and Maria Gruending, Elisha Denburg, Erica Denburg, Esther de Bruijn, Lisa Di Diodato, Kathryn Esaw, Mairead Filgate, Stacey May Fowles, Kate Holden, Kelly Jack, Ramsey Leung, Jess Romero,

Adele Phillips, Rhya Tamasauskas, Jada Van Vliet, Suzanne Watters, and Laura Wills. I am so grateful for the years of love and friendship. Thank you for believing in me and in this project even when I couldn't.

To my extraordinary neighbours: Theresa Frost, Victoria and Angus Berry, and Mike, Judy, Drew and Owen McKinnon for the sidewalk camaraderie and weekly happy hours.

To my incredible family who always have my back—Katie, Mike, Finn, Rhys, Mom, Robin, Dad, Sandy, and all of the Berards. Thank you for loving me hard and believing in me and my work. It means everything.

To Jack and Claire—my beautiful, extraordinary children. Thank you for always listening to Amelia stories, identifying biplanes, tracing Amelia's flights at two years old, and visiting plane museums and airports with more enthusiasm than I could ever have dreamed of. And napping—Claire, thank you for napping.

And to Adam, your love and unwavering support makes all of this possible. I love you.

ABOUT THE AUTHOR

Lindsay Zier-Vogel is a Toronto-based writer, arts educator and the creator of the internationally-acclaimed Love Lettering Project. After studying contemporary dance, she received her MA in Creative Writing from the University of Toronto. Her writing has been widely published in Canada and the U.K. Since 2001, she has been teaching creative writing workshops in schools and communities. Her hand-bound books are housed in the permanent collection at the Thomas Fisher Rare Book Library in Toronto. As the creator of the Love Lettering Project, Lindsay has asked people all over the world to write love letters to their communities and hide them for strangers to find, spreading place-based love. Lindsay also writes children's books. Because of The Love Lettering Project, CBC Radio has deemed Lindsay a "national treasure." *Letters to Amelia* is her first book.

COLOPHON

Manufactured as the first edition of
Letters to Amelia
In the fall of 2021 by Book*hug Press

Edited for the press by Meg Storey
Copy edited by Shannon Whibbs
Proofread by Melanie Little
Text + design by Tree Abraham

bookhugpress.ca